FRAME-UP

Also by John F. Dobbyn
Neon Dragon

FRAME-UP

A Novel

John F. Dobbyn

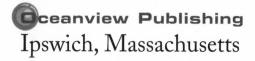
Oceanview Publishing
Ipswich, Massachusetts

ISBN: 978-1-933515-63-2

Published in the United States of America by Oceanview Publishing, Ipswich, Massachusetts
www.oceanviewpub.com

10 9 8 7 6 5 4 3 2 1

PRINTED IN THE UNITED STATES OF AMERICA

Dedication

Ninety nine percent of the great joy and excitement of seeing this story born into a book is seeing that joy and excitement in the eyes of the one whose faith, when it was needed most, made it possible — and who wrote the two hardest words of the whole book, the title — my love, my adventuring buddy, and, thank God, my wife — Lois.

FRAME-UP

CHAPTER ONE

For the life of me, at that moment, if I had to decide which side of the line I was on, I'd have had to flip a coin. The first clue that I was still on this side of the great abyss was a distant rustling of cloth. There were other clues, like a migraine that ran from every hair follicle to wherever my toes were. It seemed to ripple like "the wave" at a Patriots' game.

I opened my eyes a crack and found that they just let in more darkness. The debate became whether or not to call out. It could bring help or heaven knows what.

I heard a voice close to my ear. It was coarse and as gruff as the bark of a pit boss, but it sounded like an angel of God to me.

"Michael, can you hear me?"

It was Zeus in a stage whisper. Only Lex Devlin, senior partner of the law firm of Devlin and Knight—of which I was the junior partner—would ask that. They could hear him in Toronto.

"Mr. Devlin."

I was less surprised at how throaty the words sounded than the fact that they came out at all. "What are we doing here? And where is here?"

"Lie still, son. You're in the Mass. General Hospital. Do you remember anything?"

I was beginning to get flashbacks, but first things first.

"My eyes. Are they—?"

"You'll be all right. You had a roadmap of lacerations around the face. That's why the bandages. The restraints are to keep your hands away from the bandages."

I settled back in a quick prayer of thanks. That was the big one. "Anything broken?"

"No. Concussion was the biggest worry. You've been out a while."

"How long?"

"Two and a half days."

I tried to flash back through my trial schedule to see if I could afford the time.

"How long have you been here, Mr. Devlin?"

"Two and a half days." The voice that said it was different. When the bandages came off later that day, I was able to match the new voice with a male nurse.

"We couldn't get him to leave. I wanted to give him bedpan rounds just to see him move."

The vision of Lex Devlin, lion of the criminal defense bar, doing bedpans, and the joy that might bring to every assistant district attorney in Boston, brought a smile to my cracking lips.

Slowly the pieces started coming back. It must have happened three days earlier, Friday afternoon. I remembered coming down the steps of the federal courthouse about five o'clock in the afternoon. I could feel the cool fresh air untying knots in every gangle of nerves after a two-day trial before the right honorable and certifiably loony Judge Chauncy Hayes.

The Friday afternoon surge of humanity was at its peak. I had five minutes to make it to the parking garage on Devonshire Street. My usual Friday lunch partner, John McKedrick, had cancelled that day for the first time in seven years. He'd offered the alternative of a drive to the North Shore that evening for dinner at the General Glover. I accepted the offer as full payment of a wagering debt he'd owed me since the Bruins had eliminated the Toronto Maple Leafs in four straight.

My legs were in overdrive up Federal Street. I was catching the glares and snarls of a crowd never known for pedestrian collegiality.

I remembered rounding the bend at the entrance of the parking garage in full lather, a mere three minutes late. I climbed to the top

level of the parking garage and saw John in his Chrysler Sebring, top
down. He caught sight of me and began making an elaborate mime
of examining his watch. John and I had been close friends since we
graduated from Harvard Law School seven years earlier. I figured
that entitled me to suggest where he might relocate his watch. In restraint, I did it in mime. I caught the grin on the face of the garage
attendant watching these full-grown three-year-olds. I could hear
John's infectious laugh as he reached down toward the ignition. I
glanced over at the still grinning garage attendant, and the world
cracked in two.

The last thing I could remember was being hit with something
that felt like the defensive front line of the New England Patriots. An
instant later, it seemed, Lex Devlin was telling me that I had coasted
through two and a half days.

CHAPTER TWO

Tuesday was a day that could wring joy out of the heart of an incurable optimist. The shivers that seized every one of us gathered around that bleak pit came not just from the dank, depressing drizzle. The box we were about to lower into that black hole held a body that had exuded wit and brilliance and lightness of spirit before the car bomb put an end to it all. We knew that our John McKedrick was in the peaceful embrace of the Lord. We also knew that we'd never again in this life ride high on that laugh that must now be delighting the angels.

Physically, I was back in the game. With the exception of a temple gong in the back of my skull and lines of facial stitches that gave me the look of a Cabbage Patch Doll, I was able to sit up and take nourishment and attend funerals.

Father Tim McNamee handled the tough part from the church ceremony to the gravesite. He had known John much longer than I had. They had shared an Irish upbringing in South Boston and a great deal more in the way of friendship. I felt for him as he choked out the part about "Ashes to ashes and dust—" He belted out the words about resurrection with the Lord with conviction, but I could tell that he was, like the rest of us, in the grip of a deep mourning for his own personal loss.

I had spoken to John's parents at the church, so there was no need to match manufactured smiles again. There were, however, a couple of standouts in the crowd. I was somehow surprised, for reasons I can't quite define, to see the poker-faced, sharkskin-clad figure of Benny Ignola lurking on the fringe of the crowd. It was drizzling rain and dark enough to show slides, but old Benny was, as always, hidden behind a pair of shades that must have rendered him legally blind.

Benny had carved a semihandsome living out of being legal counsel to the lower-to-middle-level Mafia. The big shots in the North End of Boston hid behind the talents of the more prestigious graduates of Ivy League law schools. It was, however, one of their overhead expenses to throw Benny into the pit on the side of the prostitutes, drug runners, kneecap mechanics, and what are euphemistically called "cleaners." Word had it that he was actually on retainer by the Boston chapter of the Mafia.

Somehow the fact that he was at the gravesite sandpapered the part of me that should have been the first to admit that it was none of my business. The truth is that it had been grinding away at me for seven years. When we graduated from law school, John McKedrick accepted a job as Benny Ignola's sole associate.

I remember saying, "Johnny, stay away from that parasite. If you lie down with dogs, you get up with fleas."

He told me that he was a big boy, and that I could do him the favor of treating him like one. I remember him saying, "I'll get experience in court from day one. While you're still arguing motions, I'll be trying jury cases."

I gave him a look that at least wrung a concession. "Listen Mike, I'll give him two years, three maybe. Then I'm on to cleaner pastures."

I reminded John of that conversation on each anniversary of the three years. The flea quote was more truth than poetry. Every year spent with Benny Ignola reduced the chances of any respectable law firm touching Benny's protégé. John was locked in, although I never completely lost hope that he'd escape. In fact, there was something in his voice when he invited me to the North Shore for dinner instead of our usual lunch that Friday that smacked of a news bulletin. It was probably wishful thinking, but I'd been grasping at that particular straw all day Friday — until it became moot.

Looking beyond Benny, I caught sight of a much more inspiring vision. There was a young lady at the fringe of the people waiting for a chance to speak to John's parents. I wondered why I had wasted three looks at Benny when I could be analyzing why that face made the clouds and the drizzle disappear.

There was not a chance that those sparkling blue eyes and reddish auburn hair were any less Irish than John McKedrick himself. She carried herself with that smart, perky confidence that let her forget herself while she charmed everyone around her.

The longer I looked, the more I wondered if she could have figured into the news bulletin that I would now never hear from John. Only one way to find out.

I crossed between gravestones on the only path that would intercept her before she left. It took me directly behind Benny, who kept the shades pointing straight ahead. The voice, however, reached around to catch me in mid-step.

"Knight. See you a minute."

I stopped, but that was the only recognition I was up to. He turned just enough to be able to glance at me over the shades. Then it was the back of his head again.

"We should talk."

I stayed where I was. "And what would we talk about, Benny?"

He pushed the glasses back to full mast. I could visualize a sardonic grin creeping across his lips.

"You're very superior, aren't you, Knight? Very above all this."

"Not superior, Benny. We walk different paths."

"And you don't approve of my path. Somehow I'll find a way to live with that." The sarcasm was flowing over the top of my shoes.

I started to move off. He caught me again.

"Nevertheless, Knight, we should talk."

"I'm still at a loss to think of a subject we should talk about, Benny."

I could hear the smug grin in his tone. "You'll think of one, Knight. One of these days you'll ask yourself why this terrible thing should happen to a sweet boy like John McKedrick. You'll come to me to talk. And you know what, kid?"

"No, what, Mr. Ignola?"

"Maybe I'll talk to you. Because I'm too big a man to carry a grudge."

With that exit line, he moved his self-satisfied little carcass in the direction of a sleek, black Jaguar. I washed all trace of Benny from my mind with the vision of the auburn-haired colleen who was just leaving John's parents.

I reached the edge of the crowd in time to see her beginning to pull out of the line of parked cars in a Volkswagen bug. I sprinted at the best speed my recently sandblasted joints could muster and rapped on the driver's-side window.

She was somewhat startled at the intrusion. In fact, one look at my face at the window and she showed signs of shell shock. When I caught a glimpse of my stitches in the rearview mirror, I realized she must have thought Dr. Frankenstein's handicraft was hitching a ride.

I smiled and backed off enough to induce her to roll the window down an inch.

"I'm sorry. I just — I'm Michael Knight. I was —"

The shock turned to embarrassment. The angel had a voice.

"Oh, dear God, I'm sorry. You were in the accident with John. Are you all right?"

"Oh sure. Just a little healing time — I'm not sure why I stopped you. Did you know John well?"

Whatever she said was muffled by a rising growl of thunder, and the heavens began to open. She rolled down the window. I could make out, "Can I give you a lift somewhere?"

I shook my head and pointed to my car.

"Is there a way I can talk to you?" I was shouting above the rain that was revving up to a torrent. She wrote something on a card and passed it through the window. I stuffed it into an inside pocket and slogged back to my waiting Corvette.

The river that ran down the driver's-side window made my last look at John's grave seem as unreal as everything that had happened since I stood making idiotic mime signs to him on that Friday afternoon.

CHAPTER THREE

Wednesday was my first day back in the office since the "accident." I was sure there were enough calls and e-mails stacked up to scratch off a week. My secretary, Julie, was off on a court run when I got in. With no live voice to nag me about returning calls, I decided to finesse them for the moment and check in with the boss.

Lex Devlin was my partner, but if the day ever dawns when I don't consider him my superior in every respect and thank God that I can claim him as my mentor, I'll check into McLean Hospital for retuning.

I gave a couple of quick raps when I walked into his office. Whoever he was talking to on the phone got the quickest sign-off they were likely to get that morning. He gave me a hand signal that brought me to the edge of his desk. He leaned his six-foot-two-inch frame, amply padded for combat, over the desk to check out the facial scars. I heard from the nurses at the hospital that he had cashed in a rather large favor to get the head of cosmetic surgery of the Mass. General Hospital off the golf course to do the embroidery.

His only reaction was a low "mmmm." The tone of it indicated that I could appear in public without frightening small dogs and children. I was surprised myself at the amount of healing that had taken place over five days.

We chatted a bit about the cases that needed attention, but I could sense edginess. He kept checking his watch, which was out of character for a man who could intuitively tell you the time within two minutes, day or night, without looking.

By the fourth check, the hands of the Movado his deceased wife,

Mary, had given him on their fortieth anniversary had apparently reached the time he was waiting for. He leaned over the desk.

"Michael, take a ride with me."

Mr. Devlin drove. My questions just bounced off his play-'em-close-to-the-chest demeanor. The best I could get was a few words on keeping an open mind.

"Like how open?"

"Quite."

I waited for more, but that was it. Communication was Mr. Devlin's strong suit. But then, so was stone silence.

I sensed that there was no point in asking why we were taking Causeway Street past the ghost of old Boston Garden. As always, I bowed slightly with a prayer that, wherever they were, Bobby Orr, Larry Bird, and a few others would be rewarded for the memories that still lit up my daydreams.

Silence prevailed while we cruised over the Washington Street Bridge. As we penetrated deep into that bastion of the Irish working class called Charlestown, I noticed a good deal of neck swivel by my partner at the wheel. Most of the city around Bunker Hill is now toned up to yuppie standards, but when we got into the old section, there wasn't a shop or second-story window that didn't catch a glance.

"Are we on familiar turf, Mr. Devlin?"

I hit a nerve sensitive enough to break the silence.

"There isn't a spot in this town that I couldn't find blindfolded. Lean over. See that second-floor window on the corner? There with the lace curtains? I was born in that room seventy-two years ago."

I kept silence for the memory that was clearly playing behind those eyes that I had never before seen misted. There was no traffic, so we could slow to a crawl.

"Those curtains are a symbol. There were the 'shanty Irish' and the 'lace-curtain Irish.' My father was a lieutenant on the Boston Police. He didn't make much, but my mother saw to it that there were lace curtains on the windows. It wasn't a brag. It was a tone, sort of a goal for us growing up. My wife, Mary, kept lace curtains on our bedroom as a reminder of where we came from till the illness —"

We rode up Monument Avenue and pulled over in front of a church the size of a small cathedral. It was ten thirty a.m., and the sun was just beginning to take the chill out of the air.

I was totally in the dark except for knowing that this was no sentimental homecoming. The muscles in Mr. Devlin's jaw that locked his teeth together were pulsing. I caught sight of two Lincoln Towncars parked between the more usual vintage of Chevys across the street. The windows were dark, but the vapor on the windshields said both were occupied. The warmth of my body turned to a chill with the unpleasant feeling that whoever was inside was giving us their full attention.

The church was silent and, apparently, vacant. On another day, it would have brought peace and prayer. Today it just multiplied the tension.

Our footsteps resonated back to the choir loft as we approached the front altar. Halfway down the aisle, I caught sight of a massive dark figure in the shadows of the entrance to the priest's vesting room. I heard a soft voice call Mr. Devlin's first name in a whisper that echoed through the church.

As we approached, the figure in the shadows came forward. The folds of the black, floor-length cassock outlined the six-foot-three-inch frame of a man who was massive through the shoulders and tapered below. When he and Mr. Devlin approached each other, the only greeting was a clasping of both hands. Their eyes locked, and an electric tension seemed to flow between them.

The words were few and whispered.

"Is he alone?"

The priest nodded. I was still feeling the chill of the two Towncars in front, and I wondered what "alone" meant.

The priest was still gripping Mr. Devlin's hands.

"He's aged, Lex."

"Yeah, I know, Matt. His choice, right?"

Concern seemed to come through folds in the brow of the priest. I figured him and Mr. Devlin for the same generation. Mr. Devlin pressed for a commitment.

"Am I right, Matt?"

"Do any of us really have choices, Lex?"

Mr. Devlin just looked away. He caught sight of me and called me over. I felt like an intruder, but I went.

"My partner, Michael Knight. This is — Monsignor Ryan."

I sensed that Mr. Devlin was going to be more elaborate but decided against it. I held out my hand to a grip that could crack an oyster shell. The hand that covered mine was as gnarled and crooked as roots of blackthorn. The smile that went with it was warm, but it did not erase the lines of concern.

"Forgive me for being direct, but this is a closed meeting, Lex. You know how he is. I was to take you in alone. This could change things."

"Michael's involved. And he'll be more involved if things go badly. I'll vouch for Michael. If that's not good enough —"

I saw another figure in the dark corridor that led back to the priest's room. This one was smaller and seemed to move more slowly. The voice was soft-spoken, but something in the timbre set off alarms in me I had never heard before.

"When has your word not been all I ask, Lex?"

The three of us turned toward the speaker as he walked slowly, arthritically, out of the shadows. Every physical sense left me. I was riveted to the floor. For that moment, I could not have moved to run out of a burning building.

The third man kept moving on until the three men were within an arm's grasp of each other. He and Mr. Devlin stood face-to-face. Their thoughts simply passed between their eyes for what seemed like an eon. I saw the arms of the man rise tentatively from his side and extend toward Mr. Devlin. Monsignor Ryan looked at both of them with an intensity that seemed to will something to happen. I heard him whisper, "Lex, how can we forget?"

Mr. Devlin's eyes turned slowly from steel to something softer and moist. And his arms came up to embrace a man I had conceived for my entire adult life as the Antichrist. He was the reigning don of the New England family of La Cosa Nostra, Dominic Santangelo.

I sensed that the embrace had been years in coming. The great arms of the priest were around the two of them, and I looked away from the privacy of the tears that flowed across three faces. Whatever they said to each other was theirs, and it will remain that way.

When they separated, Monsignor Ryan led them back to his private office. I followed, practically unnoticed. Under Mr. Devlin's flag, I was apparently accepted as posing no threat.

The three men sat on leather chairs in a triangle while the priest poured a glass of wine for each. They were so absorbed in each other that I was able to take a seat in the corner, permitted in but not intruding.

Monsignor Ryan raised his glass and looked to each of the others to follow.

"Dominic, Lex, God brought us together as brothers a long time ago. Now He's brought us together again. It's a serious business, and it's His business that brought us into this room. He wants us together as brothers again. Let's let Him have His way."

Mr. Santangelo raised his glass, and both looked to Mr. Devlin. Mr. Devlin looked at the glass on the table in front of him as if to lift it would commit him to something he could not accept.

Monsignor Ryan rose and put a massive hand on Mr. Devlin's shoulder. The large fingers were disjointed and twisted, but the touch was gentle.

"We haven't much time, Lex. We're not three kids who are going to live forever anymore. Let's make the peace now, so we don't have to meet in anger in heaven."

Mr. Devlin looked deep into Monsignor Ryan's eyes.

"Is this the priest talking, Matt? Or is this Matt Ryan?"

"This is both of us, Lex."

It took more than a few painful seconds to cross a barrier, but Mr. Devlin reached for the glass and stood up. Mr. Santangelo stood and there was a touching of three glasses that must have been heard in heaven. I had a disturbing feeling that the compact sealed with that sound would change my life as well.

CHAPTER FOUR

Mr. Santangelo led the opening card.

"Lex, I'll put it simply. I've come to ask for your help."

The shoe dropped. So did the smile on Mr. Devlin's face. He took on a few more years.

"I know."

"How do you know?"

"It's been forty years, give or take. When Matt called me, I knew something brought it on. I'll give you the only answer I've got before you ask the question."

Mr. Devlin was on his feet. I think he needed to be standing to say what I knew was coming.

"Whatever it is, Dominic, I can't do it."

"Listen, Lex —"

"No, you listen. This is hard to say. My partner and I made an agreement." He nodded to me. I nearly jumped when I realized I was not invisible. "We represent people with blood on their hands. It's part of the trade. But we agreed never to take the case of anyone who made it their business. Dear God, man, how did you sink to this?"

Monsignor Ryan was on his feet to calm the waters. Mr. Devlin waved him aside.

"No. Sit, Matt. I've waited years to ask Dominic to his face. How? The three of us were closer than brothers. Every time I see a headline with your name connected to this filth, I die a little."

I was riveted to the face of Dominic Santangelo. I was sure that no one had spoken above a whisper to this little man for the span of my lifetime. He exercised the power of a judge and jury with the simple nod of his head. He had palace guards to carry out any order of execution without appeal.

But there he sat. There were seconds of unfathomable silence before he spoke. When he did, it was so soft that I could barely hear the words. "There is so much you don't know about me, Lex, and so much I can't tell you in half an hour. Please, talk to *me*, not to that creature the newspapers have created to sell their papers."

Mr. Devlin was searching his eyes, but I could see he was not finding the answers he was looking for. He raised his hands slightly and stopped searching. "I can't help you, Dominic."

Mr. Santangelo rose to his feet, and I held on to the arms of the chair.

"It's not for me, Lex."

Mr. Devlin waved him off. "It doesn't matter, Dominic. It's all part of the same —"

"It's for Peter. It's for my son."

The chill that passed between them filled the room.

"It's for your godson, Lex. There is no blood on his hands, and there never will be. Will you listen now?"

"What about Peter?"

"He's about to be indicted for murder."

"Damn it, Dominic!" The explosion triggered every nerve in my body. "The last time I saw you, you promised that boy would never touch any of this."

"And I kept that promise. He's my son, Lex. I swear he is as clean as this junior partner you want to protect."

That was two references to me in a conversation to which I wanted to remain a total spectator.

"Sit down, Lex. Sit down, and we'll talk."

Mr. Devlin sat with both elbows holding down the table.

"I'm certain that by this afternoon the Suffolk County grand jury will indict Peter for murder. I give you my word on his mother's grave. Peter is innocent. He's no part of my business."

The reference to Peter's mother seemed to take the fire out of the mouth of the dragon. Mr. Devlin uncoiled the spring he seemed to be sitting on and listened.

"There's a complication, Lex. Peter is accused of murdering an attorney by the name of John McKedrick."

He waited for that to sink in. Mr. Devlin looked at me, and I just froze.

"Dominic, are you aware that Michael was involved in that car bombing?"

Mr. Santangelo looked at me with pale, tired eyes. I tried to see in them all the power and the evil I had always associated with the don of a major cell of *La Cosa Nostra*. All I could find was a gentle compassion.

"I'm sorry for your pain, Michael. If I could have foreseen it, I would have prevented it if at all possible. As it is, I have no idea who's responsible."

It's hard to convey in words the sincerity that caused me to want to believe that to be true. Mr. Santangelo turned in his chair to face me directly.

"Michael, if Lex agrees to represent my son, I know you'll be working on the defense. I want to know that you have no reservations. I can only give you my word that neither Peter nor I were involved, directly or indirectly. Do you believe that?"

I knew that Mr. Devlin was watching me. I didn't look at him. I knew he'd rather I handle it on my own. Like it or not, it was my turn at bat.

"Mr. Santangelo, I'll admit that you confuse me."

He cocked his head. I knew I had his attention.

"John McKedrick worked for you, didn't he?"

He looked directly into my eyes and answered softly, "Mr. McKedrick worked for an attorney who has represented people I'm associated with. That's true. Actually, I never met Mr. McKedrick. Please ask your questions. I want you to be satisfied."

I knew his interest in me was minimal. I got the clear sense that I had fallen into a useful, if uncomfortable, role that served his purpose. I could ask the questions that would have been awkward between himself and Mr. Devlin. I accepted the invitation. "In fact, Mr. Santangelo, practically everything John did was in connection with people in your business."

"I'm not aware of that, but you'd know better than I."

"Yes, I would. John and I were very close friends. Mr. Santangelo, I can ask this delicately and be left with doubts. Or, we can speak plainly and maybe resolve something."

I had an idea where I was going, but not at the expense of another car bomb. To my relief, Mr. Santangelo smiled and turned to Mr. Devlin.

"He's cut from your cloth, Lex."

He turned back to me.

"I'm in your hands, Michael. By all means, take off the gloves."

"This is the hurdle, Mr. Santangelo. You're the head of an organization that uses murder as a business tool. Word has it that you have Benny Ignola on retainer. That means John was part of that business, legal niceties aside. John must have known enough about the inner workings of your business to make him a security risk. John called me the day he was killed with a dinner invitation. It sounded to me as if he was working up to a major announcement. I had a feeling he was about to take my advice and leave Benny Ignola and all that went with him. Am I striking any chords?"

Mr. Santangelo never moved or changed his expression. "Please continue, Michael."

"Before he could make that announcement, he was murdered. Forgive me, but car bombing is not unknown in Sicilian circles. The implication is somewhat overwhelming."

"That's not a question, Michael. Take off the gloves, and ask the question."

The softness was gone from his eyes. I was looking into two cauldrons of steel, but I was too far into it to waiver.

"Mr. Santangelo, did you give the order?"

"I did not. Nor did my son. Nor did any member of my organization so far as I'm aware. I'll swear on everything I hold sacred."

"Mr. Santangelo, I have no idea of what you hold sacred."

I could hear the nervous shuffling of Monsignor Ryan as he tried to decide when to cut off this juvenile interloper. Even Mr. Devlin was tense as a fiddle, but both held their ground. Mr. Santangelo was intent, but calmly in control. It was clearly between the two of us.

"You have my word, Michael. I have nothing else to give."

"There is something else you can give, Mr. Santangelo. I can't speak for Mr. Devlin, but for myself, I wouldn't consider representing your son without it."

He looked at Mr. Devlin, and in that fraction of a second, Mr. Devlin nearly burst my heart with swelling. Without hesitation he gave a deep nod of the head that meant that whatever in the world I was about to say would bind him, too.

"Mr. Santangelo, John McKedrick was the closest friend I ever had. If I ever learn that you or your son was responsible for his death, I'll come after you with everything the law allows. There'll be no legal wall for you to hide behind. I want not only your word. I want a full waiver of any right of lawyer-client privilege for any information that comes out of our defense of your son. You have my word that I'll use it only in that circumstance."

The air grew stone still. I thought the clock on the wall stopped. I was frozen by the thought that I was eye-to-eye with a man with more immediate power over life and death than the whole state government. Where did I get the gall to put this man to a decision on the spot? Every voice inside of me was screaming, *Get the hell out of there. You are so far over your head, you'll never see daylight.*

Only one tiny voice was whispering, *Hold your ground.* I didn't hear it. I sensed it. It was coming from Mr. Devlin. That was all the starch I needed to stay on my end of the seesaw.

I set my mental timer for ten seconds. I resolved that if he hesitated longer than that, we'd never trust anything he said anyway.

He turned his eyes to Mr. Devlin. The look he found in Mr. Devlin's eyes only confirmed the terms of the deal. Mr. Santangelo did me the honor of looking back at me with a gentle smile that was not condescending.

"Please draft the agreement, Michael. My son and I will both sign it."

Eight seconds flat.

CHAPTER FIVE

I knew the ride back to the office was going to be tense. There were a lot of ghosts in that car, crowding the front seat. Mr. Devlin was in another world, struggling with all of them. I let him keep his silence.

When we reached the Bunker Hill Monument on Monument Avenue, he pulled over and put the car in park. I think he wanted to look at me when he spoke.

"Michael, I pulled you into this, and I'm sorry. It's not your cup of tea. We agreed when we started this partnership we'd never go to bat for a mobster."

"The only agreement I care to remember, Mr. Devlin, is that whatever came along, we'd handle it together."

He looked at me as if he was about to say something, but he just nodded. All indecision was gone. The game was on. He was about to put the car in gear to propel us into a chain of events that would test the steel of that agreement when I stopped him.

"Before we go on, Mr. Devlin, that trio back there was as bizarre as anything Stephen King ever dreamed up. I don't like to ask. I know it's personal. But under the circumstances —"

He rubbed the two o'clock growth on his chin, either to decide where to begin or whether to begin at all. He finally motioned with his head up toward the window in the two-family where he had pointed out the room in which he was born.

"I told you about that one. Look at the house to the right of it. The Right Reverend Monsignor Matthew Ryan was born up there. We came up together through a lot of neighborhood skirmishes. It was different for kids in a neighborhood like this in those days. No weapons. Just bare fists. That's how this nose took on its wandering ways. I think it did more to prepare me for the courtroom than law school.

"But Matt Ryan. Matt was a natural. He took it to the ring. When he was eighteen, he turned pro. I was his cornerman. He had twenty-four fights. Twenty-three wins by eighteen knockouts. The Lord only knows how far he might have gone."

He took a second to remember the past.

"That explains you and the monsignor. You're not going to tell me little Mr. Santangelo, all five feet four of him, survived on bare fists around here."

He laughed at the thought, but then he was on me.

"Listen, don't let the suit and the chauffeur fool you. In a fair fight in those days, I'd give odds on Dominic against any two Irishmen in Charlestown, except Matt."

"So how did Mr. Santangelo get into the trio?"

"Ah, that goes back to the good days. I guess we were early twenties. Matt was fighting about every other Friday night on the card at the Boston Arena. It was a tough section down around St. Botolph Street. It's all class and reconstruction now, but in those days —" He waved his hand in a way that said "dicey."

"One night Matt fought a Puerto Rican kid from the South End. This kid had a lot of backing in the crowd. Some of them looked tougher than the fighter. Matt took him in three rounds. The kid was game. Matt had to give him a hell of a licking before the ref stopped the fight. The crowd didn't like the ref's decision. Matt dressed in a hurry to get us out of there alive.

"There was a fighter's exit in the back of the arena that led to an alley. When we came out, we could see eight of them up ahead coming for us. They filled the alley two deep. We couldn't get back into the arena because the door locked behind us. They had us, and we knew it."

He started to grin in the telling of it.

"All of a sudden comes this bat out of hell. From behind these bozos this pint-sized bowling ball comes into them like a row of ten pins. The arms are swinging. He's yelling like a banshee in Italian. Matt and I dove into them from the front. Four of them went down, and the other four didn't know whether to run or pray. From the sound of it, they did both.

"We chased them out of the alley and kept on running in the opposite direction before the cops came. That was our introduction to little Dominic Santangelo."

"Why'd he do it?"

"Who knows? I guess he didn't like the odds. Anyway, he became Matt's second cornerman. We were the three musketeers. 'One for all, and all for one.' One never moved without the others. Three years we were together while Matt climbed the ladder in the ring."

He stopped talking long enough for one last look around the old Charlestown streets. Then he put the car in gear, and we were back to silence. He slowed down as we passed through the narrow streets of the North End — the almost exclusively Italian neighborhood. He took a sharp right and cruised down Prince Street. Half way down, he pulled over in front of DeMeo's Pastry Shop.

"You better know it all, Michael. December eighteenth, the week before Christmas. Matt had fought his way up to a shot at the number-three contender. That's up there, Michael. This one was at Boston Garden. He wins this one, and he's two fights from the world heavyweight championship. He was going against a good fighter, Angie DeMarco from Brooklyn. The odds on the fight were about even.

"Dominic came into the dressing room while Matt was getting taped up. He was jumpy as a cat. When the trainers left the room, he got down to business."

Mr. D. went silent again. Suddenly he got out of the car, and I followed. We walked to the end of the block where a small alley with three houses opens onto Prince Street.

"That's where Dominic lived. He still lives around here somewhere."

I looked at the vowel-filled names on the shops, the old men sitting, smoking, speaking in Italian in groups on chairs on the sidewalk. You could almost taste the aromas of fresh sausage and tomato gravy cooking in the kitchens. We could have been on a street in Rome.

"Matt and I didn't know it, but this tough kid, this Dominic that we took as a brother, had other brothers. He was working his way up through the lower ranks of the *Cosa Nostra*. He thought he could keep his two lives separate."

Mr. D. stopped again. I was too far into it not to prime the pump.

"And?"

"They had a piece of him, but they wanted all of him. He had an assignment. Get Matt to take a dive. They knew about us three. They thought he could deliver Matt. They thought wrong. It tore the hell out of us when Dominic even suggested it. Matt and I just looked at each other. We knew nothing would ever be the same again. We gave him a message he could take back to his North End buddies. I think a piece of both of us went out of that room with him."

Mr. Devlin started back to the car.

"So what happened in the fight?"

"The first round was typical big-fight tactics. Both fighters jabbed and ducked and danced. Then in the second round, Matt was ready. He exploded out of the corner, throwing lefts until DeMarco was against the ropes in his own corner. Matt caught him with a right that glanced off his jaw. It wasn't enough to take him down, but it opened up a cut in his mouth that spouted blood like a geyser. Matt backed off. I could see by the look on his face, he knew what was happening. Since they couldn't buy Matt, they got to Demarco. He was wearing a wire."

"What kind of wire?"

"Barbed wire. DeMarco was taking a dive the easy way. He put a piece of barbed wire inside his lower lip. Any punch would open up cuts inside the mouth that looked like a major hemorrhage. The fight would be stopped because of the loss of blood. He'd get a rematch, and the boys in the North End would collect whatever they bet on Matt. Probably a lot.

"Matt knew it right away. I saw him back into his corner. He looked like everything he fought for was turning sour. The ref's hand started to go up to stop the fight. Matt grabbed the towel from around the trainer's neck and threw it into the ring in front of the ref. He conceded the fight to DeMarco before the ref could call the fight. The whole Garden went crazy.

"I pulled Matt out of the ring into the dressing room. I knew the bozos behind the fix did not suffer losses gladly. Matt dressed, and we got out of there. Neither one of us knew how this would play with the boxing commission. It turned out it didn't matter."

We reached the car, and Mr. Devlin leaned back against the hood.

"It all seemed so long ago. Then today in Matt's church it was like yesterday."

Mr. Devlin turned around and looked into the empty front seat.

"I went over to Matt's apartment the next afternoon. He was living in South Boston, to be near the gym where he trained. There was no answer to the bell. I rang one of the other apartments. When I got buzzed in, I ran up the three flights to his door. It was partly open, so I went in. Matt was there. He was on the floor. He'd been worked over pretty good, but most of it would heal. The real damage was his hands. They were broken so badly—"

I remembered the twisted knots of fingers that looked like roots of blackthorn.

"Did they ever find out who did it?"

"Maybe. Three days later, the police found three low-level Mafia hoods in a car. They each had a bullet in the back of the head, execution-style. Word had it they were the muscle involved in fixing fights. I had a hunch these three were sent to make an example of Matt. Then someone executed them."

"Someone?"

Mr. Devlin looked at me for a second. "You've got a suspicious mind, Michael."

We got in the car. Before he started the engine, Mr. Devlin said something so softly I could hardly hear it.

"I had the same suspicion. So I decided to talk to him about it. I met Dominic at a bar we used to go to near the gym. I never told Matt about it. It looked like the same old Dominic, but something was very different. We had a beer, and then I got to it. I didn't ask anything. I just said it was odd that three guys who were probably sent to teach Matt a lesson all got a bullet in the head. He didn't say a word. He dropped a five on the bar for the drinks. He put a hand on my shoulder and said what I thought would be the last words I'd ever hear from Dominic Santangelo. 'Tell Matt I'm sorry.'"

CHAPTER SIX

My trusty secretary, Julie, was there to intercept me between the elevator and my office.

"The messages are on your desk. Just break the spider webs and blow off the dust. You could call back the ones who are still alive. Some of them are probably in homes by now, but —"

"Enough, Julie. You're my secretary, not my mother."

"A fine distinction. Michael, come over here."

"I'm fine."

"Michael."

"I'm coming."

To win the argument would take longer than the inspection. Julie will probably drive me to a corner room in the state home for the incurably fussed-over. In the meantime, if she should cease to be my secretary, I'd probably retire from the practice of law.

Her only major drawback is that she is twenty-six and an auburn-haired, hazel-eyed, vital, witty, knockout. Add to that, the unfortunate fact that all five-foot-three-and-three-quarter inches of her is solid heart. That combination raises the hideous specter of marriage to someone who could take her out of professional life — my professional life.

"Michael, you look like you were attacked by a sushi chef."

"Two days ago you would have said a serial slasher. This is an improvement. The flowers were beautiful."

"You're welcome. It was the least I could do. They said you couldn't have visitors, except Mr. Devlin. I think he said he was your father."

That brought a smile to my lips that ran very deep.

"The teddy bear was beautiful too, Julie."

"That was overdoing it, but I wasn't sure I'd see you again to be embarrassed."

"Very sweet. Thank you."

"You're welcome. Would you please call four or five hundred of these people back before I say things your clients will take personally?"

"Actually, no. We've got a hot one. This is going to take up all the burners for the next week or so. Anything so overwhelmingly urgent it can't wait?"

"Yes. My resignation."

"Very funny, Julie. Just tell them all I'll get back to them ASAP. I'll be with Mr. Devlin."

I entered the corner office and quietly closed the door. Mr. D. was dialing a phone number. His square-built form looked like a block of concrete with suspenders. It only reinforced my vision of him as a solid pillar to hold onto when the winds of our practice got furious, as they occasionally did.

He saw me and punched the button for the speakerphone. His suit coat was on the table, and he looked ready for combat, except for a wearying around the eyes. It was a sign I'd begun to spot around three in the afternoon on days when the morning had been draining on the old warrior. He still sprang to his elbows in front of the phone when the voice of the receptionist of the Suffolk County district attorney filled the room.

"Good afternoon, Mary. Would you ring Miss Lamb, please?"

"Is she expecting your call, Mr. Devlin? She's in a meeting."

"I bet she's in a meeting, Mary. She'll have the war council in permanent session for the next month. Tell you what. Would you just whisper into her crusty little ear that Lex Devlin is on the phone, and he represents Mr. Santangelo. You might be prepared to catch her teeth if she drops them."

I could hear the grin in her voice when she said, "I'll deliver the message, Mr. Devlin."

I enjoyed visualizing the scene with my eyes closed. We have Ms. Lamb, five-and-a-half feet of lean, mean, calculating machine, with every obedient strand of pitch-black hair pulled so tight in a bun that her nose quivers. Nothing defined her quite so much as the fact that she was the current occupant of what she viewed as a catapult to the governor's chair, otherwise known as the District Attorney's Office. There she was, holding in her clutchy little talons the Santangelo case, a metaphor for the knife that would cut the rope that would spring the catapult. The flight would be meteoric and unimpeded. The only major question was whether to wear long or short for the inaugural ball.

Suddenly, a small receptionist is standing there telling her that between her and the goalpost has arisen the defensive front line of the New England Patriots. Mr. Alexis Devlin will be personally seeing to the dismantling of her ambitions. I could only hope that the messenger would survive the telling.

She was on the phone in thirty seconds. Her voice sounded deliberately controlled, and a pitch lower than usual. I wondered how she'd handle it when she heard that the word had gotten out about Peter Santangelo's prospective indictment by the supposedly secret grand jury.

"Lex, this is a surprise."

"I hope a pleasant one, Angela. Let's talk about the Santangelo case. What have you got?"

"Santangelo? Nothing, at the moment. Much as I'd like to personally walk Dominic Santangelo to the chamber, I don't know of anything—"

"Peter, Angela. Peter Santangelo. Let's stop playing make-believe and get down to business. I've got two things to tell you. One is that your little rowboat sprung a serious leak. Grand jury proceedings are supposed to be secret. The state constitution says something about that. And yet, here I am knowing about the Peter Santangelo indictment before the grand jury's given it to you."

That lifted her from sneaky to belligerent, two of her better qualities.

"I don't know who you've been listening to, but if you think you can bluff—"

"Angela. I told you I had two things to tell you. Now I have three. Shall we get out of the sandbox and deal?"

Silence.

"Good. The second thing is that an indictment without a trial will make you look . . . what's the word . . . inept. Not good in politics. Just keep listening, Angela. The cat's out of the bag. You know Santangelo senior's organization as well as I do. Those people can tuck Peter Santangelo away so you'll never find him. If you can't find him, you can't bring him to trial. Are you following all this?"

"I'm actually recording every word of it. I believe I have Lex Devlin on record as threatening to obstruct justice."

"Oh, Angela. How do you find the office in the morning? I haven't threatened anything. I haven't seen Peter since I changed his diaper twenty-five years ago. I have no idea where he is, nor do I intend to until we have an agreement. You know I don't play with those monkeys his father's involved with. You also know they don't exactly play by the rules. Am I going too fast here?"

"What are you proposing?"

"I'm proposing a fair exchange. When the indictment comes down, I'll bring Peter in personally. You'll get your trial."

"How can you guarantee that?"

"I've never made a promise I didn't deliver. You have my word, and you'll never get a piece of paper better than that."

"And what do you want?"

"Two things. I want immediate protective incarceration in solitary when I bring him in. I want him protected until the end of any trial, and appeal if necessary. I'll hold you legally accountable for his safety."

"That's one. What else?"

"I want you to open your file. I want disclosure now of every bit of evidence you have against Peter. You'll have to disclose it later anyway."

"You have no right to anything preindictment. I don't have to disclose anything to you."

"Angela, you're not following the conversation well at all. I know what I'm entitled to. We're not discussing that. We're talking about what you're willing to give up for a guaranteed defendant to try."

There was a gap of silence. I could almost hear the little hamsters making the wheels go around in her head, looking for a next move that would at least do her no harm.

"I'm going to put you on hold for a minute, Lex."

"That's fine, Angela. I'll be here for another two minutes."

When the music came on the line, Mr. Devlin held his hand over the speaker microphone and whispered, "She's talking as fast as she can to Billy Coyne. He's there with her. Thank God. He'll tell her what to do."

The redoubtable Deputy District Attorney Billy Coyne had been a fixture in the Suffolk County office through seven political climbers who occupied the title position. He was roughly Mr. D.'s vintage, and unquestionably the best thing that could be said about the office. He had a solid head for the law and no discernable political ambitions. He made the office tick while the newspaper headlines flew over his head to the top dog.

"What makes you think Mr. Coyne's in there."

"She may not be able to find the courthouse without a map, but she knows the political value of this case. She also knows who the lawyer is in that office. She'll be out front for the headlines, but she won't brush her teeth without Billy's okay till this case ends."

The music clicked off the line.

"Lex, are you there?"

"Yes, Angela."

"I've decided that justice would best be served if you and I cooperate. I'm ready to disclose the evidence we have on Peter Santangelo as soon as I have your assurance in writing that if an indictment were to come down, you'd turn him over to us within twenty-four hours."

"That's half the deal."

"You'll bring him to my office, and I'll agree to have him put in protective solitary for the duration of the trial."

"I can imagine. Right after a full photo opportunity for every yahoo in the media that can spell your name. No deal. I don't want him exposed till I know who his enemies are."

Mr. D. changed the tone of his voice before he called out, "Billy Coyne, Billy, for the love of Pete, are you there? Speak up, man"

There was a bit of shuffling before a different voice came across the speaker.

"Hello, Lex."

"Billy, let's make sense of this. You know what I'm talking about here."

"I know. We want him alive too. The question is the best way to keep him that way. We have to agree on a transfer point. Not this office and not police headquarters. We don't know any more than you do about the real players in this thing. You and I can work out a hand-over with people we can both trust, the fewer the better. We'll hold him well out of Suffolk County. I'll let you know when I work it out."

"Ah, Billy. The angel of reason. Give me a time frame so I can set it up on this end."

"We're looking at tomorrow around noon for the indictment. It shouldn't take any longer than that."

Angela broke in. "That's absolutely confidential!"

"Angela, get a grip. If anything about this farce were confidential, we wouldn't be having this enlightening conversation. You've got some serious plugging to do. Billy, I'll try to set things up for tomorrow afternoon or evening."

"I understand, Lex. Be careful. These are not the playmates you're used to. They have a totally different set of rules."

"I know. You know why I'm doing it."

"I take it the old acquaintances have been rekindled."

"For better or worse. Now, which one of you wants to tell me what you have?"

Angela jumped in before she lost total control of the proceeding.

"I'll give you what we have. During the week before the bombing, Dominic Santangelo was in Sicily. John McKedrick, the young man who was killed, worked for Benny Ignola. They represented Santangelo's people on criminal matters."

"I know about John, Angela, get on with it."

"We picked up one of their hoods on an extortion charge, a Mr. Salvatore Marone. He was mid-level in the Santangelo family. He was a three-timer, which meant life, so he wanted to deal. He told us that the previous week he had information that John McKedrick wanted to leave Ignola. He wanted out of the whole business. The trouble was he knew too much. He'd represented members of the mob so long that he might have had enough information to connect even Dominic Santangelo himself. He knew they'd never let him walk away. He was about to go to the FBI to get into the witness protection program. He never worked directly for Santangelo so there was no problem with lawyer-client privilege."

"I understand that, Angela."

"Since Dominic Santangelo was out of the country, Marone went to his son, Peter. He told him about McKedrick. Marone will testify that Peter Santangelo was upset, worried for his father. He said, and I quote, 'I'll take care of McKedrick. I'll do what my father would do if he were here. It's about time I got my hands dirty.' I guess we can all interpret that, Lex."

Lex swung back in his chair with his eyes closed. He had wrinkles the length of his forehead when the focus became intense.

"How'd you pick up this Marone, Angela?"

There was a moment of confused silence before Billy Coyne's voice came through. "He was working an extortion racket on the shop owners in Revere. One of them turned him in. You familiar with The Pirate's Den, Lex? It's a bikers' bar on Ocean Boulevard."

"It's not one of my hangouts, but I've been by the place."

"It's a monkey cage. It's owned by Anthony Tedesco. We've known for years that those places in Revere were under the squeeze by members of the Mafia. This is the first time one of them raised a ruckus. Tedesco came to us."

"Was this Tedesco willing to testify against Marone? That's an unusually courageous act isn't it, Billy?"

"It didn't matter. He gave us enough for an indictment. Marone was a three-time loser. This one was life. We knew he'd deal for witness protection. It'd never go to trial. Tedesco would never have to testify. We could keep his name out of it. I've got to admit, it even surprised us when Marone gave us the mother lode on Peter Santangelo."

"It's more than a surprise, Billy. This whole chain of events suddenly puts the son of the Don in your lap. Doesn't that make you a little uncomfortable?"

"Everything about that bunch makes me uncomfortable. On the other hand, you play the cards you're dealt."

"Agreed. If the deal's from the top of the deck. All right, what else have you got?"

Angela was back in control.

"Following that incriminating admission by Peter Santangelo, there was the bombing murder of John McKedrick, right on cue."

"And you're going to count on the jury making that jump, Angela?"

"They'll jump like a show pony. That's it, Lex. We'll keep investigating. I've kept my part of the bargain. I'll expect full performance from you."

"You should be as sure of reelection. Billy, I deal with you on this. No one else. I want your word."

"When did you ever need to ask for it, Lex?"

"I know. I'm sorry, Billy. I'm putting a life on the line, and I get the feeling I'm walking on Jell-O. Angela, that third thing I had to tell you. It'll make our dealings easier."

"Yes?"

"I never bluff."

CHAPTER SEVEN

It was Thursday night. That meant as inevitably as the sunset that Mr. D. would be dining at the Marliave, an authentic little chunk of Rome tucked into what seems like an alley between Bromfield and School Streets. Since the death of his wife eight years earlier, he had become the kind of creature of habit who could practically recite the menu of every restaurant he frequented.

I was still in the office when he was leaving. By six o'clock I had gone through Julie's top-ten list of calls to be returned "no-matter-what." The first three were at the screaming-fit level, but by the time I reached number eight, I was talking to people who were close to sanity. It seemed like a good place to stop. Besides, "no-matter-what" did not include passing up an invitation to join Mr. D. at the Marliave.

Having been there twice before, I expected the rotund, tuxe-doed Tony Pastore to bow a smiling welcome to Mr. Devlin and lead his friend of countless years to his accustomed corner table under an exquisite Donatelli print. The bow and smile were there, perhaps a bit more tense than usual, but instead of going to the corner table, we followed Tony up the stairs to the small private dining room. Neither of us asked the reason.

When Tony held the door open for us, the figure seated with his back to us at the single table in the small room rose. I was per-haps more surprised than Mr. Devlin to be met by Billy Coyne. They shook hands and took seats beside each other. Billy extended a hand to me and motioned to the third seat at the table. I was flattered that he had not questioned my presence at a table over which highly confidential information seemed about to pass.

Tony took care of business quickly to give us privacy.

"Your Honor, I'll be the only one serving tonight. You won't be disturbed by anyone else. May I bring you the usual?"

"I don't think so, Tony. I'd better hear what Mr. Coyne has to say with all brain cells intact. We'll order dinner though."

To my knowledge, Tony has never allowed Mr. Devlin to look at a menu. It was a friendship that went back to the old school.

"Excellent. Let me prepare something with veal. Do you feel like a veal dish tonight, Your Honor?"

I could sense from the anticipation in Tony's smile that at one word from Mr. D., he would personally wring out of that kitchen a delicacy that would make the calf in question proud to have surrendered its flesh.

Mr. Devlin returned the smile with a gentle hand on Tony's arm. "That would be wonderful, Tony."

Tony's day was made, and his heart was full. You could see it in his eyes as he withdrew and closed the door. Mr. D. looked back at Billy.

"A fine surprise, Mr. Coyne. I'd have thought you'd be taking your meals at the elbow of the Queen of Prosecution. Can she actually order dinner without you?"

"She'll muddle through."

"I expect that describes most of her waking hours. What would that office do without you, Billy? And more to the point, what's your loyalty to her?"

Billy sipped the ginger ale that sat in front of him. I knew there was no trace of anything stronger in anything he ordered. It had been ten years since a liquid escape from the pressure and burnout of the District Attorney's Office had brought him to a bed in the Massachusetts Rehabilitation Center.

"You'd laugh if I told you, Lex."

"I doubt it."

Billy took a few seconds, looking into his ginger ale while he summoned words I'd bet he'd never spoken to anyone else.

"Angela Lamb will pass through that office to better things like her six predecessors without ever remembering she's been there. No, it's not Angela. It's something I started believing a long time ago."

"Tell me."

"Every one of those hoods and rapists and arsonists and murderers I take off the street means an equal number, maybe more, of my people who won't be hurt by them again."

"Your people."

Billy nodded in the direction of the Boston streets. "They're all my people."

Lex nodded.

"Now a question for you, Lex. Our waiter, Tony. He's known you for years. That's why I arranged this through him. He must know you're not a judge. Why does he call you 'Your Honor'?"

Mr. D. leaned back in his chair with a half-smile. I'd wondered the same thing.

"Tony's from the old country. Somewhere around Palermo. It's his way of expressing respect, gratitude. Shortly after he came over here with his family, before he became a citizen, he lived in the North End. His son and another boy pulled a robbery of a delicatessen up there. They hit paydirt without knowing it. They ran out of there with ten thousand dollars."

"Ten thousand from a delicatessen?"

"Well, that was the luck of it. It was Mafia money. The butcher was one of the collection sites for the numbers racket in that area. These kids had a tiger by the tail. The police were after them, but that was the least of their worries. The big shots in the North End wanted their money plus a little blood. No offense, but their investigative techniques have yours beat in trumps. They don't worry about things like the constitution, due process, civilization."

"A distinct advantage."

"I knew Tony as a waiter here. He asked me quietly one night if

I could help his son. The boy just wanted to return the money and keep his life."

"I can see it coming."

"Right. I sent a message to Dominic Santangelo. He wasn't the don then, but he was high up. It was a straight deal. They get their money back and let it drop."

"In exchange for what else?"

"My promise not to spend the rest of my life going after everyone up to the head man if they didn't harm either of the boys."

"No offense, Lex, but couldn't they solve that problem by introducing you to the fish in Boston Harbor?"

"I guess that option didn't appeal to Dom Santangelo."

There was a light rap on the door. At Mr. Devlin's word, Tony wheeled in a cart and served three dinners of veal in a wine cream sauce with risotto, which will linger in my memory straight through senility.

When we had eaten, Tony returned with his own version of cannolis and dark Italian coffee. He carefully closed the door behind him.

Billy got down to business.

"Lex, I don't feel comfortable doing this. I'd feel less comfortable not doing it. You have a deal with Angela. That means you have a deal with my office. Whether or not she acts honorably is her concern. The honor of the District Attorney's Office is my concern. The agreement was full disclosure of everything we have on Peter Santangelo. She kept the ace of spades up her sleeve."

We both leaned in for this one.

"I appreciate what you're doing, Billy. What's the ace?"

Billy leaned close and dropped his voice.

"We have the bomber. He's in custody upstate. He names Peter Santangelo as the one who hired him to rig McKedrick's car."

"Who is this bomber?"

"'Three-finger' Simone."

"Occupational mishap?"

"No. It has to do with the amount of juice he puts in his explosives. If this crowd ever dies out, about the only thing I'll miss are the nicknames."

"Is he local?"

"No. Toledo. He says Peter Santangelo wanted an out-of-towner. Fly in, do the job, fly out. Hard to trace."

"How'd you get him?"

"Someone phoned in an anonymous tip. We picked him up at the Village Green Motel up in Danvers. Can you believe it, he stayed around an extra day to see the Bruins play the Blue Jackets. If the Blue Jackets hadn't been in town, Simone would have been out of the state and we'd probably never find him."

"What're you doing with him?"

"Angela already cut a deal with him in exchange for his testimony against Peter Santangelo. He pleads to manslaughter, takes three to five, no opposition to parole when he comes up. He serves the time out of state under a new identity."

"Very generous."

"She heard the name, Santangelo, and she opened up the store. If he asked, I think she'd have given him my job."

I could see the veins pumping blood to supply the activity raging behind Mr. Devlin's creased eyebrows. I was playing the same quiz game. If Peter Santangelo was innocent, why would Simone finger him? On another level, who was the anonymous tipster who turned Simone in? If Peter was just the bystander that we thought he was, the real lines of battle were drawn up between Dominic Santangelo and an enemy that was not listed on the program. That was clearly the don's problem. Unfortunately, it was now our problem too. The real arrows in this case could be coming at us from somebody far more dangerous than the District Attorney's Office. Billy's disclosure evened the playing field a bit, but it did nothing for the digestion.

"Billy, what do you hear about rumblings in the Santangelo family? The professional family. Any splits, power plays?"

"Nothing lately. But they don't invite me to their board meetings."

The lines deepened in Mr. Devlin's face.

"Follow me for a minute here, Billy. Assume for the moment that young Santangelo was set up, that he's innocent."

"Isn't that an assumption you never make about a client? I thought that was Rule One of Devlin's Rules of Survival. Never consider a client innocent."

"Granted. In most cases. You know the old saying about defense counsel in a criminal case, 'Whatever the outcome, the lawyer always goes home.' In this case, the lawyer could be meeting those fish you mentioned. Bear with me here. Suppose Peter's innocent. Someone disposes of John McKedrick and eliminates Peter with a frame-up in the same play. Why Peter? He's a neutral. He's never been in the game. He's a senior at Harvard."

"Oh Lex, forgive me. A Harvard man. Of course he's innocent. How could I think otherwise?"

Mr. D. held up a hand like a stop sign.

"Billy, please. Play the game with me here. If Peter's not the real target, his father must be, right?"

"Possibly."

"Never mind 'possibly.' Probably. Does that tell us that there's another player in this game who hasn't been identified yet? One who plays with bombs? One who goes outside the family to kill lawyers? That's not Santangelo's style."

"How does that change things?"

"For one thing, I want to be able to see your sorry face around here after this ends. The kid you want to have in jail is not the threat. Neither is his father. You watch your back."

"My every intent. I'll be watching yours too, Lex.

Mr. Devlin responded to the soft knock on the door.

"Your timing is impeccable, Tony. I'll have a bit more coffee and the check." He raised a hand to stop Billy's reach for his wallet.

Tony placed the check on the table, and Mr. Devlin pulled a deck of cards out of his suit coat pocket, shuffled them, and placed them on the table in front of him. Tony cut the cards and showed the ten of diamonds.Mr. Devlin cut the cards, and with a resigned smile, showed Tony the king of hearts.

Tony shook his head and picked up the check and the hundred dollar bill Mr. D. placed on top of it. He retreated to bring more coffee.

Mr. D. leaned closer and whispered.

"We've been doing this for years. After I helped his son, he'd never let me pay for a dinner. I couldn't keep coming here like that, so we reached an agreement. We cut the cards. If I win, I pay. If Tony wins, I don't."

"I get the feeling you pay most of the time, Lex.

"I shouldn't say this to the deputy district attorney, but the deck is rigged. I picked it up at the joke shop on Bromfield Street. I let Tony win once every eight or nine times so he won't suspect."

Before we reached the door on the way out, Mr. Devlin put his hand on Billy's shoulder.

"That's one more I owe you, Billy."

"It wasn't a favor, Lex. It was the right thing to do. Tell her or not, as you wish. At my age, she'd be doing me a favor to fire me. I'm getting tired, Lex."

"I'm not going to say anything. She'll have to disclose the witness after the indictment anyway."

The two old warriors looked at each other.

"Stay aboard, Billy. Let's take a run at one more windmill together."

CHAPTER EIGHT

Julie's first words when I reached the office that Friday morning were like a second sunrise.

"You have a visitor, Michael. She's waiting in your office."

The pieces of a beautiful puzzle were coming together. I had noticed a bright yellow Volkswagen bug parked close to the building.

"Julie, by any chance, reddish auburn hair, blue eyes?"

"Michael. She's pretty."

"Right. If anyone but Mr. Devlin or the pope calls, I'm in conference."

I took one deep breath for an attempt at nonchalance, and walked into my office. There she was, sitting across from my desk, even more beautiful than before. I searched for the perfect opening — something suave, intelligent, sophisticated.

"Hi!"

Unfortunately, it was none of the three, and it came with enough gusto to lift her about three inches off the chair.

"I'm sorry. Didn't mean to startle. Michael Knight."

"Yes. I know, Mr. Knight. My name's Theresa O'Brien. Terry."

"Terry. Call me Mike."

"Thank you, Mike. I think I need someone I can call 'Mike' more than 'Mr. Knight.' I know you were John's closest friend. He called you his adventuring buddy."

I could see mist forming.

"It was mutual. We went on a lot of crazy trips together. Can I get you anything — coffee, anything?"

I was dancing around my total inability to say that John spoke of her often, or even mentioned her at all. I was also groping for the reason that John never talked about her once. I finally decided to fly direct.

"Were you a good friend of John's?"

"Yes. Sort of. Actually we've known each other for some time. Since high school. I just came back to Boston a short time ago. We ran into each other at a party. We started dating just a week before his death."

The misting got heavier.

"I'm sorry."

"I'm all right. Thank you. I should be saying 'I'm sorry' to you. You had John's loss and that terrible injury. You look a lot better than the day of the funeral."

"Thank you. The power of vitamin E."

"I should tell you why I'm here. I wonder, could we close the door?"

As I eased the door closed, I could see Julie's eyebrows rise to about her hairline. By the time I got back to my desk the phone rang. I heard Julie's crisp voice.

"The pope's on line two."

"Thank you, Julie. Please put him on hold."

I hung up, and Terry had my full attention.

"I don't know how to start this. I really don't know whom to trust. I finally decided to bring this to you. I know how close you were to John."

"Whatever you say is in confidence. If it helps, I'd have trusted John with my life. I think he felt the same."

"He did. I've got to say this to someone." She took a deep breath for courage. "Every time I saw John that week before he died he was more nervous. When I'd ask, he'd only tell me that he was under a lot of pressure. You know the people he was representing. Anyway, we had lunch the day of the — the day he died."

That explained his shift with me from lunch to dinner. Perhaps.

"John told me at lunch that he had an appointment that afternoon that was going to solve everything. He was going to be free to do a lot of things he couldn't do before. I think that may have involved our relationship, although he didn't say it directly. I think he was being deliberately vague about it."

The mist became a teardrop. I gave her time and a Kleenex.

"He said something else. He gave me an envelope and asked me to hold onto it. He said he didn't want to have it with him during his meeting. He asked me to mail it the next day — that would be that Saturday — unless he told me otherwise. But then he was killed that evening."

"Did he say whom he was meeting?"

"No, he didn't. I have no idea. This is the envelope."

She handed me what we used to call a report-card manila envelope, sealed, stamped, and addressed to Mr. Anthony Aiello at an address in the North End.

"Do you know who Anthony Aiello is, Mike?"

"Yes."

I fingered this thing that could be more explosive than the bomb that killed John. There was a small, interesting, hard bulge in the envelope the size of a peanut shell.

I wondered about telling her that Anthony "Chickie" Aiello, also known as "Fat Tony," was one of those names the press loves to highlight in the large-print headlines for a quick, cheap, boost in circulation. The news articles always include the word, "reputed," followed by "mobster" or "underworld figure" or "close associate of Dominic Santangelo." They could call him a three-toed frog as long as they precede it with the word "reputed."

The more reliable scuttlebutt among the lawyers at the bars was that Tony Aiello was the underboss of the Santangelo Mafia family, the number-two man and advisor to the don, and nothing "reputed" about it.

The nickname "Chickie" sounds cute and cuddly. Nothing could be further from the truth, as any number could testify if they were still alive. The derivation of the nickname goes back to the days of his introduction of gambling on live cockfights in Massachusetts and Rhode Island. It produced a growing income until the don squelched it for good business reasons. An interesting fact of life is that Aiello could populate Boston Harbor with more human bodies than mackerel, and only the *Boston Herald* would raise a ruckus to sell papers. On the other hand, one incident of cruelty to animals — including chickens — would ignite the wrath of a sizeable and voluble section of the populace. Not good for business, and business is all that matters. The cockfights ended, but the name "Chickie" stuck.

I took the envelope. Since she didn't actually ask who Anthony Aiello was, I saw no point in volunteering the information.

"I'm curious, Terry. Why did you decide against mailing it?"

"I don't trust any of those people John worked for. After he was killed, I didn't know what to do. That's why I thought of you. I know John trusted you."

I nodded and fingered the lump in the envelope.

"Unless you have second thoughts, let's take a look."

She indicated no qualms, so I tore open the envelope. There was a sheet of white typing paper with no words on either side. It simply held a well-worn tubular key with a yellow handle and the number 134E on it.

"It looks like a key to a pay locker. Probably one of the terminals. My guess is North or South Station. It looks too old for the new lockers at Logan Airport. Probably South Station. That was closest to John's office."

"What will you do with it? Are you going to send it to Mr. Aiello?"

"Under the circumstances, I don't think that's what John would have wanted. Why don't you leave this with me? The less involved you are, the better."

She took another deep breath. This time I could sense her relief in being out from under a burden she could not understand. I put the key in the top drawer of my desk. I was about to ask her if there was anything else, when the phone rang.

"Julie, have you still got the pope on hold?"

"He hung up. This time it's Mr. Devlin. He wants you."

"Put him through."

I heard the button click, and the voice meant business.

"The indictment's in. Let's go to work."

I saw my visitor to the door, but not until after taking her address and phone number in Winthrop across the harbor — just in case anything came up. I was in Mr. Devlin's office in three minutes flat. He was on the phone with Mr. Santangelo and waved me in. He did not put the conversation on speakerphone, which didn't surprise me. The arrangements they were making were delicate and confidential, quite possibly a matter of life or death.

When Mr. D. hung up, he seemed uneasy.

"I'd like to keep this simple, Michael. Why don't you meet me here at nine tonight? We'll be going for a ride. My car, you drive."

We took Route 9 west out of the city. Mr. D. called the lefts and rights. Two hours later, we pulled up behind the back door of a small jail facility on the east side of the City of Springfield. We turned out the lights and waited. About midnight, another car pulled up across the street from us. I didn't recognize the figure that got out of the car until Billy Coyne walked up beside the window. He nodded to both of us.

"Will he show, Lex?"

"You remember that autographed picture of Ted Williams in my office? The one you always wanted? I'll bet it against dinner at Locke-Ober's. Michael included. He'll show."

Billy leaned against the side of the door in silence. I could see the red glow as he lit up a cigarette.

"Can't hear you, Billy. Is it a bet?"

"You know gambling's illegal, Lex. You're soliciting a public official to commit a crime."

"In other words, no bet."

Billy took a deep draw on the cigarette. "The bet's on. But if I lose, I'll prosecute you."

"You can't. We're out of your jurisdiction."

We waited. Twenty minutes of silence. Mr. D. slouched down in the passenger seat with his eyes closed. Billy had climbed in the back-seat. We both jumped when Mr. D. broke the silence.

"Billy, that dinner includes drinks, before and after, right?"

"Doesn't seem to matter, does it? Your innocent lamb is probably half way to Sicily."

"Before and after, right?"

"Why not?"

"Good."

Mr. D. got out of the car for no reason apparent to me until I saw in the rearview mirror a faint light from a streetlamp glint on the black surface of a limousine without running lights. It moved slowly until it slid in behind us. Billy was out of the car behind me and dialing numbers on a cell phone. He whispered into the phone, "They're here."

The back door of the lock-up opened, and two uniformed officers came out onto the platform. We all watched as four dark double-breasted suits with plenty of Italian wool material to hide unnatural bulges got out of the limousine. The men were not massively large, but from their movements and the way they filled out the suits, they appeared to be athletic and well conditioned. They scanned the area for whatever could be seen in the darkness.

Mr. D. started to walk past them toward the limousine. Two of them blocked his path until the voice of the don gave the okay. He walked between them, and the back door of the limousine swung open. Mr. D. got in. He was there for five minutes before the door opened again. A slight figure, compared to the dark suits on either side of him, walked at a quick march up the stairs and into the building, accompanied by the two uniformed officers.

That was it. It was over. Mr. D. got back in the car, and after a few words about meeting the next day, Billy went back to his car.

On the way back to Boston, now that we could get our minds on something else, I took the time to fill him in on my visit from Terry O'Brien and the key that was sitting in my desk.

"What do you plan to do with it, Michael?"

"I'll check it out tomorrow morning. I think I've seen those keys at South Station."

He gave me a nod, and he was quiet the rest of the way back to the office. I stopped Mr. D's car in front of the parking garage where I always left my car. Before I got out, he turned and gave me that look that had a message behind it.

"Michael, you've got a good mind. I want you to use it every minute of the day while this is going on. These are no choirboys. They have the morality of a sledgehammer. I don't want you hurt. Again."

"I'll be careful, Mr. D."

He shook his head.

"Careful doesn't do it, Michael. I'm talking about being constantly defensive. There's a thought that's been waking me up nights."

He had my full attention.

"We keep assuming they deliberately killed John McKedrick."

"True. What else, Mr. Devlin?"

The look was intensifying.

"That Friday, you were about to get into that car. What if McKedrick hadn't started the car till you were in it?"

Surprisingly, the thought had actually never occurred to me. Maybe I'd been unconsciously rejecting it, but once out in the open, it hit me like a linebacker from the blind side. I had no answer.

"Think about it, Michael. It was more natural for him to wait till you got into the car to start the engine. What if John McKedrick was not the target?"

I forced down the acid that was slowly rising out of my stomach, and put on a steady voice.

"An interesting thought, Mr. D. But given our different lines of work, wasn't John a much more likely target?"

"I tell myself that at three every morning. It gives me precious little relief. What I'm saying is you watch every move you make till we get this sorted out. I want you alive and present someday at my retirement party."

I smiled. "I just want to be alive and present at that dinner at Locke-Ober's."

That brought the first smile I'd seen on Mr. D's face, forced or otherwise, since the world exploded.

I woke up the next day to one of those pull-the-covers-back-over mornings. A raw, dank mist crept in from the ocean to paint everything a depressing gray. It was hard to roll out of my apartment on Beacon and Dartmouth, but after a "black eye" at Starbucks — a double shot of espresso in a cup of black coffee — my personal fog began to lift.

Mr. D. beat me to the office. It was Saturday, but we usually worked at least a half-day. He seemed to have the nervous fidgets as we discussed questions we should ask our client.

The phone rang about quarter of nine. Mr. D. punched on the speakerphone. His secretary, Mrs. Hansberry, announced, "Mr. Devlin, it's the officer from Springfield."

"Thank you, Anne. Put him on."

"Mr. Devlin, this is Captain Martin."

I've never given myself credit for psychic powers, but the voice sent a chill from the tip of my spine up to the back of my neck and down again. There was the kind of tremor in the baritone voice that gave me the feeling he'd rather lock his grandmother in solitary than make this call.

"Captain Martin. I was about to call you. Is everything all right?"

"No, sir. Not . . . No, sir. I swear we did everything. We had everything covered. I can't explain it yet, but I'll get to the bottom of it."

I had a feeling he was pleading his case to someone beyond Mr. Devlin, and I could just imagine who that was.

"Bottom of what? Is Peter all right?"

"I can't . . ."

"Say it, man. Is he all right?"

Then the shoe fell.

"Sir, he's dead."

CHAPTER NINE

"We found him dead in his cell this morning at six o'clock. The cell door was open. His throat had been cut. Two guards were unconscious in the corridor outside the cell. We're doing all we can, but that's all we know right now."

Mr. Devlin was as stunned as I was, but he fired the right questions. "What was your prisoner count last night?"

"Twelve. Eleven were in the main block. Mr. Santangelo was alone in protective solitary."

"And this morning?"

"Full count. Counting Mr. Santangelo."

"How many guards were on duty last night?"

"Two. Plus Lieutenant Lewis in the central office. We're a small-town lockup, Mr. Devlin. The facility's underequipped. We took Mr. Santangelo as a favor to Mr. Coyne. We thought the primary protection was secrecy."

"As did we. Do you have video monitoring, Captain?"

"Yes, we do, but —"

"I don't think I want to hear this, Captain."

"The cameras covering the main block and solitary both malfunctioned. We're investigating now."

Mr. Devlin looked at me with an expression of total, hands-tied frustration.

"Let me know as soon as you learn anything. Has the boy's father been notified?"

"That's been more difficult than it sounds. There's no listed number or address for Mr. Santangelo, sir. We've kept it from the press until he can be notified."

Mr. Devlin closed his eyes and rubbed his forehead. I know he was trying to absorb the blow and cover every base at the same time. I scribbled a note and put it in front of him. He read it and asked the question.

"Do you have the videotapes that covered the front and back entrances to the lockup?"

"Yes, we do."

"Have you checked them? Did anyone come into the building or leave it after Mr. Santangelo arrived?"

"That was the first thing we did. No one entered or left the building all night after you were here."

"And you haven't a clue about movements of any of the other prisoners?"

"I can only say there was a full count in each cell last night and this morning. All cells were locked during that period. As I said, the videos in the —"

"Yeah, I know. Captain, you'll be getting calls from the press in about five minutes."

"Don't worry, Mr. Devlin. I won't say a word."

"Yes, you will, Captain. You'll tell them exactly what you've told me, including the fact that Mr. Santangelo was brought in last night in secrecy. Do you understand?"

"Yes, but I'll need clearance from Mr. Santangelo."

"You have it. I'm his attorney."

As soon as he hung up, Mr. Devlin made calls to news editors at both the *Globe* and *Herald*. He also notified the three major television stations and WBZ, the major news radio station. The word was brief. Call the captain in charge of the lockup facility in the city of Springfield just west of Worcester. Be prepared for a major story.

That done, he made the call that we could both have lived a full and happy life without experiencing. The speakerphone was on, and he left it that way when Dominic Santangelo came on the line.

"Dominic, it's Lex."

There was a heavy sigh on the other end. "I'm an old man, Lex. When you call me 'Dominic' instead of 'Dom' I know you're going to make me older still."

"Did we ever pull punches with each other?"

"No."

"There was a murder last night."

A pause, then "Yes?"

"I'm sorry, Dom."

There was a silence followed by one word.

"How?"

"It was quick, Dom. His throat was cut."

There was nothing but silence. Eventually, Mr. D. spoke very softly.

"I'm terribly sorry, Dom. I wish we had more time. We have to make some plans."

"I've tried your plans, Lex. I've even tried your law. I don't think they serve me very well. I'll keep my own counsel now. Good-bye once again, Lex."

"Dom, this won't go away. Before you do anything, meet with me and Matt. What can you lose? Just listen to me, and then do what you wish."

There was a heavy silence. We were at a fork in the road. Before a choice was made, Mr. Devlin spoke once more and then hung up.

"I'm leaving now, Dom. I'll be at Matt's church in half an hour. I'll wait there one hour."

When we pulled up in front of the Church of the Sacred Heart, there was no other car parked on the road within a block. Monsignor Ryan met us at the door and took us back to his office. Mr. Devlin excused himself to use the phone in the curate's office while we waited. When he returned, it was still just the three of us.

I could hear the seconds ticking on the wall clock. We had arrived at ten o'clock exactly. I knew that we'd be leaving at eleven o'clock exactly if no one showed up. I knew there was nothing left to do but listen to the ticking and pray. I also knew that if we left that office without some agreement with Mr. Santangelo, there would be a bloodbath across the streets of Boston and beyond that would dwarf the mob wars of the sixties.

At one minute past eleven o'clock. Mr. Devlin rose out of his chair. He looked — and I'd never thought of this word in connection with him — defeated.

"Thank you, Matt. It's in God's hands now."

"It always was, Lex."

We reached the office door, when the phone rang. Monsignor Ryan picked it up, said "Hello," and handed the receiver across to Mr. Devlin.

Mr. Devlin listened for a minute and simply said, "We'll wait."

We sat again without saying anything further. In about five minutes, the door opened and Mr. Santangelo came in. His complexion was gray, and there were no smiles. He stood just inside the door opposite Mr. Devlin.

"So, Lex. I'm here to listen."

"I'm glad you're here, Dom. I wasn't sure you'd give my way a chance."

"He didn't. I did."

The voice that came from the door behind Mr. Santangelo startled us all. There was a slender, dark-haired younger man looking intently at Mr. Devlin. Their eyes were locked, and when the young man approached, they came together with their arms around each other for a long moment. I couldn't hear the words that were whispered between them, but they were soft and seemed to express an affection that had aged roots.

When he turned back to me, Mr. Devlin said, "Michael, I'd like you to meet my godson. This is Peter Santangelo."

CHAPTER TEN

I looked at Mr. Devlin. It was hard to hide my sense of lack of trust in not being let in on the game plan.

Mr. Devlin understood.

"It was an oath, Michael. Last night, when we met the car outside the lockup, only Dominic and a young man who looked like Peter were in the car. That was the first I knew of it. It was a reasonable precaution. Nobody there knew what Peter looked like. Dominic made me swear to tell no one, absolutely no one. In a few days, if all went well, Peter would take his place in the cell."

It made sense, but it needed to sink in deeper to fully dissolve my initial reaction. If nothing else, the remains of the edge that I felt made me less subdued in the awesome presence of Don Dominic Santangelo. In my unfounded confidence, I put the question. "Who was it that actually died in that cell, Mr. Santangelo?"

"A young man who worked for me. A very brave, very loyal young man. I'll miss him very much. I'll see that his family is taken care of, but the loss is very deep."

Mr. Devlin spoke softly. "They've begun an investigation, Dom. I'll let you know what they find."

Mr. Santangelo waved his hand as if dismissing the idea. "I don't need their investigation. It's being taken care of."

My imagination filled in the vagueness of that statement and sent a chill through my nervous system.

"Dom, what you're thinking about is going to play very badly in Peter's case."

"Peter's case may be going no further than this. In any event, this other matter involves treachery in my own family. It can't be tolerated. There are doors to be closed."

I could see the lines deepen on Mr. Devlin's face. I could read the disgust he felt for Santangelo's world where violence was an instant substitute for the law. If Peter had not been his primary concern, he might well have walked clear of the whole situation. I could see him narrowing his focus.

"Then at least listen to me about Peter. He's under indictment for murder. He'll have no life in hiding. We can get him into safe custody. I told you. I have an alternative. Will you listen?"

"I always listen, Lex. But I'll decide for myself what's in the best interest of my son."

"I'll stake my life on Billy Coyne. His word is like mine, and yours. I just talked to him on the phone. He'll work with people he can trust in the federal system. We can get Peter protective custody in the federal witness protection program. You must know from experience that even you can't break that security."

I recalled witnesses whose testimony had put two of Don Santangelo's capos in prison. They might not have lived to testify if the don had been able to breach the security of the federal witness protection program. Mr. Devlin added a final point.

"Hear me, Dom. I've seen to it that the report of Peter's death will be in every newspaper and television newscast by tonight. Even the DA's office, with the exception of Billy Coyne, doesn't know that Peter's alive. We can have him in safe quarters before we put out the truth. It'll take one call. If we delay, we could lose that advantage."

We all looked at the man who had built an empire and beaten the odds against staying alive by trusting no one outside of his professional family. I believe it would have weighed less heavily on his mind if it had been his own life at stake instead of his son's.

It was clear to us all that Santangelo was turning over the option of smuggling his son out of the country into friendly hands, probably in Sicily. We also knew that while it might have kept his son alive, it would deprive him of a life. Peter was an American with a promising future after college. There was no such future in Sicily.

We all looked at Santangelo, but the first one to speak was Peter. "Let's go, Uncle Lex. We'll try it your way."

We still looked to Santangelo, who had his arm on Peter's shoulder. He looked at Peter, but he spoke to us. I could see him straining under the words.

"Peter is twenty-two-years-old. He's a man now. A man makes his own decisions. One thing. Word of this goes no further than this room, and Mr. Coyne, and the federal agents in the program until Peter's safety is secured. Do we have your sacred word on that?"

We all agreed.

Mr. Devlin made the call to Billy who had already made the arrangements. The federal authorities were willing to cooperate in exchange for favors of cooperation that Billy could provide in other prosecutions. A transfer point outside of Boston was agreed on. Mr. Devlin, as Peter's attorney, was given a telephone number to memorize through which he could transfer messages to and from Peter.

The four of us, Mr. Santangelo, Peter, Mr. Devlin, and I, rode together in Mr. Santangelo's limousine to the hand-off spot. One of Mr. Santangelo's men drove Mr. D's car behind us.

During the ride, we tuned the radio to the all-news station. We were pleased to hear the report of the murder the previous night of the son of "reputed" mob patriarch, Dominic Santangelo. That suited our situation.

What was less suitable, and, in fact, considerably disturbing to Mr. Devlin and me, was the follow-up report that one night-shift guard and three prisoners in the same lockup had been found dead that afternoon. Each had thirty dollars stuffed in his mouth and a knife in his back. No one beats the Mafia for symbolism. Thirty pieces of silver was the price of Jesus's betrayer, Judas. The knife in the back underlined the point.

We listened in silence, but I knew Mr. Devlin and I were sharing the same thoughts. When we were admitted to the bar, we had sworn an oath to uphold the law. When the news report ended, Mr. Devlin continued to look out the window, but his words were slow and deliberate and carried unquestionable conviction.

"Michael and I will defend my godson, Dominic. We'll use every legal defense in our power. We'll do this because he is no part of this despicable empire of yours. When it ends, you'll do me one last favor. And that will be my fee. You will never call me again for any service as long as we live."

There was silence, until Mr. Santangelo addressed me.

"Michael, you and I and your partner, my old friend, are all from different heritages. Yes, I have power. I use the power to produce justice as I see it. Which of us is right?"

I started to speak, but he held up a hand.

"Consider, Michael. Not too long ago a man came to me, as many do. His daughter, a very beautiful young child of thirteen, the very soul of his life, just beginning her life. She was at school after classes to take part in a play. Three boys took her into an empty men's room. I needn't be graphic. When she recovered enough emotional stability to do so, with her father's encouragement, she went to the police. They arrested these boys. They confessed what they did. But your law said that their confession could not be used as evidence. Something about not warning them to remain silent. In any event they were tried. Their lawyer made this man's daughter break down when she testified. He made suggestions about this young lady's virtue that were not true. The jury found them not guilty."

"Mr. Santangelo, there are hundreds —"

"Please, Michael, just listen. I'm not talking about hundreds. I'm talking about this man and his daughter. This man who was nearly insane with grief. When his daughter was able to go back to school, these same boys taunted her. They threatened to do the same thing again. And get away with it again. Her father went to the police. They told him that until these boys do something, their hands are tied. This young lady could not bring herself to go to school, any school. She's still undergoing treatment by a psychiatrist. Whether successful or not, who knows. In any event, in all of your civilized legal system, where is the justice for this man and his daughter?"

I had no answer.

"Then consider this, before you judge me to be a complete savage. When this man came to me and put his trust in me, I gave him my word — nothing more — which he believed, and his daughter came to believe, that no one would harm her again. She's now able to attend school. The healing is going on. She has young friends around her. God willing, she'll grow to be a beautiful woman with a good life. She has had no further difficulty in this respect from anyone."

I had to fill the gap. "Did you have them killed?"

"No. They are very much alive. I'm sure they'll grow up to cause many more problems for society. But I can assure you that raping young women will not be one of which they'll be capable. Do you understand?"

"Yes."

"Then consider this. Which power, mine or yours, produced justice?"

We rode in silence. I considered making the case for a democratic republic over a self-justifying tyrant whose every unquestioned whim was enforced in blood. I considered asking the don how many times he had used that power of violence for personal profit as opposed to unselfish justice. I also considered the futility of trying to convince this little Caesar that he somehow fell short of Solomon judging the Israelites. I vetoed all of it. There was no point in turning a very dicey moment into a high school civics class. The silence that reigned was noncommittal on both sides.

We drove north to the parking lot of the Continental Restaurant on Route 1 in Saugus. By that time, the lunch crowd was moderate. In a sense, the glaring openness of a sun-drenched public parking lot was our cover.

We pulled up next to an unmarked, dark blue Chrysler Concorde at the far east end of the lot. Two federal agents in sport clothes came from the Concorde to the side of our car. Peter showed no hesitation in joining them. We let them drive out of the parking lot before Mr. Devlin and I took his car that had been driven behind us back to the office.

I only touched base long enough to retrieve the yellow locker key from the top drawer of my desk. I waved and smiled at Julie on the way out, in the futile hope that that would be the extent of any delaying conversation. She waved back. Unfortunately, there was a message slip in her hand.

On the way down in the elevator, I took a moment to scan the note Julie had handed me. It was a message she had taken over the phone. Somehow it gave me the urge to wash my hands.

Michael: It's time. And time is shorter than you think. We should talk. I'll expect your call.
Benny Ignola

CHAPTER ELEVEN

When I got back to my Corvette in the Devonshire Street parking lot, I had one of those stand-still moments when you suddenly become aware of the nerves lining your stomach and the up-tempo beat of your heart. Mr. D's advice about living defensively was good. The only question was how to do it.

I sat there with the key in the lock, about to give it that slight twist that could either start the car or blow me into pieces too small to reassemble. I told myself that unquestionably John McKedrick was the only target of the bomber. The trouble with talking to myself is that I know the fallibility of the source.

There were only two alternatives. I could hire a mechanic to search sections of my car that I can't even pronounce every time I start the engine. Or I could just get on with life. I chose the latter, but not without some stomach ripples and a prayer of thanks as I drove out of the parking lot.

I drove to South Station with that little yellow key in my pocket. I imagined that if John was hiding something in a locker, he probably chose a location close to his office, heavily populated by an anonymous crowd. It also squared with a faint memory that on the wall of the large waiting room of South Station there were rows of pay lockers, each of which had a yellow-handled circular key like that hot little item in my pocket with the number 134E.

I scanned the crowd for someone who might be waiting for some naïve goofus to amble up to that particular locker, open it, pull out heaven knows what, and walk into his arms. The problem was that I had no way of guessing whom John might have told about the location of the locker. I was sure it held more than John's lunch or he wouldn't have played spy games with Terry O'Brien. The comforting thing was that this was one situation where being defensive was something I had some control over.

I limited the scanning to men since John's business contacts were completely with one organization, and the *Cosa Nostra* has never really embraced the feminist movement. That cut the possibles to nine, of whom five could possibly fit my personal profile of a sit-and-wait Mafia soldier. I eliminated two because they were reading books. The type I was looking for was unlikely to be curled up behind anything more demanding than the sports section of the *Herald*.

That left three. There was only one sure way to eliminate the nonplayers. I waited through a succession of train departures to see who was actually there to catch a train. One left at the call for Hartford, and after a patient half hour, a second answered the call for New York.

And there sat number three. He looked like a fireplug with ears. I visualized him standing and estimated five foot eleven inches, two hundred twenty pounds of solid muscle. I had no way of physically prying him off of his watch. On the other hand, I had a couple of pieces of information.

The rows of seats backed up to each other in opposite directions. By that time, there were only a few people sitting in that section.

I bought a newspaper and slipped into the seat backing up to my new friend. I came from the direction of his back so he couldn't see my face. I turned my head till my mouth was about six inches from his left ear and whispered.

"Hey. Change in plans. You listening?"

He started to turn back to me.

"Don't turn around. Just listen. Mr. Aiello sent me."

John McKedrick's envelope with the key was addressed to Tony Aiello. That suggested that he might be the brains behind the block of beefsteak behind me.

I thought the "Mr. Aiello" was a nice touch. It suggested that we both worked for him, since no one who didn't, or who wasn't face-to-face with him, referred to him as "Mr. Aiello," as opposed to "Chickie," or, if safely out of earshot, "Fat Tony."

It apparently worked for the moment, since he stopped in mid-turn.

"Who the hell are you?"

"Keep your voice down. I'm the one who was sent by Mr. Aiello to tell you you're at the wrong station. It's North Station. "

Unfortunately, he dug in.

"Go to hell. He told me South Station. I don't know you."

"I don't know you either, but if that thing leaves the locker at North Station and you miss it, you won't be around long enough to get acquainted. You know how he is."

That left him in total befuddlement. I could feel every brain cell being overtaxed. Unfortunately, he decided to make the one move I wanted the least. He reached into his pocket and pulled out a cell phone. There was only one counter move that occurred to me. It was like a fast-draw fight in a western saloon. I pulled out my own cell phone and punched in numbers before he could do the same. I talked to him while I dialed.

"I'm calling Mr. Aiello. He can tell you himself. I wouldn't take too long to chat. He expects you to be halfway to North Station by now."

Before he could move, I started talking to my dead cell phone.

"Mr. Aiello. It's me. (pause) Not too good. I gave him the message. He said, 'Go to hell.' I don't know if he meant me or you."

That spun him around.

"Gimme that phone."

I stayed out of reach.

"Take it easy, Mr. Aiello. I'll tell him."

I shut the phone just as he was about to grab it out of my hand.

"Here's the message. He's sending two men to do your job at North Station. If you're not there when they get there, they'll have another job after they finish. I think you get his meaning. I don't think he was happy with you."

I could feel him on his feet behind me. His first choice was to take my head off at the shoulders, but somehow the message got through that his head was not sitting too securely on his own shoulders. I held the *Globe* up in front of my face as he acted on his second choice and lumbered a body not built for speed across the room at full tilt.

I was well into giving myself a mental high-five when I made a mistake I regretted instantly. The last thing he did on the way out the door was to look back just as I dropped the newspaper. He had a fleeting, but full, view of my face.

I could feel worms wrestling in the pit of my stomach, but when he disappeared, I knew the moment I wanted was there and might not last. I used the key to open locker 134E in the hopes of finding out what all the fuss was about.

It was empty, except for a small white business-size envelope. I tore it open and found a white 3 × 5 card inside with nothing on it but a series of numbers and letters printed by hand in black ball-point ink.

808PW53942

I ran outside to a nearby drugstore that sold paper supplies. I bought a box of the same type of blank white envelope, a packet of white 3 × 5 cards, and a black ballpoint pen. I used one of the cards to write the same type of code in the same way, except that I changed all of the numbers and letters. I placed the card in the white envelope and licked and sealed the envelope so it would look unopened. I put the envelope into the same locker and pumped in quarters to rerent it. I took the key with me.

For some reason not fully thought out by me at the time, I put quarters into the locker beside it, number 135E, put another white envelope with a 3 × 5 card with yet another altered number into that one. I took that key with me as well. I considered it a backup just in case of who knows what.

I'd like to say that all of this rigamarole was part of a grand master plan, but the fact is that I was flying by the seat of my pants, trying to make no mistakes I'd live to regret.

An exit opposite the one I came in brought me out into the Saturday night traffic. The night air and the ability to move at a relaxed pace felt good. It gave me time to wonder what pressure must have been gripping my old friend, John, the day he dropped that little envelope in locker 134E. It was practically the last thing he did on this earth.

On Monday morning, when I reached the office, my first check-in was with Julie. She put on a sweet, coy little smile and winked at me. She had my attention.

"You have a visitor."

My heart went into overdrive. Terry O'Brien must have thought of something else.

With one deep breath for confidence, I walked to the door of my office. I was focusing on my best entrance, suave but understated. One quick check of my tie, and I looked in. There in the seat once occupied by the auburn-haired Helen of Troy sat the unkempt lump that was Benny Ignola.

I caught myself in mid-entrance long enough to mouth the words to Julie, "You're fired."

She wrinkled her mouth and thumbed her nose at me, which was her usual response to my firings.

Benny stood when I came in. I was behind my desk before the need arose to shake hands as if we were colleagues.

"Benny, sit down. How are you?"

"Fine, Mikey. And how's yourself?"

How can an innocuous question like that be made to sound sleazy and conspiratorial? Benny had the knack.

"I'm all right. What brings you here?"

"I'm passing the office, and it occurs to me. We should be co-operating."

"Really, Benny. With whom?"

"With each other. C'mon, Mikey. We're on the same side. Johnny Mac was my boy. I loved the kid."

When he reduced John McKedrick to Johnny Mac, my temperature went up six degrees. He made him sound like one of those parasites in the bowels of society known as wiseguys. I got a grip by taking a gummy bear out of the jar that Julie kept filled on my desk and biting its little head off. Benny continued undeterred.

"For example, Mikey, did Johnny say anything before he died? Did he give you any idea who might have done it?"

"Between the explosion and the fire, there wasn't a lot of conversation."

"I mean the day before. Maybe that morning. Even if it doesn't seem relevant now, could tie into something."

"We didn't talk business, Benny. No offense, but John knew what I thought of what he did for a living. He never brought the subject up. It was mostly Bruins, Celtics, Red Sox, Patriots, whatever the season."

I couldn't tell whether he was disappointed or had had his wish fulfilled. Either way, I guess he felt he had drained this shallow well dry. He rose with a smile and extended a hand. What Benny lacked in charm, he made up in hypocrisy. It was clearly no mutual admiration society, but he played the part of "Uncle Benny" like a pro.

"Hey, Mikey. If anything comes up, you know my number. By the same token, vice versa."

When he turned to go, I let him open the door. I slipped the second locker key, the one to my back-up locker 135E, out of my pocket and pulled open my middle desk drawer. I fumbled around as if I were looking for something that had been thrown in there days ago.

"Hey, Benny."

He turned around. I flipped him the backup key. He stabbed at it with his left hand and missed. The little thing skidded across the floor under Julie's desk. Like a weasel chasing a rat down its hole, Benny went groveling on his hands and knees under Julie's desk. Julie came three feet straight up out of her chair.

She gave me a bewildered look, to which I responded with a shoulder shrug.

Meanwhile Benny emerged from under Julie's desk examining

his newfound treasure through his bifocals. I added the explanation. "John mailed that to me. I guess the day before the bombing. I got it when I got back from the hospital."

That was about as accurate as any information that passed between Benny and myself.

"What is it?"

"It's a key, Benny."

"I mean what's it to?"

"I haven't a clue. I put it in my desk till I had time to check it out. So far I haven't had time. It can't do John any good, and it has nothing to do with me. You might as well have it. It's probably got something to do with whatever you two were doing."

"Yeah. Looks like a locker key. I wonder where."

"Beats me, Benny. Looks like one of those train station locker keys. Maybe South Station. I don't know. It's no longer my problem."

I was already flipping through my Rolodex while Benny beat his little crab-walk retreat to the elevator. I could hear him poking the eye out of the elevator button to speed it up.

I dialed the phone number of Tom Burns, one-time Navy SEAL, one-time FBI, currently Sam Spade, Spenser, Mike Hammer, and every other full-varsity private eye rolled into one. His rates would make Kobe Bryant seem underpaid, but he was worth every dime of it. He was also a mere five foot ten, and one hundred sixty pounds of Brooks Brothers understated elegance. He could sip cocktails with Hillary at the Four Seasons or slip into jeans and slug down beers with stevedores at a dive on the docks, and blend.

Tom's cell phone rang while I watched through the window as Benny scuttled across the sidewalk, examining the little object of mystery in his sweaty fingers. My sincere hope was that with my loosely dropped suggestion, Benny's devious mind locked onto South Station. I was working on mental telepathy, when Tom's secretary answered. I had done enough expensive business with Tom so she recognized my voice. My tone of urgency got me through to the man in six seconds.

"Tom, am I your favorite client?"

"Definitely. Who is this?"

"Very funny. Would you drop everything to make me happy?"

"No."

"Would you drop everything to keep me alive?"

"Possibly, Mike."

"Would you drop everything if I double your rate?"

"Of course."

"Get on your horse to South Station, east wing. Call me on your cell phone on the way. I'll fill you in while you move."

My heart leaped for joy when I looked down and saw Benny double time it across Franklin Street and disappear around the corner in the direction of South Station.

The phone rang, and I had it before the first ring ended.

"Thanks, Tom. Here's what I want."

CHAPTER TWELVE

By two p.m., after soothing the feathers of neglected clients and opposing counsel, my stomach was in a perfect state of acidity to accommodate my weakness for two of those cholesterol torpedoes peddled as hotdogs by the vender a block away on Summer Street.

The level of acidity got another jolt at the thought of a meeting with Mr. Devlin, in which I could count on catching heat for even dreaming of doing what I was contemplating for the rest of the afternoon.

But if it were all put together, it would not come near the stomach clenching I was getting at the mere thought of picking up the telephone to ask Terry O'Brien to join me for dinner. For the life of me, I couldn't understand why it had that effect. It was definitely not a date. It was too soon after John's death, and I had no idea of how deeply they were committed to each other. It was just an occasion to ask a few questions about the case in an atmosphere that might give us both a little break from reality.

Having reached the foregone conclusion that she would probably turn me down, I was happily stunned when she accepted.

I set it up for seven o'clock and a drive up to a restaurant on the North Shore. When the receiver hit the cradle, I clamped a lid on the rush of exhilaration with the reminder that she was the possible fiancée of my very recently lost best friend.

Mr. Devlin took the story of my retrieval from the locker of what could be a significant piece in the puzzle of John's death with a faint grin. The news that I had passed the key off to Benny Ignola was received somewhat less enthusiastically.

"What in the damn fires of everlasting hell possessed you to give it to that microbe, Ignola? And without a word to me!"

At that point he took a breath. I jumped in with a stream of words that left no seams for him to break in.

"Mr. Devlin, just settle back and listen for ten seconds. I had a reason. Benny came sniffing around as if he thought that John had given something to me. If I read him right, I left him with the idea that I passed it on to him, and he still thinks I never saw anything but the key. On top of that, what he actually has is useless."

"And could you explain that?"

"He has the key to the wrong locker. I rented the one beside the locker John used. I put in a duplicate envelope with a white card with the same kind of code on it. But it's the wrong code. It'll lead them nowhere."

He was settled back in his tilt-back desk chair. His Irish flash temper was now replaced by dour concern.

"Would you bet your life on that, Michael? Because that could be what's at stake here. There are no rules in this game."

I was still catching up, and the look on my face must have shown it.

"Michael, that number is probably the pass code to a bank vault somewhere. Maybe Switzerland, maybe the Caymans. Is that a fair guess?"

"Chances are."

"And are the chances also that whatever is in that vault is enough to knock the socks off of whoever gets to it?"

"I'd say."

"And when your phony number code runs Benny and his play-mates into a deadend, who do you suppose they'll come looking for, and this time not to play nice?"

Events had been moving at a pretty fair clip, and I had to admit to myself that I hadn't plotted the moves that far ahead. I'd been con-centrating on the offensive game and neglecting the defense.

I groped for the bright side.

"Maybe. But didn't you tell me that the best defense is a good offense? Benny's on his way to South Station. I have Tom Burns on his tail right now. Benny's not subtle. He'll pick up the envelope and fly direct to whoever's pulling his strings. If it's not Dominic Santangelo, and my guess is that it's not or he'd have asked us about the key, we could be onto a split in Santangelo's so-called family. That could give us a lead on who's framing Peter for John's death. If we strike first, they won't have time to come back at us."

Silence reigned while we both let the air clear. The cease-fire was short lived. In about eight seconds, Mr. D. slammed the arms of his chair on his way up.

"Damn it, Michael! I don't like it. None of this is worth —"

"We're talking about something that may never happen, Mr. Devlin. I really think that whatever those numbers lead to is the ace John was about to play to buy his way out. We're the only ones who have the real code number. If John could use it to bargain, so could we."

"Could I remind you how much good it did John? And while we're at it, could you tell me, bargain with whom?"

"I don't know. John must have been meeting with someone in Santangelo's organization that day. Santangelo was out of the country. He didn't get back from Sicily until the next morning. So who does that leave?"

He turned back toward the window facing Boston Harbor, his favorite thinking position.

"You said the envelope was addressed to Tony Aiello. Word has it he's the number-two man under Dominic. Maybe this is something Aiello was handling alone. He came up through the ranks together with Dominic. Dominic climbed a little faster. But they're like brothers."

"I thought you lost touch with Mr. Santangelo through all those years."

I could see a cloud forming.

"I saw him one other time. Aiello was there."

"When was that?"

He waived the question away with his hand.

"It doesn't matter. It was a long time ago." He turned back to me. "That envelope with the number. You said it was in a public locker. John McKedrick gave the key to this Terry O'Brien. His girl-friend?"

I felt a strange jump in the stomach that I chose to ignore. "Possibly. Or fiancée. I may know more tonight. I'm having dinner with her."

That brought his eyebrows up a quarter-inch higher.

"Pure business, Mr. Devlin."

The eyebrows rose another quarter inch, and his eyes were on me.

"Where are you having dinner?"

"North Shore. Maybe the Pegleg up in Rockport."

"Uh-huh." The man was no fool, as the growing smile beneath the eyebrows told me. The hour drive up to Rockport for a conversation that could be held in my office apparently suggested sentiments that I chose not to examine.

"Anyway, you're right, Mr. Devlin. John gave the envelope addressed to Aiello to Terry. She was supposed to mail it if anything happened to John. When it did, she didn't know whom to trust. That's why she brought it to me."

The smile was gone. It was back to the war council.

"Anything make you feel uncomfortable about that arrangement, Michael?"

There was something else. But I wasn't sure I wanted to go there. On the other hand, if I didn't, Mr. D. would.

"Yes. I don't understand the game John was playing. If he was using that code for leverage, he was playing for his life. If Terry was his fiancée, or something like it, why would he get her involved in something with those risks?"

"That's the question."

"That was one of the reasons I wanted to get that key into Benny Ignola's hands with the impression that none of us, Terry included, knew what it was."

Mr. D. nodded. "Do you think you brought it off?"

I gave him a palms-up gesture. "Benny seemed to take the bait. We should be hearing from Tom Burns where he went with it. I'm going to keep an eye on Terry in case things get dicey."

"You keep an eye on yourself too, Michael. Quicker minds than Benny's will probably be asking these same questions. You remember you're a lawyer. You're not the Marine Corps."

I held up my hands in surrender. "Just taking the lady to dinner."

He looked unconvinced.

"Also, I saved a trump card, Mr. Devlin. I made up another envelope with a card inside of it. The number on that one is the wrong code too. I put it in the original locker and I have the key. If I need a bargaining chip, it might be useful. It still won't lead them to anything."

Time was fleeing, and I knew I had an uncomfortable little call to pay before picking up Terry at seven. The less said to Mr. D. about it the better. I chose that moment to take an obvious glance at my watch and bound out of the chair.

"I have to run, Mr. Devlin. I'll let you know what I hear from Tom."

"Where are you off to now, Michael?"

"Dinner. North Shore. Gotta rush."

I was into the hall and approaching the elevator

"Michael, it's four in the afternoon."

"I have one stop in between."

I was pushing the elevator button, probably with more force than necessary. Mr. D. was in the doorway of his office with every antenna getting signals that I was up to something he wouldn't like.

"What stop, Michael?"

Thank God, the elevator door swung open. I stepped inside and pushed the ground-floor button. As the door swung slowly shut, I squeezed out the words, "I'm going to drop in on Anthony Tedesco at The Pirate's Den in Revere. I think we should find out where he got the courage to be an informant on the Mafia."

The elevator door mercifully closed and muffled the explosion I had expected. I felt two senses of relief. First, I could pretend not to have heard the absolute edict of Mr. D. to stay out of that rats' nest. Secondly, I was deep-down thrilled that someone who cared knew where I was going — just in case I didn't appear in the office the next day. Or ever.

CHAPTER THIRTEEN

Revere Beach comes in two delicious varieties. On any hot summer day, the wide sandy beach is blanketed by mostly Italian and Jewish families burning to a crisp in the relentless sun. An occasional sub-teenager with the constitution of an Eskimo will plunge into those Atlantic waters that even in summer are the temperature of a barely melted glacier. For the most part, it's just families cooking themselves to anything from medium rare to well done.

In contrast, previous to the nineteen nineties, the street above the beach vibrated to the constant rumble of Harley-Davidsons. The strip of bars and pizza shops were populated by a subgroup of humanity that looked like extras from the *X-Files*. The standard uniform was leathers with sawed-off vests that bore the colors of biker gangs and skin tattooed from shoulders to fingernails.

Sometime in the late eighties, the dealers in real estate woke up to the treasure that was being squandered on cavemen. They had the money, and therefore the political clout, to clean house and put up high-rise glass condos that reaped the value of oceanfront lots with a direct view of England.

The Cro-Magnons of earlier days were squeezed into pockets of the shoreline north of the new Revere Beach. One of these establishments was the biker bar called "The Pirate's Den."

A quick phone call to an old friend in the Registry of Deeds saved some travel time in confirming Billy Coyne's statement that The Pirate's Den was owned by one Anthony Tedesco. What didn't square, and what had been jangling my sense of the likely, was Billy's statement that Tony Tedesco had filed a complaint with the police against Sal Marone for extortion.

The extortion part was self-evident. Every club on the strip, including The Pirate's Den, was reputed to be paying tribute to the Mafia to avoid an accidental bombing. Any streetwise thirteen-year-old kid in Revere could have told us that. What defied logic was that little Anthony Tedesco had suddenly summoned the suicidal courage to bring a criminal charge against one tentacle of the octopus that had had him in its grip since the club opened.

Someone clearly had to personally penetrate The Pirate's Den, and given the cast of characters, it looked as if I were the logical penetrator.

It was around six o'clock in the evening. The sun was descending on a day that had been unseasonably warm. The line of Harleys racked up on either side of the door of The Pirate's Den told me that happy hour was underway.

I pulled my Corvette, top down, to a stop crosswise in the no parking space directly in front of the door. I was flanked on either side by tattooed hulks and their hulkettes, leaning on kick-standed cycles, beer bottles in hand.

I mustered every ounce of Puerto Rican cool I could draw from my mother's ancestry and stepped out of the car without haste and without hesitation. I had changed into the most expensive, dark blue, Italian worsted wool suit I had in my wardrobe. It was, in fact, the only Italian wool suit I had in my wardrobe. My understated swagger said otherwise.

There wasn't an eye in any hairy face in the crowd that wasn't taking in every inch. I was about as in sync as Prince Charles at a slam dance.

And that was the idea. I prayed that every move of every barely-in-control feature would radiate the signal—This dude is connected. Don't touch.

I moved with unhurried deliberateness directly to the door without wasting a glance at any of the palace guard. I caught a glimpse of one of the younger ones rising off his bike and moving toward the car. An older hand with scars on every knuckle caught him by the shoulder and settled him back down. I thanked God and prayed at the same time that I'd soon find a men's room.

I passed through the door knowing that if one chink showed in the masquerade, I'd be fodder for the mackerel off the Revere shore, one piece at a time.

The inside was a dark, dank replica of some bar in Tombstone with a few touches of the *Pirates of the Caribbean*. The air, what there was of it, hung heavy with the stench of beer and sweat.

My entrance stilled the place with the pall of a sudden quiet. Every eye was on the creature from civilization. I moved slowly and deliberately to the bar without a wasted step and no eye contact whatsoever. The pool game on my left stopped, and beer bottles rested where they were. I felt a ball of acid rising from the bottom of my stomach to the back of my throat.

Without even a side-glance, I could see that this was not a random collection of misfits. Every misfit in the place wore the colors of the Satans. Even other bikers had sense enough not to wander into The Pirate's Den — only the kid in the Italian wool suit, feeling very much like an anchovy on a Ritz cracker, being served up as an hors d'oeuvre.

There was a mirror behind the bartender. It gave me a perfect view behind me of two particular masses of flesh with chains in each hand moving into position to block the door. I knew that the only way out intact was to stay the course.

When I reached the bar, I was looking into the hairy face of the six-foot three-inch bartender. He was glaring back at a gnat in a blue suit. Thank God he spoke first.

"You're a little far from Beacon Hill, ain't you, Percival?"

I returned the look and let five seconds go by in silence for whatever unsettling effect it might have on him. None was visible.

When I spoke, it was quiet, cool, and in control. I said one word. "Tedesco."

He looked around at the fifteen or so racks of muscles wearing the colors, including the two at the door, and then back at me.

"You mean *Mr.* Tedesco, Percival."

I dropped the voice to another level of softness to emphasize the point.

"Your *Mr.* Tedesco is being given other titles even as we speak by people he would not like to offend."

I caught the slightest freeze in the sarcastic grin on his face. That was enough to send my motor into the next gear. I reduced the volume yet one more notch as I played my last card. The surface was cool, but I was squeezing the Saint Anthony medal in my suitcoat pocket until the saint must have been writhing in pain.

"Tell *Mr.* Tedesco that someone he knows is very displeased with the way he carried it off. You might say I'm here with a policy of life insurance. Take your time. I have another thirty seconds to waste on this business."

The grin was gone. The mean was there, but it was mixed with a grain of confusion. That was all I could ask. He picked up a phone behind the bar and turned his back. I could hear him punch one number, which meant it was an intercom. Tedesco was on the premises.

A door at the side of the bar opened. A dark, balding figure about five foot five waddled along behind the bar. He looked like a child's drawing of a man — one large circle for the body, another smaller circle for the head without benefit of a neck in between. The bushy moustache was, to me, a thing of beauty. It meant he was southern Italian and old enough to be of the old school in his understanding of Mafia ways. That meant to me that he'd get my drift without my having to dream up specific details.

He waddled splayfoot to stand beside the bartender. I had the honest pleasure of facing off with someone I could look down to. It was amazingly comforting.

"I'm Tedesco. Who are you?"

"I'm your life insurance salesman." I'd grown to like that concept.

"You had a simple assignment. You screwed it up. He's deciding what to do about it right now."

His Italian skin lost some of its olive glow. I was apparently right about his filling in the blanks. Beads of sweat began to appear on his forehead to match the drops of battery acid that were percolating in my stomach. He leaned as far over the bar as his girth would allow.

"I did just what Benny Ig—"

"Tedesco!" I caught him in mid-sentence. "You throw out names in a public place?"

He backed off the bar like a kid with his finger in the cake icing. He snapped a command at the bartender who was by now standing slack jawed and totally clueless as to why this pissant in the blue suit was sending his boss into sweating fits on his own turf.

Tedesco snarled an order out of the side of his mouth. The gorilla in the apron retreated into the backroom.

Meanwhile, I had exactly what I came for. When he mentioned Benny Ignola's name it was clear that he was the contact. Benny was the messenger who delivered the order for Tedesco to turn Salvatore Marone over to the police for extortion. That started the chain of dominoes falling into place. Marone was then in a position to deal the name of Mike Simone to the D.A. as the bomber who killed John McKedrick. Once the D.A. made the arrest, Simone could deal his way to a manageably low sentence by fingering Peter Santangelo as the one who gave the order for the bombing. It was all part of a plan. That was why little Anthony Tedesco had the courage to buck the Mafia by ratting on Marone for extortion. He did it under orders from someone high up in the "family."

The real question was who was pulling Benny Ignola's strings and why. I was sure little Tedesco was not brought into the loop on that information. My next goal was to get my unkilled body out of Revere as successfully as I had bluffed my way in.

With the bartender gone, we could speak privately. I could see the level of panic rising in Tedesco's eyes as the possibilities sank in. His throat was so tight he was hissing the words.

"I did what I was told."

"Listen to me, Anthony. Tony. May I call you Tony?" I didn't wait for an answer. "Listen to me, Tony, and look me right in the eye. You were about to be — replaced. You understand what I'm saying? I said, wait a minute, why waste an asset? Tony's been okay for a lot of years. One mistake. Would it hurt if I met with him just once? Maybe he can fix it."

"What mistake? What did I do? I followed orders."

"Tony, are you listening to me?"

He seemed confused, but he nodded.

"This is an act of mercy. What you see on the bumper stickers, a 'random act of kindness.' He likes to do that kind of thing maybe once a week. This week you're it."

"What does that mean?"

"It means you'll meet with Benny tomorrow. Noontime. Same place."

I figured that Benny Ignola would have needed to be wearing Depends to walk into The Pirate's Den. He must have set up his meeting with Tedesco someplace closer to Benny's safe ground. Sometimes it pays to throw a wild pitch to see if the batter swings at it.

"That's the life insurance, Tony. It's a one-time offer. It expires tomorrow if you don't show. *Capisce?*"

"Yeah. Yeah."

"That's all."

I turned around to close out the longest five minutes of my entire life. I saw the two primates with the chains still barring the door. I played one more card, the last one in my deck. I looked back at Tedesco and motioned to the two slabs of beef with my chin as if they weren't worthy of a hand signal. I gave a head motion that I hoped would be interpreted as "Get those two out of here."

My newfound friend, Tony, caught the signal. One sweep of his hand and they backed off the door.

I gave Tony the coolest look I could muster on a tank that was now running on fumes.

"Noon."

He just nodded.

I began the trek across the floor to the door and freedom without a glance to either side. One thought propelled one foot ahead of the other. It was six thirty.

CHAPTER FOURTEEN

It was ten to seven when I found the address Terry had given me on Andrew Street in Winthrop on the North Shore of Boston. The small, neat house laid just a quiet stretch of beach away from the serene, rolling expanse of the Atlantic.

For a few seconds, I let my mind play with the notion that if Terry chose to live in the lap of Mother Atlantic, it might reflect a certain depth of character. Then again, what difference would it make? For the fortieth time I reminded myself that this was purely business. My dinner companion was the probable fiancée of my recently passed best friend.

Before getting out of the car, I had made a call to Mr. Devlin. After calming the volcanic burst over my recent excursion into hell, I briefed him on the news. He was less than surprised to hear that Benny Ignola was the messenger boy who pushed the domino that started with Tony Tedesco's informing on Sal Marone for extortion and ended with Peter's indictment for John's murder.

We were both aware that the real question was who sent Benny to deliver the message. Clearly it was not Dominic Santangelo. That meant that the don had a rebellion in his family that could easily become our problem in representing Peter.

I told Mr. Devlin about the imaginary meeting I set up between Tedesco and Benny for noon the next day.

"An interesting ploy. To accomplish what?"

For the first time, I realized that I didn't have a clue as to what it would accomplish. As things stood, only Tony would show up, since Benny remained unadvised of the meeting.

"I don't know. I guess I thought I'd shake the cage. Everything seemed to be standing pat."

Actually, it had been the only thing I could think of to pad my bluff in order to get my endangered posterior out of The Pirate's Den without being stuffed and mounted over the bar.

"Brilliant, Michael. And when this shaken cage of rattlesnakes decides to come after the shaker?"

"No problem. I didn't leave a name. Tedesco has no idea who I am. He just thinks I fit somewhere between Benny Ignola and the Godfather. I'm under the protection of the don, whether he knows it or not."

"Listen to me, Michael. There's not a client in this world that's worth you're getting killed. Or even slightly maimed. You start being a lawyer and stop playing the Green Hornet."

"Playing what?"

"Never mind. I forget you're an adolescent. You know what I'm saying."

I did, and I appreciated the thought. It was a nonproblem at the moment, since the rest of the evening promised a peaceful ride up the North Shore for dinner.

Just as I hung up, another thought ran across my mind. I went through information and dialed up Benny Ignola. When Benny answered, I held a handkerchief over the mouthpiece and gave my best impersonation of Tony Tedesco's Revere accent in a forced whisper.

"Mr. Ignola. Tony. Tedesco. Can't talk. Too many people. Gotta meet witcha. Same place, tomorrow at noon."

"What the hell's wrong with you? I told you not to call me."

"It's important. Gotta talk to you. I'll be there at noon. What do you say?"

There was a pause on Benny's end that sent chills down to my heels. I had no idea what the pause meant, but I had to get it off dead center.

"Or I could come to your office, Mr. Ignola. Or you could come to The Pirate's Den if you want."

I nudged Benny with two options that I knew he'd turn down in favor of root canal.

"No. I'll meet you. Same place. This better be worth it."

I could hear the distinct sound of a rattled cage in the slam of the receiver when Benny hung up.

I dialed Tom Burns's cell phone. He answered, as always, in the hushed baritone of a private detective on his private line.

"It's your favorite client, Tom. How're we doing?"

"I don't know about you, Mikey. I'm doing well."

"Could you be specific?"

"Your little mouse —"

"That would be Benny."

"It would indeed. He went directly to a locker in South Station. Do you need the number?"

"I have it. Go ahead."

"He opened the locker, took out an envelope, looked over his shoulder, and put it in his briefcase."

"And then?"

"He used his cell phone to make one call. I couldn't hear it. He got his car out of the parking garage on Devonshire and drove to the North End. He parked and went in the front door of Stella Maris, the restaurant on Prince Street. I waited a few minutes and went in like a customer. He was nowhere in sight."

"Which means either there's a back room or he went out the back door. Let's hope for the back room. If he went out the back door it's because he spotted you on his tail."

"Mikey, you know that Corvette that you love?"

"I do know it and I do love it. Why?"

"You can bet on there being a back room. Nobody spots me on their tail. Besides, I waited out front. He came out half an hour later. I followed him to his office and then broke it off. I was about to call you."

"Did anyone else come out of the restaurant?"

"A few customers in and out. Nobody recognizable. I figured you wanted me to stay on Benny."

"You did the right thing. I'll tell you, I'd give my Bruins season tickets to find out who it was he met with."

"Not in the cards, Mikey. The moment came and went. It could be anyone in the family. That restaurant is one of the places they do business. I don't see that we'll get another chance."

"Not to be so sure, Tom. I need you tomorrow. You personally, no hired help. There's going to be a meeting at noon between Benny and Anthony Tedesco. Tedesco owns The Pirate's Den in Revere. I don't know where the meeting'll be. You can follow either one of them to the meeting. You choose."

"I'll take Benny. I know his habits."

"Whatever. After the meeting, stick with Benny. He'll be running like a scared rabbit to someone up the food chain. This time I need to know who. Can you do it, Tom?"

"As long as the meter's running, I can get you a picture of Elton John in his Jockey shorts."

"I believe you could. I'll settle for the report on Benny. Let me or Lex Devlin know as soon as you have something. And would you send the bill for your excellent services to Mr. Devlin? He has a stronger heart."

Terry O'Brien was ready when I rang. She could not have been more stunning. It was the first time I'd seen her in moonlight, and the gentle rays lit her auburn hair in a way that all but toppled the mental wall I had built between business and dating.

The drive up the North Shore took us past a rocky coastline dotted with occasional white sand inlets. We passed through a succession of seacoast towns that dated back to the colonization of New England. Many of them, such as Marblehead, Gloucester, Manchester-by-the-Sea, and Salem, clung to their historical character as if the past three hundred years occurred somewhere else. I never pass along that route without a refreshment of the spirit.

The spiritual lift on this particular trip was somewhat less effective than unsual. There was a tension that I couldn't quite work out. Terry let her long hair blow freely in the open convertible, and we talked about everything under the sun except what was on both of our minds. Somehow a seat had been reserved between us for John McKedrick.

At some point, I asked a few questions about John's mental state during that last week of his life, and whether or not he had mentioned any names that she could recall. It all resulted in nothing new, but it lent a certain business purpose to the evening that made me feel a bit more at ease.

We arrived in the heart of Rockport as God was putting the finishing touches on a starlit night that could inspire poetry. We cruised slowly past the tiny sea-themed shops that line all the narrow streets. When we reached the town center, Terry twisted around to face me. She was in navy blue Docker pants and loafers with a pale blue Ralph Lauren shirt that matched the color of her eyes. She looked as if she could have arrived on one of the yachts that docked in Rockport Harbor for a shore dinner.

"Michael, how do you feel about lobster?"

I was stopped for a light, so I could lock eyes with her.

"It's the reason we're here."

Her grin broadened. "No, I mean, is it a passion?"

I never thought about it that way, but when I did, the answer was yes.

She moved closer without even thinking about it. "And can you go one-on-one with a lobster without instruments?"

It had the ring of a challenge. I was so totally captured by the moment, I would have said yes to one-on-one with a Komodo dragon.

We parked just off the square and started walking up a side street. I followed her lead in the direction away from my original idea of the dining room of the Peg Leg.

The street darkened as it wound away from streetlights toward a cove nestled into the rocky shore. One blue gray, weathered shack stood just shy of the sand's edge. Just inside the open door, a cauldron the size of a skiff was steaming over an open gas fire. The only other object in the room was a glass tank the size of the cauldron. About fifty of those prehistoric creatures with the claws that excite the taste buds stood in a torrent of bubbling cold saltwater being pumped in and out of the tank.

Terry looked at me with that smile that never seemed to leave her lips. "Trust me?"

I nodded. She leaned over the glass tank and pointed out four pound-and-a-halfers to the sweating, bearded man in a rubber apron. He clutched each one by the hard shell above the legs and shovel passed it into the steaming cauldron.

We stepped outside while the boiling seawater put a glowing red coat on those sublime crustaceans. Within ten minutes a call that was saturated in the flat, North Shore accent brought us back inside. We left with a heavy brown paper bag that was too hot to touch except at the folded top.

The three-quarter moon lit a path to a rocky plateau just above the cove. Terry opened the bag and laid out the four gleaming red creatures. She took a seat on the rock with her legs tucked under her and looked up at me.

"Well, Mr. Lawyer-Man, are you a New Englander or a tourist?"

I answered the challenge by half-reclining with the lobsters between us. Let the games begin.

I let her make the first choice and watched as she began the ritual dissection practiced as an art form by anyone born east of Connecticut.

When I realized that her lobster was in the hands of an artist, I began my own ritual with one of the most succulent specimens I had ever engaged in battle.

When that first lobster was history, we both drew a deep breath and lay back on the warm rock that insulated us against the cool east wind that had come up off the ocean. We had smiles that locked onto each other, and the world of Benny Ignola and Dominic Santangelo and even John McKedrick seemed almost not to exist.

There were long minutes without conversation that would have been difficult with anyone else. I felt as if we were climbing to the top of a roller coaster for that first plunge into something more than a restrained friendship.

Terry was the first to sit up.

"Are you still in the game?"

I nodded, and we took our leisure in each devouring the second lobster. When that last morsel of claw meat passed into memory, I stretched back and lay against the rock and just let the taste linger. Terry moved over and sat next to me. I could feel her warmth as a shield against the ocean breeze. Both felt pleasant and comforting.

She looked down at me and just nodded. I nodded back, and I think we were both saying, "This is good."

Maybe too good. I felt stung by a ripple of guilt. John was back between us. She saw it, and I could sense the pain flow from me into her. I sat up, and I wanted to hold her and comfort her and tell her it's all going to be all right. But John was there, and I couldn't do it. She was two inches away from me, but it felt like a mile.

Terry was the first to summon the courage to face it.

"Michael, I want to ask you a question you don't have to answer. It's probably out of line."

I felt a door slightly open, and every nerve froze with anticipation of what might be on the other side. There was no choosing the moment. This was it. I pushed the door the rest of the way open.

"Nothing's out of line, Terry. Go ahead."

"Where are we going, Michael? I wouldn't ask, but I think we're at a fork in the road. I don't want to take the wrong road alone."

I knew what I wanted to say, but I could still feel the ghost of John between us.

"Can I ask you a question I have no right to ask?"

"I wish you would, Michael."

"Was John in love with you?"

Terry looked away to the bobbing dots of skiffs and sailboats at anchor beyond the cove. When she looked back, the moonlight caught tiny trails of moisture at her eyes. Her voice was soft but clear.

"You're asking the wrong question, Counselor."

I was at a loss for a moment until I felt a ray of light burst through my mind.

"Were you in love with John?"

The tears had stopped, and she looked at me directly.

"No. Not like that."

She had broken a barrier, and the rest flowed more easily.

"John and I had been old friends. We got together again just a little while before his death. He was terribly distracted by whatever was going on that last week. He couldn't share any of it with me. I don't know what he had in mind for the future. He never got to tell me. I don't even know if it included me."

She stopped, and I needed one more answer. I had to know that I wasn't robbing John of something he might have had, for whatever sense that makes. She must have seen the question in my face, because her look said, "Ask it."

"If it did include you, would you —"

The words caught in my throat, but she answered it anyway.

"No. I didn't feel that way about John."

For the first moment since I'd seen Terry at John's funeral, I felt free to let John go to his new world. I didn't know what to say, but words turned out not to be a problem. However it happened, we were in each other's arms, and for some reason, the tears of both of us flowed through that first kiss.

We stayed for countless minutes alone on that rock plateau, holding on to each other as if we were really holding onto a gift that had just been given to us. Time suspended, until the moment when I realized that we were not alone.

Whether a twig snapped, or a pebble fell, or whatever, something spun me around to face a shadow the size of a bear at the edge of the rock ten feet behind us. When it climbed onto the rock, it took human form. There was no light on the features, but it just stood there staring.

There was a heavy wheeze in the rapid breath that came from lugging that bulk up the slope.

The best I could do was. "What do you want?"

The voice was guttural and hard.

"You're a smart-ass, aren't you?"

The world we'd left was back like gangbusters. I could see nothing but a shape, but I knew in my bones that it meant to kill us.

"I don't know what your problem is with me, but the girl is out of it. Let her go."

Through the wheezing I heard, "First you. Then I'll take care of the girl."

The tone was even more chilling than the words. The hulk moved farther onto the rock, and a tiny beam of light picked up the barrel of a handgun.

It was time to be cool and count options. The first thought was to charge him in the gut. One look at that frame and I realized I'd have better luck moving Mount Rushmore. That left just one option with no time to take a vote.

I grabbed Terry's hand and dove backward off the rock bluff. We spilled through the air for a brief eternity. We hit the packed sand of the beach a dozen feet below with a double thud—first me and then Terry on top of me. I landed flat enough to absorb the impact. Terry came down elbow first and caught me square in the right eye socket. I think it was shear willpower that kept me conscious.

I remembered hearing two shots fired while we were falling. I expected more any second from above.

I pulled Terry as close to the base of the rock as we could huddle. I listened for sounds above to hear which side he might be coming down. There was nothing.

When I knew Terry was able to move, I led her on hands and knees next to the rock. It was fifty-fifty either way, so we went to the left toward a stand of dune grass. I waited for a wisp of cloud to douse the moonlight before we made the scramble into the tall grass. Once we made cover, I left her hidden and worked my way through the grass up the sandy bank. I took a wide sweep in the hopes of coming up behind him.

My right eye was swollen nearly shut from the impact of Terry's elbow. I needed the light of the moon to grope my way up the craggy rocks. At the same time, I needed to move in darkness as cover against the next shot.

The motion was slow in bursts of climbing, broken by long pauses splayed against the rock when the rays of moonlight through broken clouds would find me out.

At some point, I was overcome with panic at the thought that he might be moving down the bank on the other side of the rock, leaving nothing between him and Terry. It seemed reckless but necessary to scramble to the back of his rock to get a fix on his position and head him off before he could reach her.

The in-and-out cloud cover helped in a way, but I was mostly moving blindly. Every few steps I seemed to run into an unexpected jutting of rock that would tear skin from an arm or leg. I tried to stifle any involuntary noises, but at one point I fell headlong across a face of jagged rock. The sound was out of me before I could squelch it.

I had lost the cover of silence, so there was no point in stealth. I stood upright and ran the last short quarter-circle to come up behind him. I was sure I'd be walking into open gunfire, but there was no other way.

When I reached the back edge of the rock, I was astounded to see the shape of him still stretched out on the rock ahead of me. He had the gun in his right hand, and he was focused on the stretch of beach below. I had no idea why he had hadn't fired at the sound I made when I fell. Maybe he was too locked onto the beach below, or he just couldn't hear. Whatever the reason, I rode the hope that he had no idea that I was behind him.

The cloud moved, and the cold light of the moon covered the three of us. If Terry moved, he'd have her in his sights. She had no way of knowing what was going on above her. That meant she could get up and become a running target at any moment.

Time was not on my side, and neither was my size against a human tank with a gun. The only things I had going for me were speed and surprise.

I felt around the ground behind me until my hand touched a

dead branch the size of a baseball bat. It was not much against what sounded like a thirty-eight, but under the circumstances, it seemed to come from my guardian angel.

I was no Navy SEAL, but much as I hated it, what had to be done, had to be done. I took a silent deep breath and counted. When I hit three, I drove like a linebacker on a blitz. My right foot slipped and I wound up driving my right knee into the rock. The pain forced a sharp sound out of my lungs that he couldn't miss. Before he could spin his bulk around with the gun, I put every ounce of energy into my left leg and dove the six feet to the target. My body hit the solid mass of his body, and I swung the club at his head with everything I had left. I could hear the shatter of wood and bone. I rolled off of him and held my breath. He lay still and cold.

I took a few seconds to let the pain in my knee stop screaming. There was no motion beside me. I called Terry, and she scrambled up to the rock beside me.

We made our way back to the Rockport Police Headquarters. I explained what had happened, and two officers followed us back to the rock ledge. As we approached it, I half expected to find nothing there. Either he'd have crawled away or it was just a nightmare to begin with.

No such luck. The officers went out ahead on the rock and scanned the body with their flashlights. They bent down and checked it over from head to foot before one of them came back to where I was standing. He called me aside and spoke in a low tone.

"Mr. Knight, this didn't happen the way you said it did."

I wasn't sure I understood his meaning.

"Why would I lie? I told you I probably killed him. He fired two shots at us. The gun was still in his hand. He was waiting for us to move."

The officer took me up toward the front of the rock.

"In the first place, Mr. Knight, his gun hasn't been fired. In the second place, you didn't kill him, at least not the way you said."

My look of confusion and silence said it all. He took me closer.

"Look at this."

He shined the flashlight on the gaping wound in the back of his head where my club had crushed his skull. Oddly enough, there was practically no bleeding from the open hole. He lowered the beam of his flashlight to the back of the dead man. The light picked up two clear bullet holes in the center of his back between his shoulder blades.

"My bet is the coroner'll find that he was dead sometime before you hit him."

I sat down on the rock to try to pull the pieces together. Who could have fired the two shots that saved our lives? I was too tired to think. I heard the voice of the officer bringing me back.

"Mr. Knight, I'd like you to see if you could identify him."

He rolled the body slightly and shone the light on his face. I went numb when I realized I was looking at the fireplug-shaped gangster I had taken off of his watch at South Station.

CHAPTER FIFTEEN

I woke up the next morning with one eye swollen completely shut. It was the color of a rare tuna steak. Terry's elbow had the clout of a weapon of mass destruction.

As I shaved, I swapped questions with the Cyclops in the mirror. How did the fireplug identify me, let alone find me? Bigger question — who was pushing his buttons, and whoever it was, why me? Whatever happened to that wonderful old adage, "The lawyer always goes home"? Biggest question of all — what was the button pusher's next surprise?

Through all of those disturbing negative questions, one positive question popped up. How did I acquire a protector kind enough to put two slugs into the fireplug where they'd do Terry and me the most good, and at the same time — no small matter — save me the whipping I'd be taking from my conscience for taking a human life.

It was nine-thirty a.m. I decided to reach Mr. Devlin by phone at his apartment before he left for Sunday Mass. He filled me in on his meeting the previous day with our client Peter. Since most of the world was under the salubrious assumption that Peter was dead, and his actual whereabouts were kept to a need-to-know circle, which, for the moment, did not include me, all contact was through Mr. D.

As I imagined, his meeting netted a goose egg. Peter could have been a great deal more helpful if he had actually been guilty of bombing John's car. As it was, he knew less than we did.

When Mr. D.'s news ran out, it was my turn. He asked about what I was now willing to admit was an actual date the night before.

I could hear a paternalistic grin in his voice when he asked. He was like a parent waiting up till I came home.

The grin dropped when I told him about diving off a rock to avoid a double murder accented by a likely rape, bullets flying from heaven knows where, and the smashing of an already dead gorilla's skull like a piñata.

"My God in heaven, Michael, can't you go on a simple date like anyone else? Are you all right?"

"Yeah, fine, Mr. Devlin."

"And the girl?"

"Terry was all right when I left her last night. I had Tom Burns put a man outside her apartment just in case. I'm going to call her right now. I'm certain he was after me, but I want to be sure she didn't get sucked into the game."

"That must have been one hell of a first date. Michael, this game is getting out of hand. We need to reestablish the rules. I want a meeting with Santangelo."

"I want to be there."

"Let's make it noon."

"Monsignor Ryan's church?"

"I'll set it up."

Our unlikely little foursome — Mr. Devlin, Monsignor Ryan, Mr. Santangelo, and myself — gathered in Monsignor Ryan's study. This time, the burning discontent was on our side. Mr. D. had me recount the events of the past couple of days, with heavy emphasis on the attack the previous night by the fireplug from South Station. My left eye, which was practically glowing in the dark, gave a nice emphasis to the story.

I covered the facts and left the follow-up to Mr. D.

"This crap must cease, Dominic. I'll do everything I can for Peter, but I'm not going to lose this boy over it."

I don't know about the others, but I heard the word "boy" as carrying a lot of the word "son." I'd begun to believe against all odds that Mr. Devlin had actually begun thinking of me that way, whether consciously or not. That conceit so filled my heart that, right or wrong, I knew I'd never let go of it.

I watched the lines deepen on Santangelo's face. I'm sure he took Mr. Devlin's meaning, but something far deeper and more personal seemed to be weighing on him. I'm sure he saw the threat to me as an equal threat to his own life, and perhaps more to the heart, the life of his son. But there seemed to be something even beyond that.

"Who is this man, Dominic? You heard Michael's description. Is he one of yours?"

Mr. Santangelo spoke quietly. He measured his words carefully. He seemed to be suppressing pain rather than the truth.

"Yes. As you say, one of mine."

"Why, Dominic? I know it wasn't under your orders."

Mr. Santangelo just waved his hand as if the very thought was an impossibility. We all knew that he owed us more than that, so we waited. We gave him long seconds that dragged into a minute to get control of what he must have been thinking.

When Mr. Santangelo spoke, it was muted by what appeared to be deep sorrow.

"This man . . . How do I explain? Vito Respa. He was also like a son in a different way."

Mr. D. started to speak, but Mr. Santangelo held up a hand.

"Please, Lex. It's important that I say this."

Mr. D. nodded and gave him the silence he wanted.

"I have to go back. My grandfather was a very powerful man in his region of Sicily. He had workers for his property, and he also had soldiers for protection from his enemies. This man, Vito Respa, was the son of one of his workers. Vito was, what can I say? mentally slow.

"About fifteen years ago, there was a rape of a young girl in my grandfather's village. My grandfather's enemies spread the word that Vito had done it. He was arrested. These enemies spread the word that my grandfather would buy Vito's freedom. One thing led to another and a mob formed in the square. You have to understand the Sicilian's pride, especially in matters of dishonoring a daughter of their town. With the help of a few inciters, the mob was ready to storm the jail and take Vito.

"My grandfather was home alone when he heard about it. He went to the town square, this little old man on a cane. He climbed up on the platform, and everything went quiet. I heard this from people who were there.

"Picture this old man facing that mob alone. He never raised his voice. He never made an open threat. He just raised his cane and one by one he pointed at each of the men in the mob and spoke his name. 'Aldo Baldini, Antonio Presotti,' and so on. That's all. One by one they went away. When they were all gone, he went home.

"Vito watched it from the jail cell. When he was tried, he was acquitted because there was no evidence. About a year later, they found the real rapist and got a confession.

"But from the day of that mob, Vito lived by unquestioning devotion to my grandfather. When he got out of jail, my grandfather was afraid that an assassin might come after him, so he sent him to America and asked me to look after him. I did, for the last fifteen years. He was as loyal to me as he was to my grandfather."

"What did he do for you, Dominic?"

"Odd jobs. Whatever he was capable of."

"Like murder."

"Never! He was never part of the business."

"Would he have killed if you'd asked him?"

Mr. Santangelo dropped his head and his voice.

"Yes. I'm sure of it."

"And someone took advantage of that loyalty."

Mr. Santangelo looked at me. "I'm sure that when he went after Michael, in his heart, he believed he was doing it for me. I hope you know, Michael, that he wasn't."

I could only nod in recognition of his sincerity.

"Then who do you supp —"

"Wait a minute, Lex. I want to say this." He looked directly at me. "Michael, I know this doesn't mean much under the circumstances, but he would never have dishonored that girl." He shook his head to emphasize it. "Never."

It was hard to break the silence, but there was more business on the table. Mr. Devlin picked it up.

"Who's behind it, Dominic?"

"That's for me to find out and deal with. I clean my own house."

Mr. D. and I reacted at the same instant, but he was in a position to act on it. He was on his feet.

"Not this time, Dominic. Not this time. Your type of house-cleaning could leave us with bodies and no live sources of information. I want every threat to Michael found out and cut off. Someone killed your friend Vito while he was attacking Michael. We have no idea who or why. This goes beyond your so-called family. We work together on this, or you find another lawyer for Peter."

Before Santangelo could react, I felt my cell phone vibrate. I saw that it was Tom Burns, so I stepped outside the room and took the call. Tom had followed Benny Ignola to the meeting I had brought about with Tony Tedesco. They met on a bench on Boston Common. Tom could see Tedesco doing the talking, and from the hand motions, he seemed to be describing someone — most likely the dude in the blue suit from The Pirate's Den. At some point, Benny got the picture and blew up. He turned crimson. He began shouting with accompanying gestures. Tom couldn't make out the words until Benny turned and steamed off. His last invective, with expletives deleted, was "And keep your mouth shut!"

"What's our Benny up to now?"

"Benny's in his car. I'm tailing him. I saw him make a call on his cell phone. I'll bet my fee he's heading for the Stella Maris Restaurant for a meeting. I want to put a man at the restaurant before he gets there to see who goes in and goes to the back room. I don't want to be an hour late again."

"Good idea, Tom. Do it."

"I already did it, Mike. My man is there having lunch right now. He knows the players by sight. I'll call you as soon as I get something."

"Do it by text. I'll be in a meeting."

I went back into the study. The discussion was still going on. Mr. D. looked over at me, and I gave him a "sit tight" signal and mouthed the words, "Tom Burns."

Five minutes later, I got the vibration signal from my cell phone and flipped it open. I nearly choked when I read the two words Tom sent.

I held the phone over for Mr. D. to read the words. I gave him a look that said, "You're the quarterback. You call it."

Mr. D. looked at Santangelo, and we both knew that what was about to be said would change the lives of more people than we could imagine.

"Dominic, I think we have the name of the traitor in your organization."

Mr. Santangelo froze in his seat. I could see the Sicilian flame of vengeance flaring in his eyes.

"Tell me."

"I need your word, Dominic."

"This is my business, Lex. Tell me the name."

"This is not your business. This is the lives of us all, including Peter. I don't give a damn about your business. This is beyond you. We need time to get this thing in order. That means you take your own precautions, but you leave the rest to us."

I could see Mr. Santangelo's eyes burning like coals, but his voice had the calm of an experienced combat general.

"What do you want, Lex?"

"I want five days minimum."

We waited for an answer. When it came, it was so soft it could barely be heard.

"I've built my entire life, my family, my business on loyalty. I don't take betrayal lightly. I'll show restraint for three days."

"It's not negotiable, Dominic. I need your word. Five days."

Mr. Santangelo looked down at the floor. He was a man who knew nearly absolute power. In one morning he had suffered the death of his faithful friend, Vito Respa, and now a betrayal that ran deeply into the inner circle of his most trusted people, and he was being asked to give his word to do nothing. The lines on his face radiated the conflict that was raging in his mind.

It was seconds later. He never lifted his head. We could barely hear the words. "Five days."

Mr. Devlin nodded to me, and I opened the cell phone that held the name of Santangelo's trusted second in command, Anthony Aiello.

Mr. Santangelo read the name. It was as if a curtain was drawn across his eyes. He was in his own world that had suddenly become disordered and terrifying and unimaginable to one who lived by his Sicilian code.

In a short time, he stood up like a man who had added ten difficult years to his life. Monsignor Ryan took his arm to steady him. He smiled faintly at Monsignor Ryan.

"Thank you Matt. I'm glad you're here."

That was all. There were no more words until he reached the door. He didn't look back at any of us, but I knew he was addressing Mr. Devlin.

"Five days. No more."

CHAPTER SIXTEEN

The tall, balding man with squinting eyes sat motionless in a rented Russian-built sedan on the edge of a remote runway on the outskirts of St. Petersburg. Thumbnail size flakes of snow were being scattered across the windshield by a wind off the coast of the Gulf of Finland.

Alexei Samnov was described by his colleagues on the faculty of the University of St. Petersburg with two words — erudite and cautious. Erudite without question. His reputation as a scholar of seventeenth-century Dutch painters was international, and on the subject of the work of Jan Vermeer, his word was the ultimate authority.

It was this preeminence that brought him to the edge of a bleak strip of tarmac ten miles from his comfortable lodgings at the university. It was a lifelong proclivity toward caution that brought him there an hour and a half before the appointed meeting time.

He knew that the others would have traveled to their individual pickup points by armored limousine in the company of armed bodyguards — precautions well beyond his means. A passing wave of envy gave way to the resolve to dig in behind the only defense his circumstances permitted, his alertness to the path of least personal danger.

The meeting to which he had been summoned was about to take place at twenty-five thousand feet above his beloved Russian soil. He narrowed his focus to a scrupulous consideration of which of the three men who would be aboard that plane he needed to fear the most.

He squinted through snowflakes that were periodically swept aside with a flick of the wiper blades until he finally picked up a dot on the scrub-oak lined horizon. The dot grew and took shape as a private, two-engine jet set down and rolled to his end of the runway.

He half-ran up the staircase to the door that opened out of the side of the plane to swallow him up. A uniformed attendant took his coat and offered him a seat at the table in what appeared to be an airborne boardroom.

Within minutes, he was the sole passenger in the aircraft climbing through the low scud of clouds that blanketed the region.

The passenger chamber was expensively appointed, with plush seating for four around an oval table. Once the plane had leveled off at cruising altitude, the attendant entered the room to offer Beluga caviar and the finest Russian vodka. He accepted both, but only sampled the caviar. The others had the protection of violence at their fingertips, but since his wits were his only security, he never blunted them with vodka.

Within two hours, the plane had crossed into the airspace over Belarus and set down on a small landing strip several miles outside of Minsk. Alexei watched as three heavyset men in dark suits emerged from the darkness of a hangar. Two of them waited at the door of the hangar, while the third walked to the plane and climbed the lowered staircase to the opened door of the aircraft. Without entering, he scanned the inside of the passenger compartment, bowing slightly to the seated Alexei.

This third man then descended the steps and gave a signal to the two stocky individuals at the hangar. They began crossing the twenty yards to the aircraft with handguns at their sides. A fourth man, older than any of the others, fell in step behind them.

When this group reached the man at the bottom of the steps, the four began to climb the steps in formation. A man in a pilot's uniform emerged from the cockpit and stood in the open door of the plane.

"No farther, gentlemen."

The three stopped in unison at the bottom of the steps. The two with weapons raised them slightly. The pilot held up his empty hands. He bowed to the older man behind.

"I mean no disrespect. You come alone or not at all."

The older man, more overweight than merely stocky in contrast to the others, smiled and moved up the staircase.

"If we can't trust each other —" He shrugged and said over his shoulder to the three at the bottom of the steps, "Stay here. Stay awake."

Inside the plane, the two passengers greeted each other with smiles and a handshake, but each eyed the other like two chess combatants looking for any telltale weakness before the match.

A serving of caviar was offered to the new passenger, and a second bottle of vodka was opened and placed in front of him. He accepted both and poured the vodka. Alexei took some small comfort in seeing him down two shots in rapid succession.

Alexei broke the silence first.

"His taste still runs to the finest, Sergei."

"And why not, Alexei. Can he not afford it? Do we not deserve it?"

Both laughed. The man called Sergei offered to pour from his bottle of vodka. Alexei waved him off.

Sergei grinned and waved a finger at him.

"Ah, my comrade, if you don't mind my using that term. An old habit. Still the cautious."

Alexei shrugged. "I have other pleasures."

"Such as?"

"*Staying alive,*" he thought to himself. He gave a palms-up gesture. "Little amusements. Harmless."

Sergei poured and drank another small glass of vodka. He appeared relaxed, as if the alcohol was having its effect. Alexei reminded himself from previous experience that Sergei could finish the bottle and another after it and still have a mind ready for combat.

"Cautious Alexei. No chinks in the armor even among friends?"

"*Especially among friends,*" he thought. A smile sufficed for an answer.

Another two hours and the plane found an equally isolated runway north of Moscow. The stairway dropped. Two additional passengers came aboard. The first through the door was a man of unusually muscular build, apparent even through the heavy winter apparel. The taut, gaunt features of his face sent a chill rippling down Alexei's spine. The one word that always leaped to his mind when he was in the presence of Lupov was "wolf."

Alexei's first sense was that of the three, Lupov was the one to be feared most. Experience had taught him, however, that although Lupov was a machine of violence, he was harmless until the machine was set in operation by another.

The man with Lupov was a contrast to all of them. He was a short man in his seventies, white-haired, reddish-complected like Santa Claus. He had an easy smile and an affable manner that suggested one beloved by his grandchildren. It was he who had recruited Alexei to harness the benefit of his special knowledge at a rate of compensation that put retirement from his duties at the university within reach.

This was the fourth meeting between Alexei and this man, and in that time, Alexei had never heard him referred to by name. He was simply referred to as "the gentleman," and the tone used when the word was spoken was always subdued.

Another bottle of vodka was opened by the attendant. He poured a round for each of the four at the table and withdrew. The gentleman at the head of the table raised his glass. Each of the others followed.

Sergei beamed a broad grin and proposed a toast.

"To crime, gentlemen."

The man at the head of the table smiled through a mock scowl.

"Gentlemen, rather a toast to 'business.' Let the outside world call it what it wishes."

They all laughed, as they always did at the gentleman's lighter moments. They all drank. Even Alexei knew he could not afford to disdain the toast. He took one sip, as did the gentleman at the head of the table.

The smile diminished on the face of the gentleman at the head of the table. "An inconvenience has arisen."

Sergei interrupted his reach for the bottle of vodka. "Trouble?"

The gentleman smiled, but looked sharply into Sergei's eyes.

"For the moment, an 'inconvenience.' I imposed on your time to be certain it does not become what you call 'trouble.' Alexei —"

The turn of attention gave Alexei a muscular reaction in the stomach that he did his best to conceal.

"Alexei, when we acquired the painting, it was at no small cost. I might say, at no small risk. You recall that."

"Of course." His voice sounded hollow on the inside. He forced himself to sound more confident than he was.

"And when we invited you to join our little venture it was with the understanding that you could ensure that the painting was genuine. You recall that too, Alexei."

"I can still assure you of that. The painting is an absolutely authentic Vermeer."

"Yes, but you see, Alexei, I'm not the one who needs to be assured. The funding of our . . . operations around the world comes from people who loan money on the basis of unquestionable collateral. That painting is the basis on which great sums have been placed in our hands. And consequently great debts assumed by each of us."

"If it's a matter —"

"Don't interrupt, please, Alexei. I want this clearly understood. These people we deal with are not stupid Mafia thugs. They are men of international standing and power. When they become . . . concerned about their investment, we do well to allay their concern before it ripens into something more serious. Are we all in agreement?"

Each head at the table nodded, except for that of Lupov, who merely grinned in apparent anticipation.

"Alexei, these people have approached me. They're troubled by the appearance of another painting, another Vermeer, apparently the same painting. As they pointed out with a certain distress, these paintings cannot both be the original. Does this disturb you, Alexei?"

Alexei knew that his life could depend on the composure with which he answered. He also knew that there could be no hesitation.

"If you mean do I doubt my original conclusion, no. There is no doubt whatever. We have the original."

"And that is because?"

"Nothing has changed. The painting has not changed. You say there is another. There are probably several others. In Vermeer's short life, he produced thirty-five paintings that are known to exist. That's all. The originals are priceless, as you know. Each of the thirty-five has been copied and sold by frauds time and again. There will probably be more. But we have the original. Nothing will change that."

Sergei bustled a little in his chair. Alexei felt the sense that Sergei was enjoying the fact that Alexei was under the microscope. Sergei leaned in on both elbows to face him directly.

"And what have we, or these financiers, but your word to back that up?"

Alexei continued to address himself to the gentleman at the head of the table. "There are three ways in which a painting is authenticated. The first is called provenance. It means we trace the painting from an indisputable source. In this case, gentlemen, if we may speak frankly, the painting was stolen from one of the most reputable art museums in Boston. You are all aware of the means by which we acquired the painting from the original thieves. I don't think I need to recall the details to your minds."

The gentleman at the head of the table nodded.

"The second method is more scientific. Do I need to go into the chemical analyses, the dating of the paint, of the canvas, of the stretcher frame and fasteners? The tests for the exact age, for the consistency of the colors of the paints used by Vermeer, for the genuineness of the cracking of the paints, etcetera.? May I simply say that I conducted every test myself. They all attest to genuineness. But, forgive my lack of modesty in this instance. None of these methods is the most conclusive."

The gentleman at the head of the table began to show his grandfatherly smile. "Please continue to convince me. The third?"

"The third is the word of one who has devoted his life to a study of the thirty-five paintings of Vermeer. It is intangible, but the most certain. I know every nuance of stroke, of shading, of subject matter of every original of the master. It's easy for a skilled artist to copy shapes and colors. Only Vermeer himself could produce the luminescence, the single-minded emotion of the original that to me is now second nature. I can simply look at a painting and tell an original Vermeer from a fraud the same way that you gentlemen can look at a signature and know instantly if it is your own."

Sergei bent over to look him in the eye.

"And you cannot be wrong?"

Alexei looked at him for the first time since his exposition began. "No."

The gentleman at the head of the table broke the tension with a hearty laugh. Alexei's stomach became unclenched for the first time since the discussion began.

"That look! That look in Alexei's eyes. That's the reason these people opened their pocketbooks to us."

"No. It's actually more than that."

All eyes were on Alexei for daring to disagree in the smallest matter with the gentleman.

"Normal modesty again makes this difficult to say. But it's a fact. No one else has so devoted a life's study to the work of this one master. I have — I speak immodestly, but truthfully — the trust of the entire art world. I'm sure these people you mention became well acquainted with my reputation among those who know more about art than they do. You can assure them that nothing has changed. I will stake my entire life's reputation on it."

The look in the eyes of the gentleman became slightly more intense.

"You will, Alexei, and a great deal more than that."

The import of the gentleman's words were not lost on anyone at the table. It was not the first time Alexei had regretted leaving the secure serenity of his academic niche.

Sergei poured another glass of vodka while keeping the focus on Alexei.

"And this imposter, this other painting. Who stands behind it?"

The gentleman's attention was riveted on Alexei, since Sergei had anticipated his next question. Bells of caution were going off in Alexei's consciousness. Nothing of significance occurred in the art world regarding Vermeer that did not come to his attention. He had, in fact, heard the rumor of a recent attestation of genuineness to a copy of the painting in question. He would have dismissed it with all of the others but for the fact that the authentication came from a former colleague at the university, now teaching in the History of Art department of Harvard University.

Alexei's respect for the eye and credibility of Professor Leopold Denisovitch gave him pause when it first came to his attention. There could be only one original. Why had Denisovitch compromised himself by certifying a painting that he must have known to be a fraud?

Some intuitive alarm told Alexei that this was not the moment to place Denisovitch's name on the table. He looked directly into the eyes of the gentleman.

"I'll make inquiries."

There was an uneasy pause that was difficult to read before the gentleman said quietly, "Do that."

Sergei was riding a crest of confidence in siding with the gentleman against Alexei. "And do it quickly so that we can eliminate this nuisance."

Sergei looked with a grin at Lupov who returned the grin at the word "eliminate." The smile was gone from the gentleman's lips when he turned his focus to Sergei.

"This 'elimination' you speak of without hesitation. It would certainly be the most self-defeating course we could take. It would be clear to the people who matter exactly who had taken this step and why. I can imagine nothing that would more effectively shatter their confidence in our position."

Sergei held the glass of vodka halfway to his lips. He was suddenly frozen by the turn of the spotlight on him. "I only meant — of course, you're right. We must be . . . cautious."

The word "cautious" forced upon his colleague brought a certain satisfaction to Alexei.

The gentleman continued in a soft tone, but no one in the room mistook the seriousness behind it. "My dear Sergei, when we began this venture, it was you who brought us to these particular contacts of yours in the financial world. It was you who negotiated a very sizeable loan on the basis of the painting's validity. It was you —"

"That's true, but —"

"Please!" The tone of the gentleman changed and his look silenced Sergei in mid-sentence. "It was you who committed us to this very significant debt on what now appears to be a fragile confidence in the authenticity of some work of art. We are committed to this debt on your advice."

"I know. Please allow me to —"

"What we shall allow you to do, Sergei, is to explain why I needed to bring this crisis of confidence to your attention. These people are your contacts. Why was this not handled before it ever came to my attention?"

Sergei all but turned to liquid. He took a large swallow of vodka for stability. When he could speak, he began pouring out meaningless apologies.

Alexei sensed that the questions asked by the gentleman were more rhetorical than information seeking. There seemed to be more to the gentleman's accusation than was apparent from the conversation.

Alexei chose to remain silent, out of the line of fire. He listened as the heartfelt apologies of Sergei seemed to be absorbed by the grandfatherly figure at the head of the table with no effect whatsoever. Something deeper that Alexei could not understand was playing behind the expression on the face of the gentleman.

Alexei watched as the gentleman glanced at Lupov to his right and gave an all but imperceptible nod. It was received with an equally slight grin on the lips of Lupov, and it crossed Alexei's mind that he might never see their comrade, Sergei, alive again.

CHAPTER SEVENTEEN

The plane was scarcely in the air after leaving Sergei Markov with his retinue at the landing strip outside of Minsk. For all of the self-preserving insidiousness of Sergei, Alexei felt less secure without him.

Once they were airborne, the gentleman at the head of the table leaned back in a relaxed posture. He focused the deceptively kind gaze of his soft hazel eyes on Alexei. "This fraud. This second painting. Who do you suppose has it?"

Alexei tried to put nonchalance into his tone, but he measured every word for possible consequences. "I don't know. That's not surprising. If it were authentic, I could narrow it to three people who would acquire it simply to own it. It would be a stolen art object worth much more than a hundred million if you had to put a price on it. Priceless to a real collector for its own sake. But it would be recognizable all over the world. It could never be shown. There'd be no bragging rights, no displaying it. Only three that I know would want to own it themselves on those terms. And could afford it. Any of the three would recognize a fraud."

The gentleman's eyes narrowed slightly, and Alexei's caution quotient rose to the next level.

"And what of people like us? People who would buy it to use as collateral. They could be fooled?"

Alexei shrugged.

"Speak frankly, Alexei. People like me?"

Alexei knew he was on thin ice. He also knew the gentleman was no fool.

"Yes. It happens. Particularly if the authenticator has a reputation."

The gentleman smiled. Alexei anticipated being questioned further on the source of the authentication of this new painting. He quickly shifted ground, giving more than he had hoped to expose.

"I believe the painting in question is in Amsterdam."

That brought a smile and raised eyebrows.

"Oh you do? This painting you've never heard of."

"The use of a stolen painting like this as security to borrow money, it's not a simple matter. You know yourself. If the debtor defaults on the loan, the creditor has to be able to get money for the painting or it's no good as security. That generally means selling it to the insurance company that insured it without being prosecuted for possession of stolen property. That's a delicate business."

"As we know, Alexei. So?"

"There are not many that would make a loan of this sort. We can exclude the people we're dealing with. They could be fooled by a forgery, but they'd know there can't be two originals of the same painting. The others I've heard of work out of Amsterdam. They'd want the object close by, perhaps a vault requiring two signatures, the owner's signature and the moneylender's. It's a guess."

The gentleman closed his eyes and appeared to be in repose. Alexei knew that nothing could be further from the truth.

"Do you have names?"

"No. It's all rumor. I deal in art, the real thing. I have no interest in the rest."

The gentleman's eyes opened a slit.

"And yet, dear Alexei, you were quick enough to join our little caravan."

Alexei felt the sting that returned periodically when he let himself realize that he too was misusing the thing he cherished most. He nodded.

"This once."

The soil of St. Petersburg felt reassuring beneath Alexei's feet. He walked through the blowing snow to his car and drove to his office at the university. It was getting close to midnight. All of the other faculty offices were in darkness. He kept his coat on while he dialed a number. The voice on the other end of the line was that of a secretary.

"This is Alexei Samnov. You'll be kind enough to tell Professor Denisovitch that I'll be in London on Tuesday. The club. He'll know. Ten a.m. London time."

"Did you want Professor Denisovitch to call you there?"

"No. I want to see him there. He knows I would not call if it were not — tell him I want to discuss with him a certain concert."

"I'm sorry. Should Professor Denisovitch call you back to confirm?"

"No. I don't need a confirmation. I need him there. Tell him — just tell him to be there."

CHAPTER EIGHTEEN

We had five days to pull something together before Dominic Sant-angelo began painting the town with "family" blood. I had no real proof of who it was that sent Vito Respa to shorten my lifespan, and even less of a clue as to why. On the question of who, Anthony Aiello, Santangelo's subboss, was at the top of my shortlist. I figured Benny Ignola was involved, but it was unlikely that he was trusted to make policy for the organization.

Much as I hated to admit it, Benny was right about one thing. It was time he and I talked. My first move after we got back to the office from our meeting with Mr. Santangelo was to make a phone call to Benny's office.

His secretary took my name and managed to enunciate in nasal East Boston English without missing a beat on a wad of gum, "I'll see if he's in."

That meant he was in. Benny's suite of offices was composed of a room with two desks — one of them formerly John McKedrick's — and a broom closet for the secretary/receptionist/pizza retriever. I was sure she was waving hand signals to Benny while she was snap-ping her gum in the phone. The next sound I heard was Benny's in-credulous tone.

"Who's this?"

"A voice from the dead, Benny. You'll be tickled to death to hear he missed me."

It was cards on the table time. No fooling around.

"Mikey, is that you?"

"Would you believe it, Benny?"

There was a pause just long enough to tell me that old Benny was knocked off balance. That meant that he had been in on the play by Vito Respa and was stunned to find me still on the planet. It was time to throw him another curve.

"You screwed up, Benny. Obviously. Now it's make up time."

"What? I don't —"

"I know you don't, Benny. You're in way over your head. The good news is that your wish is coming true. You and I are going to have a meeting."

The pause meant that a meeting on my terms no longer had the appeal that it did when he was calling the shots.

"Why — ?"

"Because if you give me one second of grief, the next voice Fat Tony Aiello hears will be mine. In your worse nightmare, you couldn't imagine what I'll tell him. On the other hand, I bet you can guess the kind of misfortune he'll order up for you. Do you need to think about that, or can we just get to where I make plans and you say yes"?

Pause. He was being pulled along faster than his brain cells could connect. The worst thing I could do was to slacken the pace.

"One half hour, Benny. You and me. You hear me?"

I could hear the little wheels spinning in his devious mind. Would a half hour give him time to set me up for another attempt at the job Respa botched? I thought I'd head him off at the pass.

"No, no, Old Pal Benny. Forget what you're thinking. You alone. Understand this. It'll look like I'm alone too. Not true. There will be high-caliber firepower aimed at your scurrilous heart the whole time. If I so much as grimace under a hiccup, you'll be just an unpleasant memory. *Capisce?*"

"Where?"

"Just so you'll feel at home, let's make it the first park bench in Boston Common up the walk from Park Street Station."

I knew the spot from Tom Burns's report of Benny's meeting with Anthony Tedesco. On a normal day, he probably could have fig-ured out how I knew, but after what had just come before, beginning with a voice from the not quite dead, Benny didn't know if he was afoot or on horseback. Good time to close. Click.

As I passed Mr. Devlin's office, the thought of checking out my next move with him floated through my mind. My experience with his approval rate of my unorthordox plans convinced me that what he didn't know couldn't hurt me.

I had one other dilemma. I could cruise into my meeting with Benny with nothing for cover except a bluff. It was a publicly frequented spot, and had been since the 1600s when people were welcome to pasture their flocks of sheep on Boston Common. The particular spot I had chosen was the site of the "Hanging Tree," where the religiously overzealous Puritans treated the crowds of men, women, and children to three or four hangings a week of such "heretics" as Quakers, Catholics, and anyone else who disagreed with them on a point of theology.

Or I could spend more than a few dollars to have Tom Burns provide the artillery cover I had mentioned to Benny. That was a decision I'd make on the way down on the elevator.

At exactly eleven thirty, I watched Benny settle his well-padded posterior onto the designated bench in Boston Common. He looked nervous as a cat. I dialed up his cell phone and watched him bounce when the ring zapped his pre-strung nerves.

"Yeah. What?"

"Morning, Benny. Guess who?"

"What the h —"

"Benny, get a grip. I want you to walk straight out to Tremont Street."

I could see him look around to spot what must have seemed like my ghostly presence. He had a grip on the cell phone that must have had its little diodes spinning.

"Listen, Knight —"

"Benny, you always call me Mikey. Are we drifting apart?"

The silence told me he was losing his sense of humor.

"Do it, Benny. Straight to Tremont."

I watched him stand and walk his little crab walk in the right direction. He kept looking back toward the benches around our supposed meeting spot. I thought at one point he made some kind of hand gesture that seemed more than just Benny talking with his hands, but he was so spastic at that point that it could have been nerves — his or mine. When he reached the sidewalk on Tremont, he still had the cell phone to his ear.

"Now what, smart-ass?"

"Be nice, Benny. Let's not let this affect our relationship. Flag down the next cab that comes along."

I saw him look back into the Common again before he waved at the cab that was cruising down his side of Tremont Street. The cab pulled to the curb beside him.

He said into the phone, "Now what?"

"Get in the cab, Benny."

He grabbed open the door and stuffed his little sausage form into the passenger compartment. He was still looking back at the Common and jerking his head at something. When he turned around and saw me sitting in the seat beside him, he bounced about three inches off the seat, smacking his head on the door frame.

"You son of a — !"

I let the stream of curses roll over me. What was cracking me up in spite of it all was that he was still saying it into the cell phone.

"Benny, nice language, and you, a member of the bar. You can close the phone now."

He snapped the phone and his mouth shut simultaneously.

"Don't put the phone away. You'll be needing it."

I gave the driver directions to turn right on Boylston and again right on Charles toward Beacon Hill. I needed a quiet stretch out of traffic to bring off the next piece.

As we pulled away from the curb, I caught out of the corner of my eye what to my legitimately paranoid mind looked like two bulked-up forms that could have been of the Sicilian persuasion flagging down a cab behind us. I did my best to convince myself that I was letting the demons get a grip on my imagination. At that moment, I needed full focus on the proceedings at hand.

I asked the driver to get the sports-talk station on the radio and turn the volume up to eight. Once done, I slid over closer to Benny and spoke in his ear.

"You're going to make a phone call, Benny."

His eyes were like half-dollars and his mouth was half open at this point. I knew I had his attention.

"The boys in the North End let you play lawyer to keep their scum on the street. But basically, don't take this personally, Benny, to them you're an errand boy. Open up your cell phone. You're about to deliver the message of the week."

He hesitated for a few seconds of indecision, but then opened the phone and looked over for the next order.

"Dial up Tony Aiello."

He stared at me as if I had just asked for a direct connection with the *Wizard of Oz*. A second later he snapped the phone shut.

"I used to give you credit for smarts, Knight. Not no more. You're a dead man, and you run around givin' orders like you're the king of Sweden."

His mouth was closed now, and taking on the definite shape of a smirk. I was afraid of losing momentum. I knew that without Benny on a string, I had no access to the one I needed to contact.

I noticed that Benny looked back through the window at the cab that was still behind us. I checked it out too, and the sight of the two goons in the cab made everything inside of me freeze. I did my best to keep the confident look on my face, but I was dead certain that the only good news was that I was not suffering from paranoia.

We were cruising down Charles Street when the driver slowed for the stop light at Beacon Street. I saw Benny blanch. I turned around to see what he was gaping at. A black Lincoln with shaded windows pulled around the cab in back of us. It nearly sliced off the rear bumper of our cab while cutting in between us and the cab carrying the two Cro-Magnons behind us. I couldn't help noticing the coincidence of another shaded Lincoln pulling in behind that cab.

The four cars pulled to a stop at the light in tight formation. I couldn't see what was going on in the cab that had been following us, and neither could Benny. But when the light changed and we pulled away, the two Lincolns never moved. The cab was boxed in.

I told the driver to make a quick right onto Beacon and step on it. Once we were out of sight of the trio of cars standing like rocks in a row, we backed off to a slow cruise. I had the driver just drive around the labyrinth of streets that crisscross Beacon Hill.

Benny took it all in with a look of disbelief, and while I gave thanks to the Lord and whoever was riding to my rescue, Benny just stared at me like an abandoned puppy. I was back in control. I had no idea how I got there. I knew that when I left the office, I stupidly opted to go with the bluff instead of calling Tom Burns for protection. I was beginning to wonder if Tom had waves of mental telepathy. For the moment, that had to do for an explanation.

I turned back to Benny.

"Let me lay it out for you, Benny. You screwed up. My presence makes that clear. Forget the denial. For once we're going to talk straight to each other. Now picture this scene. I send a message to Fat Tony Aiello that you and I worked out a deal. More than a few bucks changed hands, and you tipped me off to what Aiello was planning for me. I could even say you did it as a matter of professional courtesy, if you can imagine that. Either way, you wind up pleading for Fat Tony's tender mercies. Are we in agreement that that's the worse of two evils no matter what the other one is?"

He just looked at me.

"This is a conversation, Benny. You get to speak next."

He blinked, and I welcomed the beads of sweat that stood out from his neck to his forehead. To his credit, he went one more round. "What the hell makes you think he'll believe you?" "I'm alive, Benny. If you did your job, you and Respa, I'd be otherwise. Respa's dead, and you and I are not. You don't think I can make Tony wonder about that?"

He took about ten seconds to factor that in before testing the waters.

"What do ya want?"

"Open your cell phone."

He froze in position.

"The first alternative is still on the front burner. I'm running out of time. Open your cell phone."

He opened the phone slowly as if he was afraid to let something out of it.

"Good. Here's the plan. You call Fat Tony. Tell him you heard from me. Apparently Vespa missed the mark. But that's good news. You tell him I said I had information about the number you found in the locker. The number you delivered to him was the wrong one. I've got the right one. I'm ready to make a deal. It's pure business, and there's no other way he's going to get to the goods. Are you taking this in, Benny?"

I put a slight emphasis on "the goods" to imply that I knew what the goods were. I figured I was on safe ground there, since the odds were a hundred to one against the insiders letting Benny know what the goods were either. I also figured that Tony Aiello was under pressure to get whatever that number led to. Otherwise, why risk killing a member of the Boston Bar with no connections to the mob — to wit, me? They say in hockey that when a goon fights a goon, it's crowd entertainment. When a goon attacks a clean player, there's hell to pay.

Benny looked down at his knees and the beads of sweat became drops that fell on his pants. I knew he had a deathly fear of Tony Aiello. From what I'd heard, Aiello would kill in a flash, at times with his own hands. I'd also heard that the one thing that could rein in his taste for violence was his own sense of what was good for business. Benny was even more aware of that than I was.

"That's the deal, Benny. When we reach the next corner, either you're making the call or I bounce you out of this cab and do some cell phoning myself."

He turned to me with a look somewhere between anger and desperation. "Listen, Mike —"

"Two choices. Pick one."

We slowed down at the stop sign at the end of the street. I told the driver to pull over to the curb. When he pulled in, I reached over Benny and threw open the cab door.

"Out of the cab, Benny. Poor choice."

Benny reached frantically for the swinging door and pulled it shut.

"All right, all right. What do you want me to say?"

I went through it again.

"All right. I'll tell him you'll meet him at his office."

I looked at him with a grin that asked him how dimwitted he thought I was.

"All right, then where?"

I'd actually been giving that some thought, and I was getting the first amusement of the day out of my choice.

CHAPTER NINETEEN

Just before Benny made the call to Fat Tony Aiello, we were on Beacon Street, crossing Charles Street. Both of us took in the scene to the left on Charles. The cab that had been following us was pulled into the right curb at a peculiar angle. The cabbie was sitting on the sidewalk yelling into a cell phone. Two police cars were pulled up in front of the cab, and one beside it. An ambulance was screaming up Charles Street from the direction of Mass. General Hospital. There were two figures in the back of the cab, heads cocked at an odd angle, neither of them moving. The final touch was that neither of the black Lincolns was in sight.

I was close to vomiting. Two more men had just lost their lives, and in some odd way, I felt responsible. This was not what I bought into when I applied for law school.

While Benny gaped at the scene, I pulled it together enough to give him an elbow.

"Make the call, Benny. You might mention that the score looks like three to nothing, my favor. It's getting expensive. We can end it with one ten-minute business conversation."

Benny hit the last number and I could hear the ring.

"Mr. Aiello, it's Benny."

Whatever was said blanched Benny's olive complexion to a new shade of white.

"Something happened, Mr. Aiello. Michael Knight —"

"Yeah, I know, Mr. Aiello. Well listen, here's the thing. Knight's here with me. He wants a meeting with you."

I didn't need the phone to hear Fat Tony's response. The words reverberated. "What the hell? You tell that son of a bitch —"

I had nothing to lose, so I took the phone away from Benny.

"Mr. Aiello, this is Michael Knight."

After a slight catch, the voice on the other end went from tear-his-head-off wild to what sounded like an almost bemused smirk.

"You got big ones kid. I'll give you that."

"Thank you, Mr. Aiello. I've heard the same about you."

Again a catch followed by a roaring laugh. I heard him say to someone there with him, "This little creep breaks me up."

Then to me. "So you got me on the phone, kid. What do you want?"

"I want you to take me seriously enough to talk business."

"Why should I take you seriously enough for anything? You got nothin' I need, kid."

"You apparently think you need me dead. You've made two tries so far. By my count, it's cost you three men. I don't think you want to keep this up. You need what I've got more than you know. And I need something from you. It's time we did business."

"Listen you little —"

I'll omit the flavorful string of allegations about my parentage and sexual orientation that was flowing half in English, half in Italian. It ended with "— You got *nothin'*!"

"Mr. Aiello, the numbers on that card that Benny brought back from the locker in South Station —"

That brought him back to earth.

"Take a look at the card, Mr. Aiello."

There was a cautious pause.

"What about it?"

"Look at the top right. See the little *mk* up there in pencil?"

"So what?"

"It stands for Michael Knight. I made up those numbers and put the card in the locker. They're all wrong. I have the right ones. You need them. Can we cut through the macho crap and get down to business?"

I could hear him cuff his hand over the phone. I couldn't make out the words, but he was talking to whomever was with him. It took a minute, but he came back. "Put Ignola back on the line."

I put the phone back in Benny's shaking hand. He put it to his ear but he was looking at me. I heard what sounded like a question over the line. Benny spoke into the phone in a hush, for whatever good that would do. "We're in a cab. Heading down —"

I grabbed the phone out of his hand. It was no time to be mousy. "To hell with that. You've had two chances. You don't get a third. If you want those numbers, we do it my way. Yes or no?"

There was a calm on the other end that could have been encouraging or terrifying.

"You know who you're dealing with, kid?"

"Yes. Do you? You're dealing with the only one in this world who can give you that code. Maybe you don't need it. I think you do. I'm ready to deal. On my terms. What's it going to be?"

I heard a discussion going on behind a hand-muffled phone on the other end. I didn't think they were planning for my welfare.

"Mr. Aiello. Are you there?"

"Yeah, what?"

"I can save the strain on that brain trust you're talking to. I have insurance that runs directly to Dominic Santangelo and beyond. So far I haven't tipped your name. If any ten minutes passes that I don't give the right signal, that will change. On the other hand, one ten-minute meeting — my way — and we both get what we want."

There was a silent pause, but a short one.

"What do you want, kid?"

"A meeting."

Another pause.

"Where?"

I gave him the time and the place of the meeting, snapped the phone shut, and settled into swallowing the lump of burning coal that had risen into my esophagus.

CHAPTER TWENTY

The Parker House, on the corner of School Street and Tremont, is one of the grand old ladies of Boston. She is the oldest continually operated luxury hotel in America. Her dining room has served Parker House rolls and Boston cream pie to political and financial titans of every degree since 1855. My favorite table in the dining room is the one at which President Jack Kennedy proposed to Jacqueline. I savored the irony in the fact that this grand old lady was about to offer the same hospitality to Fat Tony Aiello and Michael Knight.

This time I was at a far corner table, concealed behind the sports section of the *Boston Globe*, when the Aiello entourage appeared at the maître d's station. Fat Tony, aptly nicknamed, led the delegation of four sides of beef, each stuffed into a pin-striped suit that was cut to the dimensions of a more svelte form. The entire tailor's nightmare lined up behind Frederick, the maître d', who, to his credit, maintained his cool while he escorted the entire herd to the table I had reserved for them.

I gave Frederick a nod, and he delivered my note to Aiello requesting that he join me alone at the table to which Frederick would lead him. At first, Aiello balked, particularly with me nowhere in sight. Eventually he threw his napkin on the table and followed Frederick with reluctance.

By the time he reached my table, the bands of fat that gathered over his shirt collar were nearly tomato red. He was not quite in his element, and the idea of following dutifully in the footsteps of the somewhat disdainful Frederick to comply with the whims of some little pissant lawyer — me — obviously sent his blood pressure off the chart.

I savored every bit of it. The sight of that bull moose reluctantly weaving his way through the glances of the noontime Parker House diners convinced me all the more that I had some serious leverage in that string of coded digits.

When he arrived at my table, I lowered the newspaper. Leverage or not, I found myself looking into the bloated face of a man who would, with pleasure, have had me killed at the very first lapse in precautions. I nodded to the seat opposite me without a word.

Frederick, as was his custom, unfolded and placed the napkin in what he could find of Fat Tony's lap. I thought for an instant Tony was going to punch him out in defense of his manly honor. I believe Frederick caught the same signal, because he summoned a waiter and withdrew at quick march to his station at the entrance.

The waiter appeared and began describing in florid terms the chef's specials of the day. I cut him off in mid-appetizer and suggested that ice water would do for the moment. The sooner we could get to business, the more likely we could disband this little gathering of misfits. I thought I'd better take the lead, and fast.

"Mr. Aiello, I'm Michael Knight."

He gave me a nod and a glare that said we could dispense with the customary handshake.

"Let's agree on something, Mr. Aiello. We both need information."

He was up on his elbows, oblivious to where he was, and barking.

"The hell I do!"

I matched him elbow and bark.

"The hell you don't. You didn't come here for the clam chowder. Let's not shadow box. Neither of us has time to waste."

The waiter stepped in to pour ice water. We both sat back in silence. Aiello let the steam pour out over his damp shirt collar. I just thanked God that no one was dead yet. When the waiter left, I picked it up at a more subdued pitch, and the other diners went back to their schrod.

"Let me tell you how it is, Mr. Aiello. I don't give a damn in hell about you or Santangelo or any of your business. I'm defending Peter Santangelo for the murder of John McKedrick. Nothing more. I think whatever that code of numbers leads to is at the heart of his murder. When I find out how, I'm out of it. You get whatever the thing is, and you'll never see or hear from me again. That's all I want. I'm no threat to you or your business. Are we clear on that?"

Aiello reached for his ice water and took a long slug. He didn't say yes or no. I plowed on. "Here's the deal. I give you the right numbers in exchange for your telling me what the numbers lead to. An even swap."

It was his move. He was still sweating, but no longer glowing red. He seemed to have settled into his surroundings more comfortably than I wanted.

He wiped his mouth with his napkin and slowly came forward on his elbows. His voice was low. "Now I'll make you a deal, you little piece of crap. You'll give me the numbers and maybe you don't spend the rest of your life wondering when your luck runs out."

It was my turn at the ice water. The pause was for more than dramatic effect. It gave me time to regroup and realize that I was so deep in the hole that any direction was up.

I leaned forward and cut it to a whisper. "See, here's the thing, Mr. Aiello. I never depend on luck. I told you once. Maybe you didn't catch it. If I should miss giving the right signal to someone, you have no idea who, everything I know, and a few things I made up, go directly to the ear of the father of the man I'm defending. I don't know if you're ready for an all-out war with Mr. Santangelo and the families who'll back him. I can guarantee that's what you'll have."

He looked me right in the eye and I could see a grin, closer to a smirk, creeping across his face. He put his right hand on the table in a fist with the index finger pointed at my chest.

"You're dead, kid. You want to know something? I'm gonna do it myself. You try to bluff me? You bring me down to this lousy joint. Who the hell —?"

Damn it, that did it! I lost it.

"Do you know where the hell you are, Aiello?" I was spitting the words out between clenched teeth. "Some of the people who built this country did it right here in this room. People whose boots you couldn't lick. And a bum like you calls this — Did you ever have one single thought that went beyond your damn pocketbook or your stomach?"

I was seized with the abandon of one who was certain that he would not live to walk through the door. There were no wrong moves now. They had all been made.

I came straight up out of the chair as if I had been launched. My napkin hit the table and my knees drove back the chair. My feet were clearly in gear for an exit.

I had one last line. "That's your choice, Aiello. You'll never see those numbers in this life. Watch out for what's coming, Buster. *Après moi le déluge.*"

I always wanted to use that line. The problem was it went right in one fat ear and out the other. On my way by, I bent down and whispered close to his ear. "It means, when I go through that door, the gates of hell are going to let loose the beasts."

I was never in my life so certain I was going to die. I only knew that come hell or high water, by damn I was going to walk tall through the Parker House door. From that point on, I had not one single clue. I only knew I couldn't stop.

Something in that previous insane minute must have registered with Aiello. I took one more step when a hand that felt like a vice grabbed my arm. It held me in a grip that I can feel to this day.

"Sit down."

I froze.

"I'm telling you to sit down."

I turned back to the chair, and the grip loosened.

It took every ounce of willpower to walk calmly back to my seat, sit calmly in the chair, and calmly replace my napkin as if I had just arrived for luncheon with Prince Charles.

Intuition told me that the storm had passed, and we had both weathered it. This was a new game, and it was his serve.

"Like you said, Knight, this is business. What've you got for me?"

"You know what I've got for you. The question is, what does it open?"

Aiello sat there in silence. I thought it was just hard for him to make the first disclosure. Then another thought hit me. Maybe he doesn't know.

"It's the key to a numbered account, isn't it? That much I could figure out. But where is it?"

Aiello still looked at the table, and nothing came out. I was becoming more certain by the moment that Aiello had no idea of the details. That might have been one key to his vulnerability.

Then the clouds began to lift. It takes a certain amount of sophistication to play money games with numbered accounts. The bank or vault, whatever it was, most certainly was not in the United States. It could have been on an offshore island. It could have been in Amsterdam or Zurich, or anywhere in between.

I thought of the kind of people who play those games. I looked at the pathetic figure across the table, who had likely never in his life mastered a concept more complex than raw violence. He clearly could not have pulled it off.

But my old pal, John McKedrick, could.

I looked over at the table of monkeys who came in with Aiello and wondered who in all of Aiello's organization, beside John, could have managed a deal involving a foreign account. Frightening as it seemed, perhaps the most intelligent and educated member of that tribe other than John was Benny Ignola, and in the sophistication game, Benny clearly did not hold the cards.

What the hell were you up to that last week, Johnny? That week when Terry O'Brien said you were tense and distracted?

"What's in the vault, Mr. Aiello? That's the price of the numbers."

Aiello instinctively looked left and right and leaned over the table.

"A picher."

"What kind of a picher? Like for water?"

"A picher, you schnook. A painting. It's a big deal."

"What picture?"

"I don't know. It's worth a lot of money. It's by this guy, Vermeer."

I almost fell off my chair. I remembered from a basic art history course at Harvard that Vermeer's work was probably the most highly priced in the world. I knew there were a limited number of his paintings in existence, and every one of them was worth at least as much as the combined salaries of the Boston Red Sox, to put it in terms I could understand.

"How in the world did you get a Vermeer?"

Another look in each direction, and then in a whisper with hand signals. "Keep it down. Keep it down. It was hot. That lawyer, McKedrick, he heard about it. How we could get it."

I was stunned, but I had to keep the flow going.

"How would John hear that?"

"He did some business for me. In Europe. In Amsterdam."

"What kind of business? Drugs?"

I could see him pull back.

"Let's not get too much into this thing. I'll tell you what you need to know about the picher. The rest is none of your business."

"All right. So John goes to Amsterdam to transact business for you. So what?"

"So he comes back from a trip three weeks ago. He says he met these guys over there. They can arrange to get this picher and sell it to me for like a third of what it's worth. It's hot. They can't sell it on the market. Everyone knows it."

Now he has me completely baffled. A third of what it's worth is still in the high millions. Why would Aiello want to put that kind of money into it? He had even less ability to sell it than the people who had it.

"I don't suppose you want to tell me what you'd planned to do with it after you bought it."

"That's right. I don't. I told you what it is. Now come across with the numbers."

Something frightening was taking shape in my mind.

"Suppose I do, Mr. Aiello. What will you do with them?"

"That's none of your business too."

"Think about this. I give you the code to a vault somewhere in the world. Maybe Amsterdam, where John met these people. Have you thought about the fact that it could be a joint account and some-one else has to supply the other half of the code? That's not unusual."

He was looking at me as if he was getting a glimmer of where I was going.

"So?"

"I think you need to get your hands on that painting. I think you're over your head in some kind of financing deal that John McKedrick put together, and now you've got to come up with that painting. Otherwise you wouldn't be here talking to me."

I paused, and he didn't interrupt.

"That means someone's got to find out where this vault is and deal with another someone on the other side."

I looked over at the table of thugs he had brought with him. "Which of those geniuses are you going to send to do it?"

There was no answer.

"If not them, who else have you got?

Again no answer.

"I think you're in one hell of a spot, Mr. Aiello."

He started to say something, but backed off.

"I told you before. My only interest in this thing is Peter Sant-angelo. The best way to get Peter an acquittal is to find out who ac-tually killed John. I'm guessing it wasn't you. You needed John to pull this off."

I looked him in the eye and he didn't blink. Good sign.

"Suppose I go after the painting. I think it could be someone connected with that deal who killed John. If I can get the painting and find out who's involved, you get the painting. I get the infor-mation."

He had a sarcastic edge to his voice, but he didn't sound com-pletely shocked by the suggestion.

"You're gonna work for me? What the hell makes you think I trust you?"

"No offense, Mr. Aiello, but in my worst day I wouldn't work for you. Call it a joint venture. As far as trusting me is concerned, two things. One, I'm not like you, and you know it. You can ask anyone in this town. You'll hear that my word is good. Second, what the hell would I do with a stolen Vermeer? And a third thing while we're at it. What are your other options? Benny Ignola?"

He knew better than I did that he could trust Benny as far as he could throw city hall. I saw him glance over at his collection of orangutans plowing their way through the basket of rolls. It took him a minute to exhaust every other option before he turned back.

"How do I know — ?"

"You don't. You've got my word. If I get the painting, I'll give it to you. That's worth a hell of a lot more than anything else you've got going."

Thirty more seconds, and he leaned over the table.

"You take Benny Ignola with you. I need some insurance."

"For what it's worth, okay."

I figured I could loose Benny at any point in the journey. It was a small price to pay.

"And while we're at it, Mr. Aiello, I want this card up on the table. If I ever find out that you were responsible for John's death, I'll take it to the D.A. to save Peter."

He put on a half-grin and shook his head.

"I said it before. You got big ones. You talk to me like this."

"It's better you know now. I won't go back on my word."

I think it was a new concept to Aiello — keeping one's word for the honor of it rather than fear for one's kneecaps. He was struggling with it, but it was probably his last option.

"How you gonna do it? The picher."

"You've got to give me someplace to start. Give me a name. Something. Do you know anyone connected with the deal?"

He thought. I could see that John let him in on as little as possible. Finally he leaned closer and whispered.

"There's this guy at Harvard. McKedrick knew him. He's a professor. Teaches art or somethin'. Name sounds Russian. like something-ovitch."

"Was it Denisovitch? Leopold Denisovitch?"

"Yeah. McKedrick said he could tell if it was real or a phony. He's the one said it was real."

I knew the name because Professor Denisovitch had taught the course that both John McKedrick and I had taken in History of Art 102.

I looked at my watch. It was quarter of two. I badly needed to touch base with Mr. Devlin. I needed fifteen minutes to fill him in on what I'd been up to in the past hour, and half an hour to talk him out of having me committed to McLean's.

I left Aiello with the promise that I'd let him know when I was ready to make a move.

When I walked down the carpeted staircase that led to School Street, I recalled that just two weeks week ago, I had an interesting but ordinary law practice. This week I'd survived two assassination attempts, I was up to my targeted posterior in the business of the arch-enemy of all that's holy, Dominic Santangelo, and to ice the cake, I was the commissioned emissary of Santangelo's personal Judas, Fat Tony Aiello. Go figure.

CHAPTER TWENTY-ONE

As soon as the elevator ding signaled that I'd reached our office floor, it hit me that I hadn't seen my secretary, Julie, in a spell. She being the long-suffering fire wall between me and those who vent their frustration at trying to reach me at times like this, I had an idea I'd hear about it.

"Michael, what precisely could I threaten you with to get you to return some of these calls? Some of these people want to barbecue *me*, and I'm not even the lawyer."

"Give me a list of the top five. I'll do it before I leave."

"Here's a list of the eight who are forming a lynch mob."

I had one parting request.

"Julie, would you get the number for Professor Leopold Deniso-vitch at Harvard? See if you can get him on the phone."

"No."

Julie always knew how to stop me in mid-step.

"Why not?"

"Because if I do, you won't return those calls."

"How's this? Give me twenty minutes to go through this list, and then you have Professor Denisovitch on the line."

I consumed the next twenty minutes soothing feathers and arranging postponements in the sincere hope that Devlin & Knight would have a practice left when this Santangelo business was finally put in the "closed" file. I buzzed Julie's line.

"I have fulfilled all commitments, My Lady. I can only assume that Professor Denisovitch is pacing while waiting on hold."

"Not quite, Michael. He's not in his office."

"Where is he?"

"That's as much as I could pry out of his assistant or secretary or whatever she is. Do you want me to get her back on the line?"

I thought about it. This was the last thin thread that I had to follow. It had to be done delicately.

"No. Would you see if his office is still in the Fogg Art Museum? It's on Quincy Street in Cambridge. I'll be with Mr. Devlin for a while."

My first five minutes with Mr. D. were spent filling him in on my exploits with Benny Ignola and Tony Aiello. The Benny story amused him, given his passing acquaintance with the ineffable Mr. Ignola. The part about the two in the taxi on Charles Street brought scowls and the kind of grumblings that I knew were founded on a deep concern for his junior partner. The Fat Tony story got us into deeper water.

"You know I don't like this, Michael. What the hell are you planning on doing? And this time give me all of it."

In a burst of honest disclosure, I told him that I planned on getting in touch with Professor Denisovitch to try to get a lead to the painting in the coded vault. We shared the feeling that John's involvement with that painting had some connection to his death. I also told him about my commitment to get the painting for Tony Aiello. That was a mistake.

"How do you plan to get into that vault even if you find out where it is? The chances are there's another half of the code in the hands of whoever's on the other side of that painting business."

"I'm going to do what I learned from my senior partner. I'm going to follow one step till it leads to the next one in the hope the steps don't run out. I learned that from my master mentor."

"You also picked up some of the Irish blarney. I forgot to tell you. It doesn't work on another Irishman."

"I was afraid of that."

"I mean it, Michael. You're playing with the worst sort."

"Worse than Dominic Santangelo?"

"Yes. Dominic is at least predictable. And there are limits to what he'll do."

"As long as murder is within his limits, can this be much worse?"

"Yes, Michael. This Professor Denisovitch. Do you know him?"

"He was my professor at Harvard in an art history course. But I was just one of forty names on a class roster. On the other hand, it's an entrée."

"All right, Michael. Here are your marching orders. See what you can learn from the professor. That's it. We'll talk about it when you get back."

"Okay, Mr. Devlin."

I was halfway to the door when he froze me.

"Michael. Look at me."

I put on a blank expression, and faced the penetration of his glare.

"That was too damn easy, Michael. What have you really got in mind?"

"I committed myself to Aiello to get that painting in exchange for the only lead I could get. That means that I have to go wherever this vault is and tangle with whatever emissaries from hell also want that damn painting. It's like walking a tightrope with one leg. I have no idea how I can possibly get out of this thing alive. I know I'm over my head. I hate this at least three times as much as you do. But I know I have to give it my best shot in spite of your welcome concern. Maybe I'll see you Wednesday, or in the next life."

Needless to say, those words never got past my lips. What did was simply: "I'll see the professor and let you know what I get. You're the boss."

"And don't you forget it."

By early afternoon, I was cruising the back streets of Cambridge around Harvard to find one of the elusive parking spaces around the Fogg Art Museum. The Fogg is a piece of Harvard that goes back to 1895. It houses one of the world's greatest university collections of fine art from the Middle Ages to the present. It also houses the Straus

Center for Conservation and Technical Studies, with facilities for testing the physical materials of paintings for authentication. Most importantly, it housed the office of one of its luminaries, Professor Leopold Denisovitch.

I found the door with the stenciling on frosted glass that boasted the professor's name, with the legend beneath it, HELGA SWENSON, PH.D., ASSISTANT.

I rapped on the glass and heard from the inside "COME" in a voice low enough to be on either side of the male/female divide. I opened the door to a large room that would have made any art connoisseur gasp. Every inch of the walls was covered with paintings so closely packed that it seemed to form one breathtaking mural. A wild guess was that they were being warehoused on the walls until Professor Denisovitch could authenticate them.

A voice seemed to come from the massive desk against the far wall. It came from an elongated figure bent double over my side of the desk, so that it was only visible from the rump down.

Whatever was absorbing her attention did not release her for the amenities of a formal introduction. The baritone voice, tinted with what I recognized from my undergraduate days as a "Harvard accent," bounced off the rear wall.

"Place the examinations on the chair and depart. That will be all, young man."

I almost wished I had some examinations to drop and run. I closed the door, partly for privacy and partly to send a signal.

"Ms. Swenson?"

The head came up slightly but made no move to rotate.

"Are you conversant with the English tongue, young man? You may depart. There will be no tipping."

"Not even to cover my parking meter and maybe lunch?"

I thought maybe impertinence would be a surefire grabber. It was. She slowly rose to full stature and turned to face, or rather face down, this insolent pup. When totally unfolded, she exceeded six feet by at least two inches more than I did. I assumed from the name that her now white hair was once Norwegian blonde. It was baled into a utilitarian bun and fastened with some kind of a claw, consistent with the earth-toned frock and the sensible shoes.

I jumped in with a preemptive introduction. "Ms. Swenson, my name is Michael Knight. I was a student of Professor Denisovitch. That was some years ago. In any event, it's rather important that I speak with the professor."

In the same baritone, "Concerning?"

"Concerning a painting."

"Yes. I didn't imagine you was getting up a touch football game. What about this painting?"

"Actually that's rather a delicate subject. Could I speak with the professor?"

She stiffened somewhat, if that was possible, and gained another inch in height. From that higher ground, she considered me for a second or two before dismissing me with two words and turned back to her former position.

The two words were, "No. Depart."

There was a door to the right of the desk that I strongly suspected led to Professor Denisovitch's office. The problem was getting through it. I knew it meant either physically overcoming this Viking, or winning her over. The law of possibilities indicated the latter.

"Ms. Swenson, I don't want to spar with you. You've got intelligence and height on your side. On the other hand, I can't leave this office without seeing Professor Denisovitch. I hate to dredge up an old cliché, but this is quite definitely a matter of life or death."

I thought sure she'd dismiss that pathetic speech and shoot me another "Depart." I was surprised when she turned around and simply said, "Yours or Professor Denisovitch's."

"I'm sorry?"

"Whose life?"

If I said "mine," it would probably be a matter of enormous indifference to Brunhilde. If I said "the professor's," it would sound like a melodramatic trick. On the other hand, I wondered why she even suggested the latter possibility?

"Probably both. At the moment, it's very possible that the professor is in serious danger. I'm a lawyer. I've become involved with people who lead me to believe he needs someone on his side."

She seemed to soften and actually sat back against the front of the desk.

"He's not here."

"Do you know where he is?"

The pause indicated the answer was yes.

"Who are you, Mr. —?"

"Knight, Michael Knight."

I gave her a very brief explanation of what brought me to the professor's door, leaving out the sensitive details, but giving her enough to conclude that I was one of the good guys.

"He's in London. He had a call two days ago from a man with a Russian accent. He practically demanded that the professor meet him in London. I thought that the professor would ignore the message, but he cancelled his classes for the week and left that evening."

"Do you have any idea where he might be staying in London?"

"He's gone to London several times before this year. He always stays at the Grisham Hotel. It's a few blocks from Tottenham Court Station. I'm not sure of the address."

"No problem. If I get that close, I can find it. Did he say how long he'd be there?"

"No. He has classes next week."

I started to "depart," when she stopped me.

"Mr. Knight, there's another thing. Just after the professor left for the airport, there was a call from a second man with a Slavic accent. I'd say this one was from Belarus."

"How do you know?"

"Good ear for dialect. My mother was from Minsk. In any event, this one demanded to know how to find the professor."

"And you said?"

"The Grisham Hotel, London. I didn't realize at the time —"

"Did either of these Russians call before?"

"Yes. The man from Belarus called twice during the past term. He never left a name. Each time, the professor asked me to make arrangements for him to fly to Amsterdam."

"Did he say what for?"

"No. But each time the professor seemed to be under a great strain. Particularly the last time. The other man, the one he's meeting in London now, is an art historian, Alexei Samnov. The professor's known him for years."

I knew there were more questions to ask, but they didn't occur to me.

"Thank you, Ms. Swenson. You've been very open with the information I needed."

"Yes, I have, young man. And it has nothing to do with your needs."

Somehow that did not surprise me.

"I spoke as I did because I'm concerned about the professor. I thought he might have a stroke. He was beet red when he went through that door. My point is this. If — when you find him — may I assume you're going to try?"

"That's the plan."

"Good. Please notify me. I just want to know that he's . . . well."

She turned back toward the desk before that last word.

"I owe you that. One last favor. If there are any more calls, it might help if you didn't mention my being here."

She just nodded.

It was late afternoon when I crossed the Charles River on the way to my apartment. I called Julie on the cell.

"My goodness, Michael. This is twice in one day. You're becoming a regular around here."

"Next thing you know, I'll want to be paid. Listen, Julie, no badgering. Go into your super-efficient Girl-Friday mode."

"I'm always in that mode. What's up?"

"I need you to book me on a late-night flight to London. Anything that gets me into London early tomorrow morning. Second, I need a hotel room. Something around Tottenham Court Station. Anywhere except the Grisham."

"What's wrong with the Grisham?"

"Nothing. I just may need neutral ground for a retreat."

"Should I know what that means?"

"No. And speaking of which, let not one word of this pass through your rosy lips to Mr. Devlin."

"My rosy lips are sealed."

"Good. Would you call me back with the flight and hotel information at my apartment as soon as you've made the reservations?"

"All right. When should I make the return flight?"

"I hadn't thought about it. Make it one way. I'll make the return reservation. I have to be back in a couple of days anyway."

I was thinking about the five-day deadline we had from Mr. Santangelo.

I had packed lightly in a small case when I got Julie's call. I was set on the eleven thirty flight and booked into the Chesterfield Hotel.

Just when I needed a shot of assurance that life holds good things, I listened to a call on my answering machine from Terry O'Brien. She sounded wonderful. She was just checking to see if I'd been shot since our last meeting.

I called her back, but there was no answer. I actually enjoyed listening to her voice lilt through the answering machine message. I left word that I had to be out of town for a few days, but I'd love to see her. If she was free, I'd be spending my last few evening hours before the flight at Big Daddy's on Beacon Hill.

I also remembered my agreement with Aiello to let Benny tag along. Much against my will and better judgment, I left a message on Benny's machine to the effect that I would be shipping out directly from Big Daddy's. It was somewhat stingy on details, but I figured that covered my obligation.

CHAPTER TWENTY-TWO

A shower and a well-above-average lobster thermador at The Federalist just above the State House on Beacon Street brought me back to the world of the almost normal. I had a few hours before heading to Logan Airport, and I knew exactly where I wanted to spend every minute of them.

Around half a block below the State House on Beacon Street lies a stairway that winds down to my personal conception of heaven. It's small and so dark that after dozens of Monday nights spent in attendance, I could no more describe the decor of Big Daddy's Jazz Club than that of Buckingham Palace. But when I slip up onto the second barstool from the door, and Nate, my personal favorite bartender, splashes four or five fingers of Famous Grouse Scotch on the rocks, I'm halfway to the pearly gates.

But what lifts me the rest of the way through those gates and immerses me totally in heavenly raptures is the heart-driving sound of a stand-up bass in the mammoth hands of one Big Daddy Hightower.

One never knows who's going to be crowded onto the miniature stage with Daddy on any given night. No jazz musician worthy of recognition from New York, Chicago, New Orleans, or San Francisco would consider passing through Boston without paying a call at Daddy's with the hopes of sitting in with the big guy. In his day, Daddy was a regular at such New York clubs as Birdland, the Blue Note, and the Village Vanguard, as well as being a welcome drop-in at such soul-deep jazz clubs in Harlem as the Lennox Lounge and St. Nick's. When headliners on any jazz label in those days were planning a recording session, Daddy was frequently the first sideman they called.

But that was a while ago. At some point, Daddy's calling as a musician fell victim to the surge of rock music that squeezed out of business many of the venues and record labels that provided Daddy with a living. When he couldn't earn an income on his talent, he did it with his size. He became a bouncer in one of the rock clubs in Boston's South End, a bit of a dicey neighborhood in those days. His efforts to break up a broken-bottle fight resulted in severed tendons in his hands that prevented him from playing bass with the varsity team.

At some point, a group of the musicians who knew him in the old days staked him to the establishment of Big Daddy's on Beacon Street in Boston.

While my eyes were adjusting to the dark, and that first sip of the Famous Grouse was startling my taste buds into blissful consciousness, I recognized the sweet, gentle brushwork of Paul Maxwell, one of Boston's elite jazz drummers, behind Daddy's driving bass. A saxophone player whom I recognized from several visits to a Harlem club called "Smoke," but whose name I couldn't bring back, was weaving imaginative webs around an old Jimmy Van Heusen tune called, appropriately enough for the moment, "It Could Happen to You."

By the time I took the level of the Grouse down to two fingers and let Daddy's pulsating bass massage the knots out of nerves strung like piano wire, the world was taking on the deceptive glow of normalcy.

After the set ended, I felt a mammoth hand on my shoulder. I could sense the six-foot-five, heaven-knows-how-many-pound mass of Big Daddy behind me.

"Missed you Monday night, Mickey. I assume you were out savin' the world."

"Right, Daddy. Otherwise I'd have been here. What is that, the second Monday night I've missed in six years?"

"Yeah, you gettin' to be a regular, son. I expect we should make up for lost time."

"I don't think so, Daddy. I have to catch a plane later tonight. Actually I'm kind of expecting a young lady."

"Well now, I think we can take care of that."

A hand the size of a catcher's mitt slipped off my shoulder and under my arm. I found myself rising off the barstool and threading a path between the tables toward the well-worn piano stool on the stand. Daddy turned back to Nate on the way.

"Anyone comes in looks like she might be lookin' for Mickey, table two, up front."

I slid up onto the stool and felt for the keys of the old but well-tuned upright piano. The only illumination was a two-watt bulb down close to the keyboard. Daddy liked it almost pitch-dark during the sets to induce a focus on the music and dampen any inclination of the audience to chat.

Daddy started something on the bass and yelled over, as he frequently did, "Hey, Mickey, you know this one?"

I let my mind ride with the eight-bar introduction Daddy was thumping out. I picked up the delicious chord structure that Hoagy Carmichael wove into his exquisite "Skylark." On the ninth bar, I came in on the melody with Daddy carrying me on the bass as solidly as he carried me to the stand. I noticed his grin when he caught my first few notes and knew we were on the same frequency. I always looked for that grin.

We did exchanges of somewhere between ten and twelve choruses before Daddy gave the fist up signal to bring it in for a landing. A round of applause reminded me that other people were in the room.

I glanced down at the table just off the stand, and my breath caught. An aberrant beam of light traced a familiar figure at one of the two seats. I'd have leaped off the stand to join her if Daddy hadn't launched into his particular favorite, "Cherokee," at full ramming speed, and I couldn't abandon ship.

When the set ended, the lights came up slightly, and Terry was still there. It was my first chance to do more than phone her since what could justifiably be called an unusual first date.

"Michael, that's great what you were doing up there."

"Thank you."

She touched the edge of my eye that still showed the imprint of her elbow.

"Ouch. Is that new?"

I had forgotten that the black eye blossomed the morning after our last meeting.

"Actually, a young lady did that."

"Oh?"

"She has a dynamite elbow, but only if you pull her off a cliff."

Her mouth fell open. "You mean I did that?"

"Not to worry. I took it in the spirit in which it was intended. Thanks for coming tonight. I've missed you."

"Likewise."

"I wanted to see you right away, but things got a bit out of control."

"You mean work?"

I couldn't find it in my heart to classify the lunacy of the last week as "work."

"This one's a special case."

"If it's all right to ask, does this have anything to do with that key I gave you from John?"

"You could say that. That little sucker's tied me up with a biker gang, a Mafia thug and his goons, and whatever form of human mutants deal in stolen art. I've survived two murder attempts, and I'm now in partnership with Fat Tony Aiello, the Prince of Pain."

That was what leapt to mind. What I said was, "Only indirectly."

"I'm sorry if I got you involved."

"You didn't. I was involved from another angle. It's just something—"

I realized that Terry's eyes were locked on something across the room.

"What, Terry?"

"That man who just came in. I've seen him. One night that last week, I was at dinner with John. He came up to us in a restaurant. He started whispering. Then suddenly he started yelling at John."

I followed her focus, and what should appear at the bar but the rumpled sack of laundry that was Benny Ignola. He apparently got my message.

"Excuse me, Terry. I'll be right back."

I moved over next to Benny at the bar. I noticed he'd taken on an additional five hundred pounds in the form of two accompanying goons.

"Benny. We keep meeting. How delightful."

"Yeah, smart-ass. We're gonna keep on meetin'. I got orders from Tony. I don't let you out of my sight. So where we goin'?"

"That accounts for you. What about Bevis and Butthead over here?"

"They go too. You might say they're security. Where we goin'?"

I had trouble visualizing a meeting with Professor Denisovitch with Benny attached at the hip. Benny plus two water buffalo? Not a chance.

"You wait here, Benny. I'm going to play one more set before we go to the airport. Keep Tweedle-Dumb and Tweedle-Dumber here with you."

"The hell, you say. I ain't lettin' you get two feet away from me. That's what Tony said."

"Benny, open your eyes. There's the stage. Here's the door. You and the Bobbsey Twins are in the direct path. Sit. Stay."

Benny analyzed the situation and settled back on the barstool.

"All right, Knight. Make it quick."

"One set."

"Hey, Knight. Where we goin'?"

"Paris."

I picked up Daddy and brought him to the table for a quick introduction to Terry. I explained to both of them that it would be the best thing for all concerned if Terry and I could be on the outside of Daddy's Club while those three at the bar were still on the inside.

Daddy nodded, and Terry looked puzzled.

I explained what I had in mind, and Daddy and I stepped up on the stand. Paul and the sax player, Freddie, were already there. We settled in, and Daddy called the tune. Never let it be said that he lacked a sense of humor. The tune was, "Get Out of Town."

The lights came down, and Daddy provided eight bars of intro at a medium clip. It must have been a good fourteen choruses later when Daddy brought it to a close. I'd have given my two seats at any Bruins playoff game to have seen the expression on Benny's face when the lights came up, and he saw that the piano player was little Julio Gianotti and not me. When the lights had gone down to darkness, Julio had accepted my invitation to sit in, and Terry and I slipped out through Daddy's office in the back of the club.

I put Terry in a cab with the promise that when I got back, we'd go out on a date like two normal people, whatever in the world that might be like.

Before I closed the cab door, a thought occurred. I asked Terry if she could remember any of what Benny said to John the night she and John were having dinner.

"Yes. The important part. They whispered for a while, then that man pulled back and yelled, 'You ain't gonna get away with it. I'll stop you cold.'"

Interesting. Just like that, Benny joined the list of suspects for John's death. I was surprised that I hadn't mentally added him earlier.

I saw Terry off with a kiss and a promise that I prayed God I'd live to keep. I caught a cab for Logan airport, and a plane for London. As far as I knew, Benny and the boys were at some other counter at Logan, scrounging three fast tickets to Paris. I only wished I'd told him Singapore.

CHAPTER TWENTY-THREE

The Tolstoy Club, as it was known in translation of the Russian, was located three blocks from the small Grisham Hotel in the Tottenham Court Square district of London. Its membership included not only authors, but practitioners of all of the fine arts. The only requirement for membership, other than an initiation fee, was a heritage from one of the former Soviet republics. That rule was self-fulfilling since the only language spoken within its walls was Russian.

Alexei Samnov rose quickly from his seat in the large library when he saw Leopold Denisovitch appear in the doorway. They greeted with the embrace of old friends, followed by habitual quick glances around the room to see who might be taking note.

Alexei led his friend to chairs in a far corner. Although they had the room to themselves, nothing was said by either until they were seated close to each other, and then only in hushed tones.

"I knew you'd come, Leopold."

The smaller man leaned closer.

"Did you leave me a choice, Alexei? I had no idea what to make of your message."

"I know. There was no time for invitation, refusal, persuasion. You correctly read the urgency of my message."

"And so I'm here."

A waiter in a white jacket approached with an offer of tea or vodka. Both declined, and waited for him to leave the room before speaking. Alexei sat stiffly forward on the leather chair.

"Leopold, this is uncomfortable. I don't know how to begin. Time doesn't permit delicacy. So I'll simply say it. What are you doing?"

There was silence for several moments while Leopold looked blankly at Alexei.

"I have no idea how to respond. You bring me across an ocean to ask a question like that?"

Alexei leaned closer still. He rubbed the bridge of his nose with his thumb and forefinger, at a loss for the words.

"Leopold, I've come a long way too. I think you know what I'm asking about. If I let this go with a coy denial— Leopold, I can assure you that you are in serious danger. You remember how it was in the old days? This is worse."

"The old days? You mean the Soviets? What does that have to do with me? I'm an American citizen now."

"And you believe that will protect you. Your American citizenship. Your comfortable position at Harvard."

Alexei shook his head. Leopold looked in his eyes.

"Protect me from what? I'm a professor of art history. It's not a dangerous profession, Alexei."

Alexei paused for a moment before speaking quietly and calmly. "If you won't say it, I will. You've placed your name behind the authentication of a painting attributed to Vermeer. *The Concert.*"

There was a slight hesitation before he replied. "Yes. It's what I do. You do the same."

"You do realize that *The Concert* was stolen from a Boston art museum years ago?"

"Who would know better than I? I live across the river from the museum. So what? My function was simply to certify its authenticity. I was told it was for the benefit of the insurance company. That it was part of the process. The painting would be returned through the insurance company. This happens."

"I know it happens. And you know that none of that is at the heart of the problem. Again I ask you, what are you doing, Leopold?"

Leopold raised his hands with a shrug to indicate confusion.

"Damn it, Leopold! I'm telling you that your life is in danger. Mine as well for telling you this. Answer the question."

"I would if I had any idea —"

"That painting is a fraud. There is no one on this earth, including Vermeer himself if he were alive, who would know that better than you do. You've broken faith with everything you've put your life into. Why, Leopold?"

He held up his hands and merely shook his head.

"All right, Leopold. If I can't appeal to your pride, maybe I can rouse your sense of self-preservation. There are those whom you have caused — serious inconvenience with your lies. One solution to the problem, which is you, is to do away with you. This is being considered. Does this get through to you? I owe you this warning out of our friendship. Understand, it places me in danger as well."

Alexei could see the change in his friend's countenance from naïve denial to honest fear.

"I ask you again, Leopold. What are you doing?"

His friend covered his eyes and withdrew against the back of the chair. Alexei gave him time to compose his thoughts.

"It began so simply. A former student came to me. He said he represented an art collector. He wanted a good reproduction of Vermeer's work, *The Concert*. An honest, admitted reproduction, you understand. As you said, the original had been stolen from the museum, but there were plenty of photographs of the painting to work from. I produced a reasonable reproduction for a fee."

"You painted it?"

"I did. An admitted reproduction. Not for fraud. I was later told that I would be required to certify that it was the original. I refused, of course."

He hesitated.

"So what changed your mind?"

"They came to me with pictures of my grandchildren at school, at play, in their home. What they said they would do to them — The pictures were to prove they could get to them anywhere." He paused. "I gave them their certification."

Alexei leaned back into the high leather chair. He could feel his breath flowing out of him when he heard the confession, even though he knew before it was spoken.

"Why did you call me, Alexei?"

Alexei held up limp hands.

"What I said is true. Your authentication produced ripples in the financial world. You have no idea. What matters is that there are those who believe the ripples will go away if you —"

He waved his hand, and Leopold understood.

"Alexei, this was a very private transaction. Do these people you're talking about know that I was the one?"

"I want to say no. I want to very badly. From what I'm told, they only know that the painting was authenticated. They don't know by whom. Of course I knew who it had to be as soon as I heard it. I can swear to you that I told them I didn't know. If they believed me, you're safe. It's just that — I would not bet your life or mine that I fooled them."

"What can I do, Alexei?"

"I could say be careful, but even I don't know what that means. These are terrible, vicious people. Unfortunately, unlike the old days, they are also very intelligent. I could say go into hiding, but I think they're too clever for either of us. Perhaps the best thing is to go on with your life and raise no suspicion. And pray."

"Yes."

Leopold leaned forward. "You put yourself at risk to save me, old friend, even though you thought I betrayed the thing we love."

"I knew there had to be a reason, Leopold. That's why I had to see you, and warn you. I'll say it from my heart. Be careful."

Alexei rose and held out his hand. Leopold remained seated.

"We're not through, Alexei. Sit down."

Alexei sat slowly.

"You said you knew that the painting I authenticated was a copy. How?"

"I assumed that a painting that was missing all these years would hardly turn up just like that."

"No. I don't think so. Missing paintings turn up in unexpected ways. Now it's my turn to insist. How did you know that my painting was not the original?"

Alexei sat mute.

"There's only one way you could be sure. Yes? You've seen the original. You know where it is. And why would someone show it to you? I think so that you would authenticate it for them — even though you knew it was stolen. I think it's your turn to be honest."

Alexei remained silent.

"My dear God, Alexei, our folly may be the death of both of us. Can't we at least preserve a bit of honesty between ourselves?"

Alexei placed his hand on Leopold's shoulder.

"It seems we've both played Judas. Do you remember when we were at university together in St. Petersburg all those years ago? What brought us to this confessional, Leopold?"

His friend just shook his head.

"At least you can say you did it to save your family. I did it for money. A great deal of money. I told myself that it was no lie. I said to myself that I was being true to the master by announcing to the world that that masterpiece was his handiwork. My sin was the greater. I've paid the penance in anguish, and, I'll admit it, in tears."

Leopold rose and lifted his friend by the arm. He embraced him.

"If we can't absolve each other, Alexei, at least we can know that one other person understands. I've carried this for so long. Somehow I feel like a rock has been lifted from my shoulders."

They smiled and embraced once more before Leopold put on his raincoat and walked through the chilling rain back to the Grisham Hotel.

CHAPTER TWENTY-FOUR

I'd been to London before, so I knew that it was more important to have rain gear than underwear. And still the chill rain penetrated to the skin on my walk from the Chesterfield Hotel, where Julie booked me, to the Grisham Hotel.

The "lobby," to be generous, was about the size of my bedroom in Boston. It just barely managed a front desk, room for three people to register, and two wooden chairs that might have actually supported the royal rump of William the Conqueror, if age were the test.

I coaxed the grizzled, bearded face of the desk clerk out of a worn paperback copy of a Lee Child novel with a question.

"Excuse me. Is a Professor Denisovitch registered here?"

He rose out of his seat to a diminutive height that barely put him eyeball-to-Adam's apple with me. He did it rather nimbly, considering a girth that was at least twice mine. His bulk made it a bit jolting when his voice was a good octave higher than one might expect.

"I'm sorry, the name?"

"Professor Denisovitch. He's an American." I'm not sure why I added that. It scored no points.

"No. I mean your name. Are you some form of constabulary?" The words fairly reeked of condescension.

"You mean am I with the police?"

"I mean, have you any official function that entitles you to breach the privacy of the gentleman you're asking about?"

I noticed that the officious little twit ended a sentence with a preposition. I did not stoop to comment.

"No, I'm not. Let me put it this way. Would you be kind enough to ring the room of Professor Denisovitch, who may or may not be registered here? If you reach him, my name is Michael Knight. I'd be most grateful."

He turned his back and dialed a two-digit number on his mini-switchboard. I noticed from the mailboxes behind him that there were eight rooms in all, spread over the three floors above the "lobby." Ten seconds later he turned back to me.

"I'm sorry."

"Meaning he's not in his room?"

He donned a sardonic look and tone and merely repeated, "I'm sorry."

I doubted the sincerity of his sorrow, but I got the message that he would rather have self-immolated than give me one bit more data. The professor apparently was registered there or he wouldn't have tried to call him. On the other hand, he was apparently not in. Communication sometimes works in mysterious ways.

Since I had only one purpose for being in London, I decided to wait. I took up a station on one of King William's chairs and perused the London *Times*.

It was a good twenty minutes before the front door opened, admitting rain, wind, and two weather-protected individuals. My first guess, when they peeled off an outer layer, was that they were Eastern European. That was confirmed by accents that, to my untraveled ear, could have ranged anywhere from Serbia to Siberia.

They approached our jovial host and asked for a room. He asked in his most officious tone if they had a reservation. They said "No," and he booked them anyway into one of the rooms on the third floor.

I'd been a semicasual observer until one of them pulled an envelope out of an inner pocket and asked Conrad Hilton to leave it for Professor Denisovitch. The twit obliged the paying customers by slipping the envelope into the mail slot behind him marked Room 5, one of the three rooms on the second floor.

Interesting, I thought. With one little envelope, they had acquired the information that I couldn't pry out of him with a crowbar. Why didn't I think of that?

They had my undivided attention when they carried their two valises, the size of the old-time carpetbags, to the "lift." It was a caged affair that resembled the metal boxes that run up the outside of construction sites. The floor indicator was out of the view of the desk clerk, but I dropped the *Times* and retrieved it so that it was not out of mine.

Now they had my curiosity as well as attention when the indicator said that the two rode to the second, not the third floor. I waited to see if it was a mistake that they'd correct. Not a bit of it.

Ten minutes later, the elevator descended from the second floor, and the two went back out into the wind and rain. They had the same two valises, but from the way they were carrying them, they seemed considerably lighter than when they'd arrived.

Anyone who was not paranoid from assassination attempts and nerve jangled from jet lag would say, "Of course they're lighter. They took the stairs the rest of the way up from the second floor to the third floor and unpacked." There was, however, no one that normal sitting in one of King William's chairs. Personally, I was engulfed in a sea of raging theories and suspicions.

At six o'clock in the evening, a drenched but familiar figure walked through the front door. Professor Denisovitch went directly to the desk and asked for the key to Room 5. I was on him with enough pent-up angst to cause him to back off a few steps.

"Professor, it's all right. My name's Michael Knight. I was a student of yours in History of Art 102. Harvard."

The exuberance of his ex-student did nothing to prevent him from steadily retreating backward. I thought perhaps he was expecting me to ask him to raise my grade.

"Professor, I need to speak with you. I'm sorry to do it here, now, but I can't overstate its importance. Could we come over to these chairs for a minute?"

I remembered him as a relatively short, slight man, which he was, but standing there in an oversized dripping raincoat, he also looked pathetically vulnerable. The look on his face shifted from mere trepidation to outright fear combined with an urgent desire to get out of my presence.

"No. Not now, young man. I'm — No."

He headed at double-quick-time for the lift. I was on his heels, pleading, but he had closed his ears to me. He pulled the door of the lift open just enough for his wan body to slip inside. I grabbed the door, pulled it open the rest of the way, and slipped into the tiny space beside him.

From the look on his face, I had a genuine fear that the panic in his eyes could be the precursor to a heart attack. He was punching the button for the second floor as rapidly as his little fist could poke.

The clangs and squeaks of that industrial dinosaur were mixed with the high-pitched demands of the twit below. "Come down this instant or I shall summon the police."

"Summon the queen if you want. Just keep everyone off this damn elevator for the next ten minutes!"

We reached the second floor in what seemed like half an hour. The professor wanted nothing more than to spring loose and lock himself in his room with me on the outside. It was time to use the one advantage I had over him. I was bigger than he was.

I grabbed him by the shoulders and pinned him to the side of the elevator and told him in a tone that I could not have conceived of in History of Art 102, "With all due respect professor, shut up and listen."

He was so far beyond terror that he did just that. I had the stage and an attentive audience of one.

"Professor, I am not going to harm you. I firmly believe I am about to save your life. Two men, Russians I think, came to your room this afternoon. I think they left a surprise package for you. We have to be extremely careful. Are you hearing me?"

His eyes were like letter *O*s, and he couldn't seem to speak.

"Just nod. Are you hearing me?"

He nodded, and for the first time that day I felt I had communicated with someone.

"Good, professor. We're going to get out of the elevator. Stay behind me. Give me your key."

He did. I walked ahead to the room marked 5. The door and lock were as ancient as every other part of the building. I looked for any kind of marks on the door and thought I saw a scratch on the outside where the latch fit into the groove. I felt the tiniest vindication. On the other hand, the mark could have been made four hundred years ago.

I slipped the key in the old-fashioned lock and turned it until the tumbler clicked into the open position. I thanked God that it predated spring-loading.

I guided the professor down the hall to a position outside of Room 4. I pushed him against the inner wall and told him not to move. He behaved like an obedient cocker spaniel.

I went back to the door to Room 5. I moved as carefully as a bomb squad in turning the knob just enough to leave the door free to swing open. I took off my raincoat and plastered myself as far down the corridor as I could and still have a shot at the door. I rolled my raincoat into a tight ball.

One check of the professor, who had not moved an inch, and I hurled the raincoat with the best sidearm pitch I could manage.

The raincoat hit the door and sent it flying open. In that fraction of a second, I realized that if nothing happened, I would feel as if I had just walked naked into a meeting of the Ladies' Abstinence Society.

The concern was short-lived. In a fraction of a second, I found myself grabbing the sides of my head to dull the double percussive shock that nearly blew out both eardrums. I fell to the floor with the instantaneous pain in the ears and forced my eyelids closed against the cloud of plaster that filled the corridor.

When I could open my eyes, I saw that the wall opposite Room 5 had been blown away. I was still on the floor when I checked back to see the professor in the same place but down on his knees, holding his ears. He looked up at me, and I signaled him to stay put.

I crept up to the open doorway and looked inside Room 5. The two Russians, or whatever they were, did nothing halfway. Two shot-guns were strapped to chairs five feet inside the room. They were wired to go off when the door was fully opened so that the person entering, assumedly the professor, would get the full benefit of both blasts.

I kicked open the door to Room 4 with a shot from the heel of my still water-soaked shoe. I pulled the professor inside and told him to "sit on the bed and don't move" till I come for him. At this point, if I'd told him to stand on the window ledge and do the Macarena, he'd be up there.

I closed the door to Room 4 and raced down the steps. The twit was in full fluster. The double blast must have blown to pieces what little grip he thought he had on the situation.

He had the phone in one shaking hand, and was stabbing at and missing the digits with the other. I grabbed the phone out of his hand and hung up.

"Get a grip. What do you dial to get an ambulance?"

His body was shaking in rhythm with his hand.

"I want the police. Right now." His voice was half an octave higher yet. One more disaster in his evening and only dogs would hear him.

"First the ambulance. What number?"

He fumbled for a sheet of paper with emergency numbers, and I picked the one marked "Hospital/Emergency." I called it and gave the address of the hotel. They sounded efficient, and to my delight, within three minutes I heard that yodeling wail ambulances make over there.

I watched them pull up to the entrance, and two uniformed medical technicians rushed through the door. I left them to make whatever sense they could out of the rantings and whimperings of the clerk.

I took the stairs on the fly back to Room 4. I grabbed the professor by the hand and led him like a chimpanzee down the stairs. The lobby was now full of confused guests milling around and asking each other questions that none of them could answer. Another siren indicated that the police would soon be taking control. It was time to leave.

I found a back entrance. Still grasping the professor by the hand, I quick-marched down the alley behind the hotel until we reached a cross street. Fortunately, the rain had let up. In two blocks, we slowed to a breath-catching walk.

My ultimate destination was my own hotel, the Chesterfield. A block short, I could not resist a left turn into a warm, dry pub. We found a table in the back where the noise level let us talk but not be overheard. I settled the professor into a seat while I went to the bar. I prescribed a brandy for the professor and five fingers of the Famous Grouse for me.

I gave us time to medicate before beginning a conversation. Three fingers into the Grouse, a spurious thought crossed my mind. Wouldn't this be the darndest time to actually ask him to reconsider the B he gave me in History of Art 102?

I resisted.

CHAPTER TWENTY-FIVE

The pub was beginning to pulse with the after-office-hours clientele. New arrivals gave dripping evidence of the heavy rainfall. The professor and I huddled in our remote corner, nestling the Grouse and brandy in our increasingly warm little mitts.

I was reasonably confident that the panic had passed, unless, of course, the professor's two Slavic visitors chose this out of all of the pubs in London.

They were clearly pros, which led me to believe that they undoubtedly waited around to hear the resounding percussion of their handiwork. I had called for the ambulance to give them one last visual indication that the shotguns had found their target, i.e., the professor. With that satisfaction, hopefully they had moved on to other duties.

I finally had what I wanted—a one-on-one with Professor Denisovitch, he being in a mood to open the store.

"Professor, you might have missed the introduction. My name's Michael Knight. Why I'm here is a long story. You don't need to hear it right now. Let's cut to the chase. First point. Your life is in danger, do we agree?"

He looked up from the brandy and nodded.

"Young man, how did you know—?"

"Michael, professor. Michael Knight. Ordinarily I wouldn't care, but I think we're going to be in close contact for a while."

"Yes, Mr. Knight. How did you know—?"

"That's part of the long story. I don't want to be rude, but we have a lot to cover in what could be a short time. My second point.

I believe your life is in danger because you probably authenticated a painting by Vermeer. You did it for another former student, John McKedrick. You probably didn't know that John was working for one of the big shots in the New England Mafia. What I'm saying is you're dealing with some dangerous people. I think you're convinced, correct?"

He just nodded his head slowly.

"How did I bring this on myself?"

"A more important question is how you're going to get out of it. If I'm going to be able to help you, I need information. I need to know every detail you can think of regarding this Vermeer deal."

The professor finished the brandy before beginning an account that I could hardly believe. Apparently John approached him and commissioned him to paint a copy of the Vermeer canvas that had been stolen from a Boston museum. When it was finished, John demanded that he authenticate his painting as the genuine Vermeer. He even brought threats to bear on the lives of the professor's family if he refused.

"Professor, did John actually threaten you himself?"

He thought for a bit, and I was glad to have him take the time to put the pieces together accurately. I took another slug of the Grouse and braced for the answer.

"No. Not personally. He came to me with the original commission to paint the copy, but it was a Russian man who made the threats. He was part of the same group with Mr. McKedrick. That's why I was confused. He was from Minsk, from Belarus. Sergei Markov. I won't forget that name. He made the threat."

"Now I'm confused. John McKedrick was working for a Mafia gangster in Boston by the name of Tony Aiello. Did you ever hear that name?"

"No. I never heard whom Mr. McKedrick represented. He and Markov seemed to be working together."

"All right. To whom did you give this authentication?"

"There was a meeting."

"Where?"

The professor's energy was draining fast. I figured that I better squeeze it bit by bit to get everything in one sitting. There may not be another.

"In Amsterdam."

"Who was there?"

"Mr. McKedrick. This man from Belarus, Markov. And two men with whom they seemed to be negotiating."

I signaled the barmaid for another brandy for the professor to keep down the nervous fidgets that seemed to be starting again.

"This is important, professor. Do you remember their names?"

He gave it his full concentration. I thanked God that he didn't come up empty.

"Van Drusen. That was one. He was a financier of some kind. 'Jan' they called him. We met in his office. The other was, I'm not sure, Van Arsdale I think. They were partners."

"Do you remember where their office was?"

"No. It was my first time in Amsterdam. It was beside a large canal."

"And you gave them your opinion that the painting was a genuine Vermeer?"

He went silent on me.

"Professor?"

"Yes. I did. I'm ashamed."

"Under the circumstances, you really had no choice. Were these financiers buying the painting?"

"I don't think so."

"Why don't you think so?"

"After I signed the authentication certificate, they took the painting to a bank in the same block. They placed the painting in a vault. Mr. McKedrick and Van Drusen each took a separate coded number. They had me come along to certify that the painting was not switched before it was put into the vault."

"Did you have any idea what they were doing?"

"I think so. I've seen it done before. I believe the painting was security for a loan."

"Loan to whom?"

"I suppose to whomever John McKedrick was working for. I'm very tired."

The second brandy had him more relaxed than I'd hoped, but at that point I probably had all he was able to give me. I got the two of us bundled up, more for disguise than for weather protection in case the two Russians were still lurking about.

I hustled him through the rain to the Chesterfield Hotel and up to my room. While he took a hot bath, I made some calls. My first was to Helga Swenson to let her know that the professor was alive. I decided to tell her about the incident at the Grisham Hotel. I didn't want to alarm her, but I wanted her to take seriously my plea that she tell absolutely no one where the professor was, or even that he was still alive.

My second call was to Mr. Devlin. I decided to tell him everything, particularly in view of the fact that I had the Atlantic Ocean as a buffer between us. What could he do, fire me?

"Michael, damn it, you're fired. If that's the only way to get you to stop putting your neck on the block, you are no longer engaged as an attorney."

"You can't fire me, Mr. Devlin. We're partners. Besides, you're not my client. If you'll be kind enough to remember, I represent the Prince of Evil, the Godfather of all malevolent Godfathers, thanks to your boyhood reunion. Besides, who else will put up with your intimidation?"

"Intimidation? When the hell have you ever followed one bit of my good advice to keep you in one piece?"

"I'm definitely starting now."

"Good. I'll expect you on the next plane to Boston."

I decided to finesse that one. Instead, I told him what I'd learned from the professor. I had one final point.

"Mr. Devlin, can you find out from Santangelo if he knows anything about this deal with the Vermeer? My guess is he doesn't."

"That's my guess too. It looks like Aiello was going big league behind his back."

"It's going to look that way to Mr. Santangelo too. Without tipping too much, can you try to squeeze a few more days of truce out of him? I think I'm getting close."

"I'll see what I can do. And you stay out of danger."

"No problem. I'm just dealing with stuffy art dealers from here on."

"All right. Remember, the next plane to Boston."

"I'll be on it. Just one small detour."

"Michael, where the hell are you going now?"

"Boston, Mr. Devlin. And straight to the office. As soon as I get back from Amsterdam."

That seemed a propitious moment to hang up.

My next call was to Tony Aiello. There was one card I needed to get on the table. He answered graciously as always.

"Yeah. What?"

"This is Michael Knight. Is that you, Tony? May I call you Tony?"

"Oh yeah. Call me Tony. Like we're old buddies. How's about I call you son of a bitch, you little bastard. What'd you do to Benny?"

I had to cover the phone piece to prevent choking on a laugh. It had to be for Fat Tony that the phrase, "piece of work," was invented.

"Benny? I haven't seen Benny since yesterday. Besides, he's the least of your problems."

"The hell he is. That little shyster's spendin' my money runnin' all over Paris. He says you sent him there."

"Paris? I've never been to Paris in my life. Well, the good news is he's probably eating very well. I hear there are wonderful restaurants in Paris."

"Well that just tickles the ass off me. That bum's gonna pay back every dime if I have to skin him alive."

"You've gotta do what you've gotta do. Meanwhile, there's something I need to know. This painting I'm after. Why do you need it?"

"You got cement in your head? I told you once. It's none of your business."

"Yes, I heard that. See, here's the thing. I'll be dealing with some very intelligent, very dicey people. When they ask questions, if I look like some gofer, you won't get your painting, and I won't get to live. Let me make it easy. This much I can figure. John set up some kind of deal where you acquire the stolen Vermeer. I assume at a good price. You borrow money, a lot of money, using the painting as security. Professor Denisovitch authenticates the painting, which satisfies the lenders. The painting is kept in a vault with two codes. You have one. Actually I have it from John. The lenders have the other code. Am I on track so far?"

There was silence for a few seconds before Tony came back in a whisper.

"Are you sure this line ain't tapped?"

"No. But what the hell's the difference? Where I am, I can't just drop into your office, and I need some information."

"That's another thing. Where are you?"

"I'm out of town. Here's what I need to know. Why do you need to get your hands on the painting?"

"To sell it, you schmuck. What the hell do you think, I'm gonna start a museum?"

That was what I needed to know. He obviously couldn't repay the debt. He had to use the security to square it with his lenders. That told me a couple of things. One was that John McKedrick apparently never let Fat Tony know that the painting was a fraud.

Holy mackerel, John. How many games were you playing?

My second guess was that if Tony couldn't come up with what must have been a horse-choking wad of cash to pay off the lenders, he was in seriously deep and dangerous waters — a fact that could give me more leverage than I thought over Tony.

"How much do you need to raise?"

"More than you'll ever see, wise-ass."

"Come on, I need to know what we're playing for. If it's as much as I think, you're not dealing with some low-level Mafia loan sharks. This is big time. Probably international. Give me a number."

I heard him mumble something that sounded like "sixty."

"Sixty what?"

"Mm-nn."

"What? Speak up."

"Million, asshole."

That number staggered even me.

"Okay. That's what I needed to know. I'll be in touch. And Tony—"

"Yes. *Mikey.*"

"I'll do what I can. I know it's important. But there's something even more important."

"Yeah, what?"

"That you and I be nice to each other."

I gave him time to get out six words before cutting off the line. The five words were, "You little son of a bitch."

CHAPTER TWENTY-SIX

My plane touched down early the next morning at Schiphol Airport, outside of Amsterdam. I had left the professor in my room at the Chesterfield in London to eat, sleep, and generally hang out inside the hotel for the day or two I might be gone. A chance meeting on the street with the boys from Belarus could be his final social encounter.

The travelers' advisory service at the airport put me into the most expensive hotel in Amsterdam, the Amstel Intercontinental Hotel, a truly five-star operation, luxuriously covering a city block beside the Amstel River. I wanted to present an up-scale address to the financiers I was about to deal with.

It was also easier to get an immediate room during the high tourist season at a hotel that drained the bank account than it would be at an economy hotel, and I didn't particularly mind that it was Dominic Santangelo's bank account that was being drained.

My first move was to scan the phonebook for a Jan Van Drusen. There were a few. Then I checked for a Van Arsdale who had the same business address as a Van Drusen, since the professor thought they were partners.

Bingo. There was a match. I called the number. I gave my name, and asked the female voice that switched in an instant from Dutch to English for Mr. Jan Van Drusen. She asked, "To what was it in reference?"

I noted that this linguistic foreigner was sharp enough to place the preposition before the noun instead of at the end of the sentence,

and realized that if this was the level of intelligence of the receptionist, I'd better be hitting on all cylinders.

"Would you tell Mr. Van Drusen that I'm only in town for the
day. I represent the American gentleman who owns a certain painting by Vermeer. I'm staying at the Amstel Intercontinental. It would
be in both of our interests to meet as soon as possible."

She politely put me on hold and was back in thirty seconds.

"Mr. Van Drusen would be happy to meet with you at your con-
venience, Mr. Knight."

"Good. I can come to his office directly."

"Mr. Van Drusen would be pleased to send a car for you."

"Thank you. That won't be necessary. I'll be there shortly."

The car idea was probably a courtesy, but a little paranoid voice
was repeating my mother's warning against getting into a car with
strangers.

The address of Van Drusen's office was on Herengracht, between Leidsestraat and a street that I couldn't pronounce if I had
three tongues. As the professor suggested, it was on a canal, which is
as much help as saying "look for the fish somewhere in the water."
There are over a hundred canals. Everything in Amsterdam is on a
canal.

I got a map of the city from the concierge and followed his
advice on the best route to walk there. I asked how long it would
take. He said with a big, good-hearted grin, "About twenty minutes
if you make it at all."

I grinned back and took to the street, wondering if he just had
strange speech patterns. In thirty seconds I realized that he knew
whereof he spoke. I waded into the automobile traffic with the certain conviction that they couldn't show this boy from Boston anything he hadn't survived on his home turf. What I soon learned was
that the car traffic is just a distraction. It's the bicycles in barbaric
hordes that will leave treads right up your back.

Against all odds, I found the address, an impressive white
marble three-story office building facing the canal. The inside offices

carried through the theme of tasteful opulence. Mr. Van Drusen's suite of offices was on the second floor, all facing a view of the canal and its interesting variety of aquatic traffic.

The receptionist created the same impression as the building, as did everything about the office. You sensed before even meeting Van Drusen or Van Arsdale that you might lose your shirt in a business deal if you were not on top of your game.

Mr. Van Drusen met me at the door to his office with a smile and a warm handshake. He was tall and well proportioned with one of those faces that seems to smile even when it's at rest. His hair length suggested that his attention would be on the business at hand rather than on himself. His suit and silk shirt were equally under-stated, although I could tell from the tailoring that the ensemble rep-resented enough to pay off my Corvette.

He introduced Mr. Van Arsdale, whose proportions around the center were more indicative of the allure of Dutch cooking. He looked a bit like the Michelin Man.

I liked the fact that both proceeded to drape their suit coats around the backs of chairs. They were ready to play.

"Play," however, as I'd heard about the Dutch, began with strong coffee and chocolate pastry. The conversation was light, witty, and unfortunately, time-consuming — a commodity I couldn't afford to spend lightly. Much to my regret, I had to break the mood.

"Gentlemen, I'm going to be direct. John McKedrick set up an arrangement with you that involved the loan of a considerable sum of money."

They each nodded with a smile, but the glint in their eyes said that they were fully tuned in. With the exception of myself, there were no rookies in that room. I hit it again for emphasis.

"A *considerable* sum of money."

Again they nodded.

"We all understand that the security behind the debt owed to you gentlemen is a work of the great master that is clearly beyond price."

I thought an appeal to their sense of pride in the Dutch master,

Vermeer, might be a nice touch before wading into deep waters. If it had an effect, they hid it completely.

"What might or might not have been disclosed by John McKedrick is that he represented the interests of an American by the name of Anthony Aiello."

This time the nods meant that they were aware that the loan was, in fact, made not to the suave, sophisticated John McKedrick, but to the overstuffed hood with whom I was now on a first name basis.

"Mr. Aiello's business —"

"Mr. Knight." Mr. Van Drusen cut mercifully to the chase.

"We're aware in a general way of Mr. Aiello's business. The loan was arranged, as you say, on the basis of very sound security. How Mr. Aiello chose to invest the money is something we don't care to know or discuss. I don't mean to be rude."

"I can accept the ground rules, Mr. Van Drusen. I do, however, bring you this word. Unfortunately, Mr. Aiello is not in a position to repay the loan and probably never will be."

Looks were exchanged between the two Vans, which I read as expressing concern but not panic. The intensity level of the conversation just rose three degrees, and I detected a layer of steel beneath the previously jovial hospitality of the two.

"Please go on, Mr. Knight. I'm sure that's not all you came to say."

"No, it isn't. At this point it is certainly in the interest of both you and Mr. Aiello to look to the security, the painting. May I speak freely here?"

Both raised two hands with the comforting implication of "How else?"

"Good. Frankly, we need to sell the painting. Would you agree?"

Mr. Van Drusen was about to speak, I believe, in agreement, when a door opened at the rear of the office and a third gentleman entered the office. He had the Slavic features that suggested a Russian lineage, and a manner that clearly indicated that he was now assuming control of the other side of the negotiation.

I could feel the gentility of the atmosphere drained from the room. There would be no pastry and hot coffee on his watch. Every sensory alert in my makeup went directly from green through orange to red.

"Mr. Knight, may I introduce Mr. Sergei Markov?"

The security color code jumped from red to ultraviolet without even passing through purple. I remembered Professor Denisovitch saying that it was a Sergei Markov who conveyed the cold-blooded threat to his grandchildren.

I stood to shake hands, but Mr. Markov moved directly to a vacant seat across from me without speaking.

"Mr. Markov, I assume that you're involved in this transaction."

"You assume correctly. May I assume that you speak with authority to act for this Aiello?"

"Yes."

"And just how does this Aiello propose to meet his obligation? You come into this office and say he won't repay the debt."

"I say he can't repay the debt."

"To us there's no difference. Does he think he's dealing with fools?"

The volume was steadily rising.

"No. Do you?"

The tone was as cutting as I could make it. The jolt produced a pause. I pressed the point, lest he mistake my tone.

"Do you think you're dealing with fools, Mr. Markov?"

He was not off guard for long.

"Frankly, yes. This Aiello is so far out of his depth —"

"You're not dealing with Aiello. I represent his interests, but I'm not his errand boy. Neither was John McKedrick, with whom you arranged the loan. Now, if we're through judging each other, I'll say what I came to say."

Markov was steaming. I sensed that he dealt in intimidation and had a short fuse when his upper hand was challenged. Mr. Van Drusen came forward to put a firm, but settling, lid on the pot before it boiled over.

"Please, gentlemen. There's business to be done here. I assume you came with a proposal, Mr. Knight. I believe we should hear it. And then we'll decide what course to follow."

He was speaking to me, but he was looking at Markov, who retreated for the moment into a smoldering silence. I backed off to a businesslike tone with a prayer that I could carry it off.

"Gentlemen, you knew whom you were dealing with when you made the loan. I can't for a moment believe that you had the slightest confidence in Tony Aiello's ability to manage that sum of money to the point of repaying it. He is what he is."

I noticed that Markov had come out of his pout to the point where I had his full attention.

"Which raises the question of why you made the loan to him in the first place. Shall we be honest with each other, gentlemen? Tony Aiello was a pawn. Mickey Mouse would have done equally well. You were dealing in a Vermeer painting. You didn't want to own it. That's risky. A stolen masterpiece? No. But you saw the chance to make a sizable fortune in interest on a loan that was securely backed by an object of immeasurable value without soiling your hands by touching the object directly. So let's drop the feigned shock at the mention of Tony Aiello's inability to repay the loan. Are we ready to talk business?"

Markov was glaring, but he sat in a pool of silence. Mr. Van Drusen not only followed the discourse, but smiled when he nodded his assent. I made a note never to play chess with him for money.

"Mr. Aiello owes you a principal in the area of sixty million dollars. With interest, the figure is close to seventy million. Are we in agreement?"

The figures were based on the scraps of information I'd squeezed out of Fat Tony. My only interest was in fixing the upper level of the debt, interest included, to set up my next step.

If I allowed myself one fraction of a second to think of the meaning of the numbers I was spewing out with abandon, I'd have needed more underwear than I'd packed.

The Vans nodded, and the Russian sphinx failed to correct me. On with the show.

"There is no question that the value of the painting covers that figure and much more. There is, however, one minor complication. The painting is the most recognizable piece of stolen property on the face of the earth. If one hint of what's being said in this room got beyond these walls — I'll leave it at that. We all value our freedom."

The Vans were both taking this in with an equanimity that convinced me still further of the steel subsurface, while the Russian sphinx remained in deep freeze. Van Drusen urged on the next step.

"You wanted to talk business, Mr. Knight. I assume you didn't come this distance without a proposal."

"I have something better than that. I have a buyer."

I read the reactions of the Vans as cautious relief, if not incipient optimism at the thought of pulling off the deal as they had planned. I hoped they caught a whiff of cleanly laundered cash.

Markov, on the other hand, sat with an expression that was impossible to read. He was the joker in the deck. What had to be affecting his reaction was the fact that he knew that the painting was a phony. In fact, he was in on the original scam on the Vans to secure the loan to Tony Aiello.

The wild card was that I had no idea whether or not Markov believed that I thought the painting was genuine.

"And the name of this buyer, Mr. Knight?"

"Is known to me, Mr. Markov. I've given certain pledges of confidence. The question is whether or not I have your approval to proceed with the sale."

"At what price, Mr. Knight?"

"That's Mr. Aiello's business. He is, you remember, the owner. You have half of the code to the vault. That's your leverage. That assures you that the painting won't be released without a price paid in cash or credit that covers the full amount owed to you gentlemen. Anything over that amount will, of course, go to Mr. Aiello."

I walked to the window with my back to the three. I counted boats and barges on the canal while I let them exchange looks and signals behind my back. It could have been a mistake, but I was making up the moves as I went along. Van Drusen was the first to speak out loud.

"Mr. Knight, I think we need to know more about this buyer of yours."

"That's a coincidence, Mr. Van Drusen. The last thing he told me was that he wanted to know more about you and Mr. Van Arsdale. And now Mr. Markov."

That spooked Mr. Van Arsdale into jumping in without checking with Markov for permission. I knew I hit a nerve.

"What did you tell him about us?"

"The same thing I'm going to tell you. When I take on a confidence, I keep it. The question comes down to this: Do I proceed with this sale, or would you gentlemen like to try peddling this stolen item on the market?"

The Vans both looked at Markov. Markov looked me in the eye and searched my inner soul for a clue. I knew that if I looked away, or even blinked, he'd own me. I put every ounce of grit and steel I could muster into returning the intensity of his glare.

I can't say that he folded, or that I won. I only knew that we'd moved on to the next step when he said, "You interest me, Mr. Knight. Let's see if you're more than words. As your Mr. McKedrick used to say, 'What have we got to lose?'"

CHAPTER TWENTY-SEVEN

When I hit the street, I crossed to the railing on the bank of the canal. I decided to give myself two full minutes of respite on a bench in front of the constantly moving canal traffic. Thirty seconds into the respite, a tiny internal voice whispered, *For his next trick, he shall pull a buyer of a stolen masterpiece willing to pay seventy million dollars right smack out of his ass.*

I must admit, however, that when I had dropped that particular bomb at the meeting in the upstairs office, I was not totally without a plan. I had a pretty good idea of whom I was going to suck into this little disaster. I'd done it before in another disaster, and still he considered himself my friend.

There are so many things I could say about Harry Wong, every one of them a superlative. But one thought sums it up. If I were in a foxhole in heavy combat, and I could pick the one person to be there at my back—no question—Harry Wong.

Harry came from China about five years before we met as classmates at Harvard College. We were fellow residents of Kirkland House in our freshman year and teammates on the house wrestling team. We were cemented by the fact that at that time, there were a number on that wrestling team who did not exude a tolerance for those of either the Chinese or half-Puerto Rican lineage. The fact that Harry, a scrawny, six-foot Chinese beanpole, could pin any member of the team to the mat did nothing to assuage their discrimination, and as Harry's half-Latino buddy, I caught my share of their discrimination as well. While it separated us from them, it bound us more closely together.

When I went on to Harvard Law School, Harry began acquiring degrees in the sciences until he was on staff as a resident brainchild at M.I.T.

Our primary contact after college graduation had been our annual Thanksgiving dinner with a Latino twist at the home of my mother. If the original pilgrims did not serve *pollo con arroz* to the Indians at the first Thanksgiving, we were none the wiser.

Just as I had done the previous winter at a moment when I was engulfed in a very dicey situation in Boston's Chinatown, I dialed Harry's number in Cambridge. True to form, he was there when I needed him.

"Harry, it's good to hear your voice."

"Michael. Likewise."

"You'll never guess why I'm calling."

"Sure I will. It's either for Thanksgiving dinner or you want me for something that could kill the both of us. Could I hope for Thanksgiving?"

"Wrong month, Harry."

"Was I right about the second part?"

"Yes. God didn't make you a genius for nothing. I'll give you an option. You can hang up right now. We'll still be on for Thanksgiving. That's probably what I'd do."

"That's the hell of it, Mike. You wouldn't. You'd come through for me. God help me. Here we go again. What is it this time?"

"I need you to buy a painting."

"Really. How dangerous can that be? What painting?"

"The Vermeer that was stolen from the museum in Boston."

Silence.

"You there, Harry?"

"Not really. Mike. That painting was never recovered. How the hell did you get involved with a priceless, may I say, *stolen* Vermeer?"

"That depends. Are you game to hear the rest?"

"I'm thinking that for just engaging in this conversation, I could pull down, what, fifteen years in Walpole Prison?"

"As I say, Harry, are you game to hear the rest?"

"Why not? If you're still alive, you can be my defense counsel."

"I'll lay it out, and in the words of Nancy Reagan, you can 'just say no.' Just listen. They can't indict you for listening."

I brought him up to speed on the painting and then dropped the bomb.

"What I need, Harry, is a suave, sophisticate to play the part of the prospective buyer of the Vermeer."

"Dare I ask, at what price?"

"In the neighborhood of seventy million."

"That's one hell of a neighborhood, Mike. I don't live anywhere close to there."

"Not to worry, Harry. The offer is a phony. And so, for that matter, is the painting."

"That's a great relief, Mike. Now we're up to what, twenty years for fraud?"

"If it's any consolation, we'd be defrauding a defrauder, who is probably part of the Russian Mafia. I'm not sure of that last part."

"So instead of the FBI, we'd have the Russian Mafia after us."

"Actually, we'd have both. But if we handle it right, we'll never see either one."

"Uh-huh. One more question. Who are you doing this for? Who's your client?"

"The Godfather of the Boston Mafia, Dominic Santangelo."

There was a brief moment's catch before Harry broke into a laugh.

"Mike, you son of a gun. This is a joke. Isn't it? You had me going till you threw in that Godfather part. That was over the top. Do you really have nothing better to do than jack up my blood pressure?"

"It's not a joke. I'm deadly serious. Forgive the choice of words."

"Oh crap. You really mean it, don't you?"

"I do, Harry. So?"

I could hear him take a deep breath.

"Why waste time, Mike? We both know I'm going to say yes. Just fill me in."

I did. At least in regard to his role in the fake purchase of the

fake Vermeer. I let him know that the point of it was to get the painting out of a vault that required two codes of which I had only one. It
was the best plan I could come up with to make good on my promise to deliver the painting to Aiello. Needless to say, I had additional
motives other than making Fat Tony's day.

"So how do we start, Mike?"

"You get yourself to Logan Airport. Pick up the ticket for Amsterdam in your name on KLM. It leaves tonight. Take clothes for
about three days."

"You conman, you already bought the ticket. How'd you know
I'd do it?"

"I know you're a good friend, Harry. When you get into the airport here, take a cab to the Amstel Intercontinental Hotel. I'll have
your reservation. Just one complication. I'm booking you through
London. It's a quick stop. I need you to bring someone with you."

"Sounds like the easy part."

"Not entirely. There are people out to kill him. Just keep a low
profile. They think he's already dead so you shouldn't have any
trouble."

"That's a comfort. Exactly who is he?"

I filled in the details.

"One last thing, Harry. While you're here, you get your choice
of names. Who do you want to be?"

He thought for a moment before coming up with "Qian An-
Yong. Can you spell it?"

I recalled he ran a fine Chinese herb shop in Chinatown.

"I believe I can spell it. Good choice. See you in the land of
tulips."

On my walk back to the hotel, I made cell phone calls to book
Harry's flight and hotel reservation and also the flight from London
for Professor Denisovitch. The flights had to be in their own names,
since they always check passports before boarding. Same for the hotel
reservations, since they usually check passports on check-in. I made
a third hotel reservation in the name of Qian An-Yong.

Once back at the hotel, I settled in for one of the most sumptuous lunches Dominic Santangelo ever paid for at the world-renowned La Rive Restaurant in the Amstel Intercontinental Hotel.

I was early enough to get a table by the window. The sun was playing on the gentle river, dotted with boats of every description. It was actually soothing to watch people who were not risking their lives every time they opened their mouths strolling along the banks of the river.

The choice of wine I wisely left to the waiter. He came through with a carafe of angelic ambrosia.

My defensive antennae sank slowly into repose with each sip — almost to the point where I would not have noticed the three Russian types who sat down at the adjoining table. Once tuned in, I spotted bulges under the heavy Eastern European suits that did not correspond to any human musculature. Both "repose" and my intake of wine went on hold.

I cruised quietly through the first course of the meal in a conscious effort to quell any signs of panic. That worked well until peripheral vision told me that the largest of the hulks was standing at my elbow. He spoke quietly with a pronounced Slavic accent.

"A very fine restaurant, is it not?"

"It is." I continued to look at my plate. I could hear him take a deep slow breath before speaking in a low voice.

"I think it would be well not to disturb these fine people enjoying their lunches. I think we could do that if you just quietly stand up and follow me."

I remained seated and silent. He spoke in a bit lower tone and closer to my ear.

"I think perhaps you did not hear. If you wish, this could be done differently. Either way —"

"Sit down."

It was not what he expected, and he wasn't sure he heard me. I spoke without looking up at him.

"Sit down."

I nodded to the seat across the table from me. I'd have bet everything I owned that Larry, Curley, and Moe were emissaries of Sergei Markov. I continued in a soft, even tone.

"Think about it. I'm not going anywhere. You've got me outnumbered three to one. What can you lose? Sit down."

While he stood there trying to fathom a response to a turn of events he hadn't been briefed on, I called over the waiter.

He hissed in a whisper. "No police."

I ignored him and said to the waiter, "Would you bring another wine glass?"

I looked in his general direction, still avoiding the indignity of looking up. "It's an invitation. Sit down. This wine is better than anything you'll taste in Mother Russia."

He slowly took a seat. His eyes were fixed on me like a goalie watching a forward on a breakaway.

The waiter brought a glass and poured from the crystal carafe.

"Try it." He slowly took the glass. I reached over and gave our glasses a salutary clink.

"Your health."

And mine too, I added in silence.

He poured that ambrosia into his thug-like face as if he were tossing down a shot of vodka. I doubt that he even tasted it. On the other hand, who cared? I had him in a position to talk face-to-face.

I slowly opened my suit coat and reached with my thumb and forefinger into the inner pocket. He stabbed his hand inside of his coat at one of the bulges as expected, but I moved so slowly that he went no further.

I took out my cell phone with two fingers, flipped it open, and handed it across the table to him.

"Call him. Do it now. Do you see that maître'd over there? Tuxedo? By the desk? If I should get up to leave with anyone like you or your boyfriends, he'll have the police meet us at the door."

My wine-tasting companion watched as I gave a hand signal to the maître'd that everything was cool so far. He signaled back that he understood, but continued to keep an eye on us.

I wish I could say that I had actually been clever enough to fore-see what was happening and had prearranged the whole signal code with the maître d'. Unfortunately, I'm no Spencer. I did, however, on the way in, give him an enormous tip, enough to induce him to stay alert to my every desire. I'm sure the hand signals baffled him as much as they did the thug at my table, but he did his best to give back whatever response the crazy American at table two wanted.

My luncheon companion seemed perplexed enough to sit tight.

"Shall we do this without anyone spending the night in a Dutch jail? You know his number. Dial it."

He was on shakier ground than I was for the moment. I think he welcomed the chance to put the situation into other hands. For whatever reason, he dialed a number. I took back the phone.

A voice answered in gruff Slavic syllables. I didn't understand a word of it.

"Mr. Markov, I presume."

What sounded like a Russian curse came through the muffled mouthpiece.

"A pleasure to talk to you too, Mr. Markov. I'm enjoying a glass of excellent wine with your trained ape here. He seems to want me to leave with him. That's not going to happen. Do you want to keep playing spy games or can we act like adults?"

There was a pause filled with raspy breathing. I knew he was using it to get a grip on a temper that he was not used to keeping in check.

"Let me make this easy, Mr. Markov. I want a meeting with you as well, let's say out of the hearing of your partners. We have a few things to discuss that might well be kept between us. Am I making sense?"

I noticed a distinct shift in the direction of civility.

"A meeting is what I had in mind, Mr. Knight. My associates there in the restaurant are merely there to offer you transportation."

"I see, Mr. Markov. You're the soul of generosity. I think, on the other hand, that we'll do this differently. I suggest that we meet this afternoon at three o'clock. Is that convenient?"

"That would be excellent. May I suggest —"

"No, Mr. Markov. It's my turn to do the suggesting. I have your phone number in my cell phone now. I'll call you at quarter of three."

He didn't jump at it, but after a bit of thought, he agreed.

"One last thought, Mr. Markov. I have something you want even more than you can imagine right now. No more games or I close the shop. Are we absolutely clear on that?"

"And what do you have that is so important to me?'

I was thinking of Professor Denisovitch whom I was sure Markov believed to be dead, but I wasn't ready to play that card yet.

"Let's meet at three. I hope you like surprises. I'm going to hand the phone back to your gentleman's gentleman here. It would definitely grease the gears if you would instruct him to pick up his playmates and take the whole troop back to the home."

I handed the phone across the table. I could hear a flood of Russian coming through the receiver that could blister the paint on the Kremlin.

My tablemate bolted straight up and gave a brusque signal to the two at the next table. They beat a direct retreat.

I'd have finished the carafe of wine, but I had some serious homework to do if I was going to live to keep the reservation I planned to make at the same La Rive for dinner that evening.

CHAPTER TWENTY-EIGHT

I had an hour before my meeting with Sergei Markov, and a couple of phone calls to make for personal life insurance as well as to propel the whole charade to the next level. The most secure place for phoning was my exquisite suite on the sixth floor. I made the calls on my own cell phone rather than the hotel phone, just in case.

First up was a check-in with Mr. Devlin. Given the time difference, I reached him at his condo on Storrow Drive just before he left for the office.

I fully appreciated having three thousand miles of Atlantic Ocean between us. I thought he was going to come through the phone bodily—not an unexpected response since I'd cut him off in mid-sentence when I announced my side trip to Amsterdam

"What the hell are you doing in Amsterdam?"

"It's tulip season. Where else would I be at this time of year?"

I could have said that, but I didn't want to find him expired on his kitchen floor with exploded arteries.

"That's what I want to explain, Mr. Devlin. I think we're making progress."

I filled him in on my meeting with the two Vans and Sergei Markov. That went well right up to the point where I told him about my offer of a buyer for the phony Vermeer.

"Michael, damn it! Are you smoking something over there? You don't have a buyer. What the hell are you going to do when they call you on it? I don't even want to think about who 'they' are."

"It's all right, Mr. Devlin. I do have something to back it up."

"And that would be?"

"You remember Harry Wong from last winter. He's flying over tonight. He's my buyer. At least that's the story."

"Michael, that's it. This is not going to happen. Next plane back to Boston. You hear me? I'm still the senior partner of this circus."

"Yes, sir. I understand."

"Don't give me this 'understand' business. I want you back on safe soil."

"Yes, sir. Right away."

"Damn it, Michael! Every time you agree with me without a fight, I know you're going to do just the opposite."

"Yes, sir."

"There. You see that."

"That's because I think the safest soil is right here till I get this thing put together."

I was recalling what Aiello and his legions of death might do if I came back without the painting. For that matter, even Benny Ignola was probably ready to do the job himself. And both of them were back on the "safe soil" of Boston.

"It's going to be all right, Mr. Devlin. I think I have it under control."

That was an extension of the truth so far it could leave stretch marks.

"But I do need your help."

I could tell he was not thrilled with the idea of aiding and abetting my lunacy.

"Like what?"

"It's important that we push this purchase by Harry to get our hands on that painting. It's in a vault here in Amsterdam, and those three are the ones with the other half of the code."

"I'm only asking as a matter of curiosity. What is it you want me to do?"

"I need some money. I've got to put up more than Harry's handsome face to put this across."

"And we're talking how much money?"

"I think I can do it for three million dollars."

"Oh, well, that's no problem. I'll take it out of petty cash. You are smoking something. I've heard about those places in Amsterdam."

"You didn't let me finish, Mr. Devlin. I'm thinking you could talk to Santangelo. I'm absolutely convinced that if I can get my hands on that painting in the vault, I can use it as leverage to break open the case against Peter. I can explain when I get back. It's still in the hunch stage, but it's a very strong one. And to be honest, we don't have much else."

"And exactly how do I sell this three million dollar hunch to Dominic? Again, just curiosity."

"Like this. He never actually loses the three million. He uses it to set up a line of credit with a bank here in Amsterdam in Harry's name. Harry writes a check for the three million to show his sincerity in buying the painting. He makes it out to two names jointly, Van Drusen's and mine. That works since we're both on the side of the seller of the painting. It would be like money in escrow. It would set Harry up as a serious purchaser of the painting, but they couldn't cash it without getting my signature. If things work out the way I hope, I'll be out of here before that happens. Then Mr. Santangelo can just cancel the line of credit, and he has his three million dollars back."

There was absolute dead silence on the other end of the line.

"Mr. Devlin?"

I could sense the rumblings of an eruption from Mount Vesuvius. A large part of me would have welcomed enthusiastically a full-scale blow that would have put me on the next plane back to Boston. Another very small part wanted to hang in there to see if Harry and I could actually pull it off. The small part did the talking.

"I really do have some leverage here, Mr. Devlin. They need this sale. It's their only chance to recoup a bad loan to Tony Aiello. If I cut and run now, it could be seriously dangerous even if I come home."

More silence. Then a calm.

"Michael, I'm groping for words to tell you how much I detest the danger you've gotten yourself into. If you get yourself—"

"I won't, Mr. Devlin." I added in a Puerto Rican accent, "I'm a tough half-Puerto Rican kid from Jamaica Plain. I've got 'em out-numbered and surrounded. They haven't got a chance."

I could sense him almost smiling.

"If you can sell that three million dollar idea to Mr. Santangelo, I think I'm on good ground."

I could hear a deep exhale of resignation.

"I'll do what I can. You be careful, son."

I could hear the deep pain of worry in his voice. I sorely regret-ted putting it there, but I have to admit, I thanked God that the man I loved and admired had come to care that much.

A chat with the concierge of the hotel gave me a lead to the safest ground for my meeting with Markov. I knew it would be like jump-ing into a tank of sharks, and I had no Tom Burns in Amsterdam to watch my back.

I made the call to Markov fifteen minutes before the three o'clock meeting to allow him as little set-up time as possible. I gave him an address anyone native to Amsterdam would recognize — 42 Stadhouderskade.

At two minutes of three, I climbed the steps of the most well-known art museum in Amsterdam — the Rijksmuseum. It was laid out exactly as the concierge had described it. It was just a matter of following the stream of tourists to the large gallery on the second floor where one of the most famous paintings in the world occupies one entire wall.

The Night Watch of Rembrandt is, in one way, a lot like the *Mona Lisa* in the Louvre in Paris. Tourists who wouldn't know a Rembrandt from a pickled herring find their way to the Rijksmuseum to be able to check it off the list of things one must see while in Amsterdam. The result is a gallery half filled with people standing in awe of Rem-brandt's colossal depiction of a company of citizen militia that would, in the United States, have been called *Neighborhood Watch*.

The room was just what I'd hoped. I could stay hidden in the crowd to see if Markov came into the room alone. It was unlikely that he or his thugs could pull off anything intimidating in the ebb and flow of dozens of tourists.

At three o'clock, I watched through the heads and shoulders surrounding me as he walked in alone and took a position in one of the corners away from the crowd. So far he was following directions to the letter. I stayed in the crowd for another three minutes to be certain none of his men came through the door.

I let him get to the fidgety stage before approaching him.

"Mr. Markov, quite a masterpiece. That fellow Rembrandt had style, didn't he? Or does your taste run more to Vermeer?"

Markov, whose taste clearly ran more to money than to either one of them, adjusted well. He wore a smile bordering on a smirk.

"Mr. Knight, I'm puzzled. Why are we here? The painting is charming, but you and I could be sitting like two gentlemen in my comfortable suite. Yet here we are standing in a crowded room with sweaty tourists. I could come to believe you don't trust me."

"Mr. Markov, I believe you and I are about to exchange secrets that we wouldn't tell to another living soul."

His eyes narrowed into a wary squint and he cocked his head without losing the smirk in a noncommittal invitation to go on.

"I also believe you would slit me from my toes to my hairline if I gave you the chance and you thought you could make a buck on it."

The grin turned into a throaty laugh.

"On the other hand, in my neighborhood, we survived on sharpened wits and staying two jumps ahead. That levels the field. Shall we do business?"

He spread his hands in a "you go first" gesture.

"Fine. Let me tell you what I know so we won't waste time sparring. You and John McKedrick have been doing business over here for some time. John was dealing for Anthony Aiello. Given the character of Aiello, it was undoubtedly illegal. What was it — drugs, money laundering?"

Markov bowed slightly without answering the question.

"You have the floor, Mr. Knight. Please continue."

"Either you or John hatched an idea to scam the two Vans, who probably have enough money to finance the World Court. And who, I might add, are probably nobody's fools. The scam was based on the Vermeer that was stolen from a Boston museum back in the nineties.

"You tell an interesting story, Mr. Knight. Is there more?"

"Oh, yes. Much more. The Vans loaned money, quite a large sum of money, on the security of the stolen painting, which John, again acting for Aiello, claimed to have. It was believable since Aiello's a big shot in the Mafia, and John had the brains to pull it off. But you needed a very serious authenticator for the painting to suck the Vans in. John thought of his old professor at Harvard, Professor Denisovitch, one of probably two or three world authorities on Vermeer. No one could doubt his reputation. How am I doing?"

"Go on, Mr. Knight. I'm still listening."

"The loan was made. I'm sure you got a share of the loan money. And the painting was hidden away for security in a bank vault with two number codes, one went to John and the other to the Vans."

He gave another noncommittal shrug.

"Now here's the clincher, Mr. Markov."

I dropped my voice and leaned closer. I knew I was showing a major hole card.

"The painting is a fake. It was painted by Denisovitch. We don't need to go into the kind of threats you personally made against his family to force an honorable man to betray his life's work."

Markov just looked at the ceiling and smiled. That gave him a major piece of the puzzle. It was now on the table that I knew that what lay in the vault was worth no more than the price of the canvas and paint. The second shoe hung suspended in midair.

"So there we are. I've anted up. Do you play poker, Mr. Markov?"

He looked back down from the ceiling.

"Perhaps."

"Good. Then you understand the concept. Now let's see if you'll ante up so we can deal the cards."

I had full eye contact.

"You knew from the beginning that Professor Denisovitch

painted the so-called Vermeer. You knew his authentication was a complete fraud. That's past history. What matters at this point is that we both concede to each other knowledge of the fact that there is absolutely nothing of value in that vault. Can we agree?"

He continued to look me in the eye, and I could see the wheels turning. We were at a threshold. I needed his admission of complicity to cross it.

"Understand this, Mr. Markov. I have no interest in using the information for any purpose other than making a deal. Let's be honest. If I ever disclose it, you'll have me killed. That's a fact of life I accept. Is that blunt enough?"

His eyes narrowed and he spoke in the slow syllables of a cautious man. "Let's say for the sake of argument, Mr. Knight —"

"Let's not, Mr. Markov. The deal is cards on the table or I'm on the next plane, and you'll never hear what I have to offer."

It was my turn to look him straight in the eye. I knew he was in discomfort, and probably planning personal future revenge on the one who put him there.

"I believe we might proceed on the assumption —"

"You can take your assumptions, Mr. Markov, I respectfully submit, and stuff them. It's yes or no. Nothing else."

I checked my watch purely for effect. I then gave what I hoped would appear to be my last look into his squinty eyes. I got nothing back.

I gave it three seconds before I looked back at the great Rembrandt on the wall ahead of us and merely whispered, "I'm sorry, Mr. Markov. My mistake. I thought you were a player. I've wasted the time of both of us."

I turned and took one reluctant step toward the door when I heard it.

"Mr. Knight, I'll give you the yes you want. And I'll give you two things more. Two pieces of advice. Don't ever try to minimize me again. And secondly, don't for an instant believe that you would live to leave Amsterdam if I choose to have it otherwise."

I turned to face him and the smile was gone.

"I never thought otherwise."

"Then what have you to offer me, Mr. Knight?"

The air between us cooled, and we were back to business.

"A second harvest from this same painting in the vault. I meant what I said about having a buyer. Mr. Qian is a very private man. The extent of his wealth is staggering, and his greatest pleasure is indulging his taste in art. He has no scruples about the source of it. How I found him is my business. I'm sure you'll do your research on him. You'll find nothing. He can afford to keep it that way."

"And exactly how do we convince this sophisticated buyer that our little painting is genuine?"

"Unquestionable authentication. I'll produce the expert. Mr. Qian has already agreed that if my authenticator says it's genuine, we'll have a deal."

"And who might that be?"

I could understand the question since I had apparently been successful in convincing Markov his assassins had killed Denisovitch in his hotel in London.

"That's my concern. I've said that Qian has agreed to the authenticator. That's all you need to know."

He hesitated on that one, but stayed in the game.

"And how do we arrange the authentication?"

"That's your part. Mr. Qian insists on being present. I'll have him and the authenticator at the bank where the vault is at two tomorrow. Your job will be to have the two Vans there with their code number. Can you arrange that?"

"Of course. And now, Mr. Knight, to the essentials. What price have you discussed?"

"Eighty million as a base. More depending on the condition of the painting. Of course my authenticator will rave about the fine condition and preservation of the painting. He may get the price over a hundred million. The Vans will be repaid their debt, and you and I will split everything over that."

"And what of your client in Boston? This Aiello person."

"He'll be satisfied to have the debt repaid. He left this in my hands. There's no reason why he should know what the painting actually sells for, is there?"

That brought a quiet smile.

"There is one problem, Mr. Knight. Why should the "Vans" as you call them place any trust in this mysterious Oriental? The painting is supposed to be stolen property. They won't open the vault to just anyone."

"Of course not. Mr. Qian and I have discussed it. I told him we need some assurance of his seriousness. He's willing to write a check for three million dollars jointly to the Vans and myself. I'll have the check in the hands of the Vans by tomorrow at the vault. They can hold it in escrow. If the painting is authenticated, and it will be, and Mr. Qian fails to go through with the purchase, I'll sign the check and they can cash it. Mr. Qian knows the value of what he thinks he's buying."

Markov took a breath and turned back to look at the nearly life-size figures in the *Night Watch*. I did the same.

"Astounding how he used light to breathe life into the figures. You can almost see them move."

"You're an art connoisseur after all, Mr. Markov."

"Perhaps."

He looked back at me and our eyes met.

"But I am most certainly a man who would be very disappointed if my confidence were betrayed. And, Mr. Knight, I would express my disappointment in ways that are by no means subtle. Cards on the table, as you say."

I gave him my most dejected look.

He smiled and just shook his head.

"Always the joker. But you take my meaning. Again, the time?"

"Mr. Qian wants his authenticator to be able to examine the painting. There are tests he'll pretend to perform. Mr. Qian wants to be there as well. We'll meet at the bank vault tomorrow afternoon at two. You'll have the Vans there with their part of the code. Satisfactory?"

"Quite."

CHAPTER TWENTY-NINE

My wake-up call the next morning pulled me right out of a bass fishing boat on a crystal clear lake in New Hampshire. The cheerful sparkle of the hotel wake-up voice did nothing to relieve the incipient terror of awakening in Amsterdam with the day I had ahead.

After fortification at the world's premier breakfast buffet at the hotel, I launched the plan that finally came together just before sleep the night before.

Mr. Devlin called to say that he had gotten Mr. Santangelo's very tentative approval of my three million dollar idea. I took it the sell was hard, since the only thing Mr. D. had to back it up was his blind faith in me.

The first step was to rent a bicycle — no great feat in Amsterdam. Years ago, the city fathers took a shot at the intolerable automobile traffic by providing hundreds of white bicycles on the streets around the city. The Dutch took to bike riding like the Swedes to pickled herring, and the automobile traffic abated. Only two problems remained — theft of the bicycles, and the menace of hundreds of kamikaze cyclists.

The city next turned the free bicycles into cheaply rentable bicycles. It was on one of these that I started crisscrossing an erratic path along the canals and through the cross streets that make up the area called the Ring — a series of concentric semicircles of canals that fan out from the harbor.

My purpose was to eliminate a tail, in case Markov decided to play dirty pool. Within twenty minutes, I felt as secure as I would in the Back Bay of Boston.

The second purpose of my cycling odyssey was to accomplish two errands before meeting Harry and the professor back at the hotel. The first was to find a specialty art shop in the museum district in the center of the city.

The second was to find the particular bank that rented the private vault now containing the fake Vermeer painted by Professor Denisovitch. Markov had given me the address, and the concierge found it for me on a map.

I did a bit of business at both the art shop and the bank. I gave the manager at the bank a tip sizable enough to insure that he would accommodate, first by not recognizing me when I returned with the group at two, and equally importantly, by doing a small favor that afternoon that did not compromise him, but was a key element in pulling off a bit of magic.

That done, I cycled back to the hotel and welcomed any tail that Markov wanted to put on me.

At exactly two o'clock, Mr. Qian, aka Harry Wong, and I stepped out of a hired limousine in front of the bank. Harry was in his finest suit — in fact his only suit, but cleaned and pressed for the occasion. The third member of our little trio was Harry's traveling companion from London. Professor Denisovitch was dressed in the style of any number of Harvard intellectuals, *a la couture* of Horace Rumpole — tweedy and somewhat ill-fitting. But that didn't matter. It was Harry who had to make an impression.

We strode into the bank and asked for the manager. He greeted us without a hint of recognition and led us to the vault room where the two Vans and Markov were waiting.

Even the Vans dispensed with the Dutch custom of preliminary social bantering. We were there for a single purpose, and an unusually large sum of money was at stake.

The Vans were pleasantly surprised to see Professor Denisovitch again. In fact, they seemed somewhat relieved, since the professor had been the original authenticator of the painting in their deal with Tony Aiello. They were obviously confident that he would not change his mind about the painting in the vault. In fact, based on the professor's previous authentication, the Vans still believed the painting to be the genuine Vermeer.

The true shock told on the face of Markov. He looked at the professor as if he had come back from the dead. I had been saving that little surprise for this meeting at the bank, hopefully to set Markov a bit off balance about his ability to control events.

The bad news for Markov in seeing the professor alive was that his boys had flubbed it in London. The good news was that the professor would be capable of setting up another profitable scam for him. Until he could get his mind around the conflicting possibilities, he stayed in the background, which allowed me to play master of ceremonies.

I introduced Harry — Mr. Qian — and got down to business.

"Gentlemen, we know what we're here for. Mr. Qian has a check for three million dollars made out jointly to Mr. Van Drusen and myself. The check will remain in the hands of the manager of the bank, Mr. Van Houten. If the painting is authenticated and for any reason Mr. Qian does not complete the transaction, Mr. Van Drusen and I will be free to cash the check. The three million dollars will go to Mr. Van Drusen and Mr. Van Arsdale, who made the loan for which the painting is the security. Acceptable?"

I looked to the two Vans, each of whom nodded assent. Markov still looked a bit nonplused, but he nodded to keep the train rolling.

"Then let's get on with it. Mr. Van Drusen, if you'll give your code number to Mr. Van Houten, I'll give him mine."

Van Drusen wrote something on a slip of paper and handed it to the bank manager. Since that seemed to be the routine, I did the same with the correct code I had memorized.

The manager located the numbered vault and opened it. With almost silent reverence, he took a roll of canvas, a bit over two feet long, out of the vault and gently unfurled it on the table. If I didn't know it was a fake, I'd have been awestruck in the presence of the masterpiece that the entire art world would give untold fortunes to locate.

Even in the form of Professor Denisovitch's copy, the painting was gripping enough to bring silence and a genuine moment of respect from this group of dealers and hustlers. I broke the spell.

"Gentlemen, shall we do what we came to do. Professor Denisovitch wishes to examine the painting before giving his authentication. He requests that we leave him alone while he performs certain tests that he's developed. I think we should respect his privacy."

That brought Markov out of his funk.

"What do you mean alone? We're to leave him alone with this?"

I knew I had to quell Markov before he got the Vans in an uproar. "It's perfectly normal, Mr. Markov. The professor says that he's developed techniques of authentication that are not generally known. What are you afraid of?"

Markov glared at me. He spit out the words. "Paintings can be switched, Mr. Knight."

"That's not a problem, Mr. Markov. I've discussed this with the professor. He'll agree to be thoroughly searched before examining the painting as well as afterward to guarantee that the actual painting never leaves this room. Would that satisfy you?"

Markov ruminated over the possibilities. He was hesitant but not hesitant enough to derail a multimillion-dollar scam. He finally agreed, as long as he would be allowed to do the searching. The Vans also consented.

It was an indignity to the professor, but the point of the precautionary search was obvious. Having survived an assassination attempt, this indignity seemed tolerable. I had warned the professor that a search might be a nonnegotiable condition of his examining the painting in private.

The professor and Markov stepped into a side room of the vault. Five minutes later, they returned, and Markov assured the group that the professor had nothing on his person with which to switch or harm the painting.

The Vans, Harry, and I, and even Markov left the vault to allow the professor to perform his "tests" in private. The bank manager, Mr. Van Houten, remained out of sight in the vault's side room.

The wait was shorter than expected. Within two minutes, the

professor stormed out of the vault, red in the face and perspiring, waving the canvas over his head with considerably less care than one might show for a priceless masterpiece.

"Is this a joke? You brought me here for this?"

To say that the group was stunned doesn't begin to describe the atmosphere. The jaws of Markov and the Vans were at half-mast. Even Harry — Mr. Qian — seemed genuinely shocked.

Van Drusen, who was closest, tried to grab the arm of the professor to rescue the painting. The professor, seeing him coming, fairly threw the canvas at him.

"Here! Take it! You insult me with this."

Markov recovered enough to seize the professor in mid-frenzy. He shrieked at him. "What are you talking about, old man?"

The professor was flying in high gear. He pulled loose and grabbed the canvas out of the hand of Van Drusen. He held it up to the face of Markov and matched him in volume. "This — this insult!"

Before the entire scene disintegrated into total panic, I stepped between the professor and Markov. "Quiet! Both of you! Professor, quietly, what are you saying?"

The professor took his cue and lowered his tone. He held out the canvas so that we could all see it and practically whispered the words. "This is a common giclee print of the master's painting on canvas. As copies go, it's a good copy. But it's a copy. Look here. There are no brush strokes. There is no elevation of the oil. You could buy this copy in any good art store in Amsterdam."

As a matter of fact, that's exactly what I had done that morning. The real trick was to substitute it for the painting that had been in the locked vault to which I had only half of the code. I let the professor in on the trick that morning so he'd know what to expect. He played his part to perfection.

The total effect on the Vans and Markov was numbing shock, considering the amount of money that had suddenly vanished from their prospects. But the shock had a short shelf life. It was time to move to scene two before it dissipated.

Harry picked up my signal. He took the canvas from the professor and looked closely at it for the first time. It was difficult to tell whether the facial expression he was registering was anger or frustration. When he spoke, it was in a heavy Chinese accent.

"I don't know what you people are up to. I find this deceit unpardonable. Do any of you have an explanation?"

Since no one did, no one spoke.

I picked up the ball in profound humility. "I sincerely apologize, Mr. Qian. I don't know —"

Now Harry turned on me. "Apparently you don't, Mr. Knight. I misjudged you, I thought you were a sincere dealer of substance. You're apparently no more than a common charlatan. You've abused my trust. I see now that you're just — a buffoon."

The more he spoke, the heavier Harry's Chinese accent grew. And out of what old movie he pulled the word "buffoon" I couldn't even guess. But before he blew the entire scene with bad dialogue, I thought it best to find an exit line.

"Mr. Qian, I'll make this up to you in our other dealings."

"You will not, Mr. Knight. There will be no other dealings. Mr. Van Houten, I'll thank you to return my check."

Van Houten, who had not closed his lower jaw since the professor's tirade began, simply held out the three million dollar check. Harry snatched it out of his hand and stormed through the front door to fresh air and silence.

Professor Denisovitch followed close on Harry's heels in a huff. They summoned separate cabs and were out of sight by the time the rest of us reached the street.

The Vans were holding the discredited canvas between them squinting at the surface lacking brush strokes. Markov was back in the vault room searching the empty vault for any trace of the actual painting by Professor Denisovitch that had apparently disappeared into thin air, while I went through the front door and hailed a third cab.

Harry and Professor Denisovitch each directed their cabbies to travel a separate route to prevent anyone from following either of them. By different paths, they arrived at the airport and went straight to the Turkish Airlines counter. I had booked separate flights for each of them to Boston, one by way of Istanbul, and the other by way of Ankara, for no other reason than to frustrate followers.

I took my cabbie on a roundabout ride to the Prinsenhof, a small hotel on the west side of the city on Prinsengracht, a short way up the canal from the house in which Anne Frank had found refuge from the Nazis. The symbolism was not lost, and I needed peaceful, obscure accommodations for one night.

I called Mr. Devlin and told him that Mr. Santangelo's three million dollars were intact, and he could cancel the line of credit with the bank.

I was delighted to add that the mission had been accomplished. I'd be in Boston the following night with the Denisovitch painting that had been in the original vault, ready to do some serious business with Fat Tony Aiello.

"Michael, how in hell did you get that painting out of the vault?"

"Ah, a magician never divulges his secrets, Mr. Devlin."

"Michael, this is your senior partner speaking. How did you get the painting?"

I was hoping he'd insist. I was dying to tell it anyway.

"This morning I went to the bank where the vault is. I gave a tip to the bank manager that will probably bring an Italian curse out of Mr. Santangelo when he gets the bill. Anyway, he played along. I rented a small box in the same vault room as the vault that was holding the actual Denisovitch painting. The box I rented had just one code so I was the only one who had access to it. I bought a good giclee print on canvas of the Vermeer painting at an art shop for about a hundred dollars. It's good enough so an amateur could be fooled if he weren't suspicious. I put it in the vault box I rented.

"That part was easy. It took a bit of acting to get them to leave the professor alone in the vault room with the actual painting. He let them search him for anything he could use to make a switch. Of course, they found nothing, so we all left him alone in the vault room. The last thing the bank manager did before he left the vault room was to leave open the box I had rented that morning. No one noticed because they were all focusing on the original vault box. When the professor was left alone in the vault room, he could just slip the painting he had done, the one he was supposed to be examining, into my rented box and close it. Then he took the giclee print that was in my rented box, and stormed out to berate us all for insulting his intelligence with the giclee print. He missed his calling. He could have been an actor. Now I just have to go back to the bank in the morning and get the Denisovitch painting out of my vault box. I should be back in Boston with the Denisovitch painting tomorrow night."

CHAPTER THIRTY

The next morning, I awoke from a deep sleep and had a hearty breakfast. I took a cab back to the bank and sought out the manager. He welcomed my approach with a cautious smile and a question as to whether or not we might be in for another "interesting" day. I assured him that, God willing, we'd seen the last of those.

I used my code to retrieve the Denisovitch painting from the vault box and closed out the rental. Another tip, sizeable by any standard, to the manager on Mr. Santangelo's account would hopefully insure discretion in case Sergei Markov returned with the odd question.

Ten hours later, I touched the sandy, salty, gritty, reclaimed soil of East Boston. It felt to me more like the emerald-encrusted Land of Oz. If they were going to do me in now, at least it would be on my home turf.

I grabbed a cab directly to South Station, where I salted away the Denisovitch painting in the locker I had previously rented "just in case."

Next stop, my apartment. With the time change from Amsterdam, it was still mid-afternoon in Boston. One shower, shave, and change later, I was ready to do business.

I called Mr. Devlin at the office. I told him that if things broke right, I'd have some real pay dirt that he could take to Mr. Santangelo by the following morning. That naturally brought on more questions that I was not quite ready to answer. I cut in with a promise.

"Mr. Devlin, tomorrow morning the rest of the dominos should fall into place. What do you say to breakfast at the Ritz Carlton? You and me. My treat."

"Michael, how the h — !"

"Great, Mr. Devlin. Nine o'clock. Your signal's fading. I can barely hear you."

Actually, you could hear him in Chelsea, but I needed an exit line.

My next call was to Professor Denisovitch's office just to be sure he was back in safe territory. Helga Swenson's stentorian tones set the little hairs in my ear vibrating. When I spoke, she recognized my voice and the change was instant.

"May I speak to the professor, Ms. Swenson?"

There was a pause as if my words had startled her. I knew I was not going to like what followed.

"Is he there, Ms. Swenson?"

"Don't you know? You were the one —"

"Ms. Swenson, I don't have much time. Are you saying he hasn't come back yet?"

"I haven't seen or heard from him since he left for London. Didn't you —"

"I'm sorry to interrupt. He was flying in yesterday. Could he be at his home?"

"I tried there this morning. Nobody there has seen him."

"Is there anywhere else? A club? Another office? I don't know. A relative?"

"No. None of those."

I held the phone against my head to think for a minute. This was a complication I hadn't counted on. I also knew there was no time to deal with it at the moment. I could hear Helga's voice on the line.

"What did you say, Ms. Swenson?"

"Should I call the police?"

Something instinctive inside was giving me the answer.

"No. Not yet. I can do some checking. I'll get back to you. If you hear anything, call my cell phone."

I needed time to work this out, and I knew I had nothing like the kind of time it might take to locate the professor. I figured that if he was dead, it could wait. If he was alive and kidnapped, the chances were good that whoever did it would be contacting me or Helga Swenson.

I pulled my thoughts together to focus all my attention on the next call. I got Tony Aiello on his cell.

"Hey, you bum, where you been?"

"Pleasure to hear your voice too, Tony. Have you been well?"

"Yeah. Peachy. What about that picher?"

"I've been fine too, Tony. I know you were concerned."

"The picher, ya bum. What about it?"

"The answer to your question, you art lover, is that I got the "picher" that was in the vault box in Amsterdam. I told you I would. Don't tell me you doubted my word."

"You are so full of crap. Get it over here. I'm at—"

"I don't think so, Tony."

"What the hell'd you say?"

"I said, 'I don't think so.' You've got to listen better."

"What're you pullin', you little bum? I get ahold of you—"

"Tony, I told you once. It's very important that you and I be nice to each other. It's important because we have business to do with each other. And it's not going to happen any other way. Let me repeat. I've got the painting. It's where you'll never find it. But other people will if anything should happen to me. And that wouldn't do you any good at all. So to go back to square one, we have business to do."

There was silence. I could almost hear him choking on his own anger, but business came first.

"So where do we meet?"

"Well, Tony, you seemed to take so well to the Parker House, I'll make reservations for eleven thirty tomorrow morning. We'll be at 'our table.' By the way, that'll be reservations for two. You and me. Leave the baboons in the cage."

This time he answered by slamming the cell phone shut, which was actually music to my ears. This was overtime in the seventh game of the Stanley Cup finals. I needed a big win, and I figured that having Tony distracted by his passion to have me sliced into his next cacciatore could be a helpful edge. Or it could lead to my actually being one of his ingredients.

CHAPTER THIRTY-ONE

The flight from St. Petersburg to Moscow is about the length of a flight from Boston to Washington, D.C. It gave Alexei Samnov's imagination time to fabricate a dozen different reasons for his being summoned to a meeting with the gentleman. None of them offered peace of mind.

When he reached the terminal in Moscow, he followed instructions to look for a limousine driver holding a sign bearing the single name, Alexei. He made contact immediately, and was ushered into a black stretch limousine that was driven beyond the city limits of Moscow and deeply into the open country to the north of the city.

The sun had been down for hours by the time the limousine pulled into the courtyard of a walled stone villa overlooking Lake Rybinsk. Alexei was greeted as "Professor Samnov" by the attendant staff and shown to a guest suite where he was invited to refresh himself before dinner.

Within half an hour, he returned to the main hall and was shown to the main dining room. He had no idea of whether to take comfort or alarm from the fact that the massive table was set for two.

He was seated at the side of the table, a short distance from where a setting had also been placed at the head of the table. Wine had been poured at each place, and a bottle of excellent vodka was chilling beside the table. The allure of easing with fine wine or vodka the tensions that were playing havoc with his entire nervous system was more than countered by his sense of velvet-clad danger that would require his clearest mind.

Alexei was scarcely seated when the door at the far end of the room was opened to admit the gentleman who had summoned him. The gentleman approached with a smile and a warm, welcoming clasp of arms. Uniformed servants seated them, and the hospitality began with a vodka toast to Mother Russia. It was unthinkable not to drink, but Alexei did so mostly in pantomime, taking in as little liquid as possible.

Throughout the dinner, conversation was light and general on three favorite subjects of an educated Russian — art, music, and warfare. The gentleman appeared to be enjoying both the meal and the company. Alexei tried to appear the same.

When the last dish was cleared and vodka was once again poured, all attendants withdrew from the room. The gentleman leaned back in his chair, his glass in hand. Alexei had observed the "gracious host" side of the gentleman, but at the same time, he took note of the fact that the gentleman had actually not consumed a drop more vodka or wine than Alexei.

The subtle shift in tone when the gentleman said, "Alexei, my friend, can I trust you?" sent a chill to the very base of his spine.

The question jolted him. He knew he had to respond quickly.

"Of course. What would make you —?"

"I don't think so."

Alexei was stunned, but recovered as quickly as possible.

"What have I ever —?"

The gentleman held up a hand that froze the words in his throat.

"By now you must at least surmise my intolerance for disloyalty, Alexei. Yes?"

"Certainly."

"Shall we say that most men would not survive one instance of even wavering loyalty?"

"But I never —"

The gentleman cut him off with a wince as if pained by Alexei's words. He reached inside his pocket and tossed a stack of photographs that splayed across the table in front of Alexei. Without sorting them, he could see that they recorded every minute of his conversation with Professor Denisovitch at the London club.

Alexei merely stared at the photos, unable to speak. He had made what appeared to be the fatal error of underestimating the tentacles of the gentleman in trying to warn his friend. He had nothing to say. He could only resign himself to whatever manner of death the gentleman had in mind for him.

"Alexei, look up at me. I said that of most men. I think perhaps you made this one mistake out of loyalty to a friend. I admire your loyalty, and your bravery. I find them both too useful to extinguish."

The gentleman leaned forward, closer to Alexei. He spoke in a more quiet, but harder tone.

"But only if they're both directed to me. Do you take my meaning, Alexei?"

Alexei wanted to say yes immediately, but fear of what it might commit him to stilled the word. The gentleman leaned back and took the slightest sip of vodka.

"Take your time, Alexei. This time your commitment must be complete. Don't speak lightly with any room for wavering later on. I can assure you that there will be no such dinner as this ever again."

Alexei wrestled with every possibility. If he failed to commit now, he would most certainly be killed in a way that would set an example. The death of his friend Denisovitch would be equally certain. If he committed now, he would at least buy time, possibly for both of them.

Alexei looked into the eyes of the gentleman and he nodded solemnly.

The gentleman smiled. He shook his finger and his head in the same slow motion.

"No, Alexei. What you are thinking would only delay the inevitable. You see, you are in fear. When a man is in fear for his life, I can read his mind, because he has only so many possibilities."

Alexei looked into his eyes.

"What more can I do than to commit my loyalty to you?"

"A great deal more, Alexei. You can commit your loyalty to me without a single thought of wavering. To have you do that, I must give you only one possible path to follow. Listen closely."

The gentleman straightened away from Alexei to remove any bodily suggestion of weakness.

"Your friend, Professor Denisovitch, is in my hands. Actually he is in the hands of my employee. I believe you met my associate, Lupov. Lupov is an extraordinary individual. He has no conscience whatsoever. If it became necessary to subject your friend to Lupov's ministrations —"

He held up his hands as if words could not express the thought that would finish the sentence. He paused to let that idea generate whatever unspeakable terrors it might engender in Alexei's already stimulated imagination.

Alexei merely said in submission, "What is it you want me to do?"

The gentleman took a deep breath and smiled at what he sensed to be complete capitulation.

"Now that divided loyalties are out of the equation, we can begin to make sense with each other. You'll be going on a trip. You'll strike a bargain with someone who apparently shares your affection for Professor Denisovitch, someone who has been causing me unnecessary aggravation. This aggravation will stop immediately. You'll see to that."

"You mentioned a bargain. What do I give in exchange?"

The gentleman broke into a jolly, full-face Saint Nicholas smile.

"Why I should think that would be obvious, Alexei. Just what will please you most. The life of Professor Denisovitch."

CHAPTER THIRTY-TWO

Eleven thirty is too early for the regular set of bankers and lawyers to have lunch at the Parker House. A spotty group of tourists, whose schedule is topsy-turvy anyway, might drop in, but it was a likely time for privacy in a public place.

I waited behind a newspaper in a chair at the far end of the classic lobby to see the lumbering bear that was Fat Tony Aiello come up the School Street steps and turn left toward the dining room.

He was a total surprise package to Frederick, the maître d', who winced at the thought of Tony's becoming a regular. I followed close behind and signaled Frederick for a table at the far end of the dining room.

Frederick forced a smile in my direction and asked tentatively, "And will you be expecting others, Mr. Knight?"

"No, Frederick. Our party is complete."

"Very good, sir." He meant it as he had never meant it before.

We sat. Frederick beat an anxious retreat. Tony grabbed his napkin before the waiter could lay it in his lap. He glared at the busboy pouring the water until the poor kid could barely hit the glass.

"Good morning, Tony."

"Yeah, yeah, yeah. Where's the picher?"

"It *is* a lovely day, Mr. Aiello. Reminds me of a morning in Amsterdam. You wouldn't believe the tulips."

That brought him scrunching his entire obesity so far to the right that he nearly toppled his chair. He was now close enough to whisper at the top of his lungs.

"Listen, you little bum, you don't know who ya playin' with here."

I stayed put and kept the tone restrained.

"Sure I do, Tony. I'm dealing with a man who's so far under water he can't even send up bubbles. I met those boys you owe all that money to. They could grind you up for Russian meatballs."

"They're Dutch, ya jerk. Ya been over there, you don't even know that?"

I looked him dead in the eye and dropped my voice. He had to lean in to hear me.

"Take this to heart, Tony. The Dutch members of the crew may be a threat to your economic well-being. The Russian contingent would take out your tonsils from the other end for a small fraction of what you owe them. And lest there be doubt, that gang of trained apes you depend on would be history in the first wave. This is the varsity team."

He had no comeback for the moment. Now, he looked me straight in the eye. I took that as an invitation to talk business.

"According to the deal John McKedrick put together, the money was loaned to you on the security of the painting that was in the vault in Amsterdam. You can't repay the debt. So your only leverage to keep them from taking the debt out of your flesh is having that painting to sell.

His teeth were clenched so hard that the words came through muffled. "So where's the picher?"

"That's where the business part comes in. I've got the 'picher' that was in the vault."

He seemed to relax slightly.

"So turn it over."

"First a question. What will you do with the painting if I hand it over?"

"What the hell business of yours?"

"Have you even thought about it? Are you going to sell it? How? What do you know about selling stolen paintings? You don't even know who these people are. Who's going to deal for you? Benny?"

"That's my business. Your business is to hand it over, which you better do fast, or you're not gonna live to see another lunch with this here fine dining. You hear me, wise-ass?"

"I hear you threatening the one person who has the key to your survival. Let's be clear about this. If I should have an accident of any kind, that painting goes into the hands of the police. Then you are really up the creek. You'll be explaining ownership of a stolen painting to the police, and a hell of a lot more to those boys across the pond. You may not love me, Tony, but you sure as hell need me."

I took a long drink of ice water.

He finally spoke in a tone that was not overheated.

"What do ya want? I'm just askin'."

"This is the way it's going to be. I don't give a damn about your temper or your bloated sense of power. I have the painting. Without it, you don't want to live through what comes next. That means I get to make some serious demands. Do we agree?"

He grabbed his napkin and wiped the sweat off of his lips.

"What demands?"

"The only thing I care about is Peter Santangelo. You set him up for the murder of John McKedrick. You got your stooge, Mike Simone, to cop a plea to the bombing for a light sentence in exchange for implicating Peter Santangelo as the one who hired him to do it."

"You're guessin'. You don't know nothin'."

"I know the whole Santangelo indictment smells like you're calling the shots. Little Anthony Tedesco over in Revere all of a sudden gets the courage to rat on Sal Marone for extortion. You and I both know the extortion money flows into your pocket, and it's been going on since The Pirates' Den was built. Why does Tedesco squeal now? Because you told him to. It puts Marone in a position to deal with the D.A. He can give them your boy, Three-Finger Simone, as the bomber so Simone can trade with the D.A. for Peter Santangelo. Just like dominos. And you set up the whole thing."

Actually that was all guesswork. I was deeply in need of some confirmation from the red-faced buffalo sitting to my left as a basis for my next move. I got none.

"So. I'm sittin' here listenin', ya mug. What do you want? A round of applause?"

"No, Tony. This isn't a show. Time is short. Your turn at bat. You either confirm or deny. If you confirm, we talk about what it takes to keep you alive. If you deny, or sit there like a lump of pizza dough, I leave. It's your call."

He shifted around like his shorts were riding up. This was not the way he was accustomed to being treated. I wondered how long I'd get to live if I didn't have that painting.

He leaned over and whispered so that it could only be heard on Tremont Street. "So listen. Is this like you're my lawyer? I mean if I say something to you —"

"Tony, if you live long enough to plant grapes on Mars, I will never be your lawyer. On the other hand, whatever you say to me stays at this table."

He looked me in the eye and apparently made a decision. I could feel the tide turn.

"What you said before, Knight. About Marone and Mike Simone. Suppose we say that's it? Maybe."

"Suppose we say, that's it? End of story, and move on."

"All right. All right. What else?"

"This is the good part, Tony. I think I know the answer, but I'm going to ask it anyway. I want to hear it from you. Did you have any part in the actual bombing of John McKedrick?"

"No. I heard about it that night. That's when the idea — what you said with Marone and Simone."

Why in this world I should believe anything that passed between the fat lips of Tony Aiello, I'd be hard put to say. Nevertheless, I believed him.

I was sorely tempted to ask him why he wanted to frame Peter for John's murder, but that would be getting deeper into Tony's business than I thought I could go. Anyway, I had what took me to the next step.

"Then here's the deal. I'll give you the painting. Do what you want with it. I'm sure you'll be hearing from the boys in Amsterdam. You'll be a hell of a lot better off with it than without it."

"Yeah. All right. So what do you want?

"I want a letter from you to Mike Simone in prison. Either I or my partner will deliver it personally. It won't go through the hands of the police."

Now I really had his attention.

"Sayin' what?"

"Orders. Directly from you. He's to recant his confession. That means take it back. He denies that he was the bomber. He denies that Peter Santangelo ever asked him to do anything. He may do some time for lying to the authorities, but they can't prove that he did the bombing, because he didn't. That's it."

I took paper and a pen and an envelope out of my suit coat pocket and set it in front of him.

He looked at the paper without moving.

"I don't need to confess nothin'?"

"No. Tell him to destroy the letter after he reads it if you want."

He just sat there, and I let the pot cook.

Fifteen seconds later, he took the pen.

"What do you want me to write?"

I gave him the ideas, but I wanted it in his words so Simone would believe that it came from Tony.

I took the letter, read it, and folded it into the blank envelope. I sealed it and placed it in my inside pocket.

I took the locker key out of my pocket and dropped it on the plate in front of Tony. He grabbed it like the Hope Diamond, but instead of stuffing it away, he sat there looking at it.

When I stood up, I looked down at him. He looked somehow smaller than I had ever seen him. I wondered if my questions about what in the world he'd do with it finally sank in, leaving him as lost and frightened as he looked.

I touched him on the shoulder, and spoke the first words I ever spoke to him that were not threatening or ridiculing.

"Take care, Mr. Aiello. We both have things to do. Take care of yourself."

CHAPTER THIRTY-THREE

When that elevator door slid closed behind me at the office, it was as if I had crossed the moat. The drawbridge had been hoisted. I was in my castle, and all the dragons and marauding beasts were outside the walls.

Then I saw Julie. She had a blanched and worried look.

"What's up, Julie?"

"You had a call an hour ago, Michael. A man with what sounded like a Russian accent."

Bad news. I'd hoped that that door was closed for good.

"And he said what?"

"He wants you to meet him. He says it could be life or death. Michael, what are you involved in?"

I was computing the possibilities opened up by that call as fast as my mind could function.

"Michael, speak to me. What is he talking about?"

"Did he say anything else, Julie? Did he leave a name?"

"No. No name. He mentioned that professor at Harvard. Denis — something. The one you called before the trip."

"What did he say about him?"

"Just that. Life or death. Michael?"

"It's all right, Julie. He gets a little dramatic. Did he say where and when?"

"Tonight at ten. Harvard Square. He says there's a coffee shop on JFK Street. It's on the left about a block and a half off Harvard Square toward the river."

"Okay. I know the place. It's all right, Julie."

"No, it isn't, Michael. That man sounded —"

"Mean, tough, scary?"

"No. Just terribly stressed and frightened."

That did not scan. Sergei Malkov was frightening, not frightened. On the other hand, Julie had nothing more to tell me to make sense of it. I could only log the time and place of the meeting, and get back to being focused on things I could handle.

There was, however, one preliminary item. I vowed that I'd never again walk into a lion's den without serious attention to my backside. I didn't care if it cost Mr. Santangelo every ill-gotten dime he owned. I called Tom Burns.

I caught Mr. Devlin on his way out the door. He did a one-eighty back into the office and told me to sit down.

"Tell me about it, Michael."

Before I started, I closed the door. It was not that I distrusted either his secretary or Julie. But the way things were going, the less they knew, the better off they might be.

"Go ahead, Michael. I want to hear it all."

I brought him up to date on my deal with Aiello that got the Denisovitch painting into Aiello's hands, and got us the letter to Three-finger Simone with instructions to tell the truth about the framing of Peter. He read the letter and nodded.

"Well done, Michael. Now we know Peter had nothing to do with John McKedrick's death."

"Did you ever think he did?"

He looked over at me with a sly look, knowing that it was a loaded question. He'd been trying to indoctrinate me into the first rule of the Devlin school of defense tactics since our first case together — don't ever assume that your client is innocent. They lie.

"He's my godson. I gave him the benefit of the doubt. Don't make a precedent out of it."

"I hear what you're saying, Mr. Devlin."

That always jerked his chain. He never failed to pick up the lawyer's distinction between my hearing what he said and agreeing with it.

He held up the letter. "The next issue is how do we use this."

"Unfortunately, Mr. Devlin, we don't take it to the D.A."

"Why not? I know it's hearsay, but we could get this in under two or three exceptions to the hearsay rule. We could at least show it to Billy Coyne. He'll do the right thing."

I shook my head. "We can't."

He raised his hands and eyebrows in a "Why the hell not?" gesture.

"I gave my word to Tony. We can show it to Simone, but no one else."

He closed his eyes and rocked back in his chair.

"That does make it interesting. Angela Lamb has Simone hidden away somewhere deeper than Fort Knox."

This was Mr. D.'s territory. I gave him time for forehead rubbing and cogitating. In thirty seconds, he bounced forward and grabbed the phone.

"We can't do this over the phone."

He got Billy Coyne on the line and set up a dinner meeting at the Marliave at five o'clock. The drinking members of the trial bar would likely be in their favorite watering holes, and the nondrinkers would still be in their offices. The confluence of Lex Devlin and the deputy district attorney in a social setting on the brink of the beginning of a highly sensitive trial would be most likely to go unnoticed at that transition hour.

At five past five, the three of us were huddled over generous servings of an antipasta in the upstairs chamber. This time Mr. Devlin did not wait for the final serving to get down to business.

"Billy, I don't know exactly how to put this."

"You mean there's something that Irish silver tongue can't get around? I don't believe it."

"You will. I need to get a message to Mike Simone."

Billy leaned back and looked at the angels painted on the ceiling.

"My dear Lex. You'd stand a better chance of communicating with Al Capone in the great beyond."

"I mean it, Billy. I know what I'm asking."

"Oh, I don't think you do. Our esteemed lady district attorney would sooner give her body to the Inquisition than risk any interference with that witness. What is this message that's going to save the world?"

Mr. Devlin looked down at the table. I could feel his frustration at the size of the hurdle he was facing, and there was not a thing I could do to help him.

"I can't disclose it, Billy."

Billy just shook his head with a smile on his face that expressed wonder that Mr. Devlin would even ask.

"Billy, there isn't a favor in the world that I could do for you to balance what I'm asking. So I'm not asking you to do it for me."

"Really."

"I'm asking you to do it because it's the only way that justice is going to be done in this case. You're trying an innocent man, and you're going to convict him of murder because you've got the perjured testimony of Mike Simone."

"Is this the Lex Devlin who never believes a client is innocent?"

"This is the Lex Devlin who knows, in this case, and no other, that an innocent man will be convicted on false testimony. And when it happens, your office will be duped into serving the interests of the *Cosa Nostra*."

"And you won't tell me the basis for this one-time belief that your client is innocent. Why in the world —"

"Because you and I are different. Damn it, Billy. We're not like some of those you deal with. When was the last time you ever broke you word?"

Billy just looked.

"And you know damned well that my word is the same."

Billy remained frozen.

"I'm not asking you to dismiss the indictment or take any action whatsoever. I just need to get a message to Simone."

"I take it this message might change Simone's testimony."

"It might."

"And is this message coming from you, Lex?"

"No. It's from — a third party."

Billy cast his eyes to the ceiling. Mr. Devlin looked at me for a reading on whether or not he could disclose that it was from Aiello. I could only shake my head.

Mr. Devlin leaned over the table.

"I can't disclose the message or the sender because Michael's word has been given. I'll give you this though, Billy, and then you've got to follow your conscience just as I'm following mine. I give you my word that the purpose of this message is not to induce perjury. It's not to deprive you of a legitimate witness. The sole purpose is to guarantee the truth in this case. I'll give you one more fact, Billy. It's the only way the truth will be served in this case."

Mr. Devlin took the sealed envelope from Tony out of his suit coat pocket and set it on the table in front of Billy. He looked at it without moving.

Mr. Devlin stood up. I followed his lead.

"Please tell Tony Pastore that we'll continue his wonderful dinner on another occasion."

We began to walk toward the door. Billy never took his eyes off the letter.

When we reached the door, Mr. Devlin spoke without turning around. "I can't make the decision for you, Billy. But I want your word that whether you deliver that letter to Simone or not, no other eyes than his — including your own — will ever see it."

Neither of us looked back. I heard from behind us Billy's voice. "Damn it, Lex."

"I know. But I need your word."

There was a significant pause before Billy spoke quietly. "That much. Yes."

CHAPTER THIRTY-FOUR

I had two glorious hours all to myself before my meeting at Paul's Coffee House in Cambridge with the nervous Russian. It was an easy guess that it was Sergei Markov. It was not a reunion that held happy prospects. The one comforting thought I had been allowing myself was that that whole buy/sell episode over the Vermeer was closed. Apparently not.

Terry O'Brien answered on the second ring.

"Michael, how's the eye?"

"Terrific. I'm even seeing in color. Quick question. Are you brave enough to try another date? Before you say no, I'd certainly understand if you'd rather wash your hair or trim the cat or anything that doesn't involve getting shot at."

"I don't have a cat, Michael."

"I know. I'm just providing a ready-made excuse if you want one. I've actually got two reasons for wanting to see you."

"One will do if it's the right one."

"Couple of questions I want to ask you about John. It's better if we do it in person."

"That's not the right one, Michael."

I could hear a very welcome disappointment in her voice, so I pulled my foot out of my mouth and gave the real one.

"I just want to see you, Terry. I wasn't sure you'd go for that one."

"That's the only one I go for, Michael. When?"

I'd have given my personally autographed Bobby Orr playing

jersey and more to have jumped in with the offer of a normal date, but you can't offer what you don't have, and I did not have the time.

"Terry, I'm thinking of a stroll through the Public Garden just before sundown. Maybe a ride on the swan boats. Possibly feed the ducks. Then a quiet dinner at the Ritz Carlton. We could walk up Commonwealth Ave to a small jazz club for drinks and dancing to the greatest jazz singer since Sarah Vaughn. Then we could drive back along the shore for a walk on the beach, and —"

"Michael, you're dreaming or hallucinating, aren't you?"

"How could you tell?'

"It's still winter. The swan boats are in drydock, and the ducks are in Miami Beach."

"Right. Actually I only have a couple of hours, and I really want to see you. How about fried clams at the Sea Witch in Danvers?"

"Sounds good to me."

I had the Corvette in gear before the phone line was fully disconnected.

The Sea Witch may, in fact, dispense the absolute caviar of fried clams, but even the owner would admit that the décor is, to be generous, seacoast rustic, and that is a euphemism. But with Terry sitting beside, rather than across from me, and giving every indication of being just where she wanted to be, we were in the Oak Room of the Park Plaza.

Time, however, being mercilessly short, I had to break the mood.

"Think of this as a one-minute break for a commercial, Terry. Can I ask you one business question?"

She had a slightly disappointed look, but she bore up.

"Why not, Michael? I'm actually counting my blessings. We haven't been shot at or even hustled out a back door to escape goons."

I liked her attitude.

"During that last week before the bombing, did John seem — frightened, as if he were in danger?"

She thought for a minute before answering.

"No. I don't think so. He was more tense, sort of exhilarated. He said he was working on something that would dramatically change his life. Those were his words. I wouldn't say frightened."

I frankly couldn't square that with the John I knew. Why wasn't he frightened? He was about to steal more millions of dollars than either of us ever dreamed of from Tony Aiello, who could and would slice and dice him for ravioli meat if he ever caught him. And Tony had the tentacles around the world to catch him. On top of that, he was pulling the art fraud of the century on two well-connected Dutch financiers. And finally, he was the tenuous bedmate in all of this with a crafty Russian scorpion, Markov. Any one of those three would have scared the everlasting crap out of me.

I started to ask a follow-up question, but Terry put her fingers on my lips. "Not tonight, Michael. This is our night, right here in fried-clam heaven."

She replaced her fingers with her lips. It was our first really meaningful kiss, and I couldn't have thought of a question if it was the answer to final *Jeopardy!*

The waitress with a North Shore accent thick enough to make it a foreign language stood behind us holding two plates of steaming hot fried clams. The smile on her face said she would have waited all night.

I wanted to remember that table at that restaurant at that moment, because I knew more surely than I knew the license number of my Corvette that a major recalculation of my priorities had just taken place. Of everything in this world that matters to me, Terry had just moved to number one.

"Terry—"

"Michael."

"Terry, I'm serious."

"I know, Michael. So am I. Your clams are getting cold."

"Terry, this has nothing to do with John or this case or anything beyond you and me. I'm serious."

"Michael, didn't you hear what I said? I'm serious too. If we're falling in love, and I certainly hope we are, our love won't cool. The clams will."

It was ten minutes of ten when I walked down the three steps that led to the slightly below ground-level outdoor patio of Paul's Coffee-house on JFK between Harvard Square and the Charles River. I'd been there more times than I could count with classmates — both college and law school.

Like Big Daddy's, it breathed nothing but happy memories. The coffee was rich, the atmosphere was European, and then there was Paul. He was a short, dark Spaniard with a smile that always said to his customers, "Thank you for coming home."

He loved good coffee, some of us students, and anyone whose life was devoted to classical guitar. He had a quick invitation for any of his patrons who spoke a word while his artist of the week was play-ing — an invitation to go to any other coffeehouse in Cambridge.

I stood quietly at the entrance while a young guitarist with Gypsy features in the far corner spun magic out of the strains of the Concerto de Aranjuez. Paul's eyes were closed as he leaned against the coffee bar on the side. I knew better than to speak or move or sit or do anything that would break the slender thread of the moment.

I scanned the crowd of about eight scattered in silence among the dozen tables. Markov had apparently not arrived yet. My stom-ach unclenched for the moment.

When the guitarist finished, I waved to Paul, and took a seat at the empty table closest to the door. Paul brought me a latte with a double shot of espresso and steamed milk without my asking.

"So, Michael," he nodded his head toward the guitarist, "when have you heard better?"

I put on a thinking expression for a couple of seconds. Paul gave me the smack on the side of the head that I half expected.

"Never! Admit it or I take back the coffee. You can go where they wouldn't know a guitarist from a torero."

"Never, Paul. I admit it. You shouldn't assault your customers. It's not good for business."

"To hell with business. His name is Garanto. He just came to this country from Malaga. I heard him there. I talked him into coming over."

"And paid his passage, right?"

He waved the thought aside as too unimportant to consider. "Who cares? Besides he'll pay me back out of his earnings."

"As a guitarist in coffeeshops? Right. That should be about the turn of the next century."

Paul grabbed me by the back of the neck.

"Michael, what are they doing to you? You used to be a musician. Are they turning you into a capitalist?"

"No, Paul. I'm just distracted."

I scanned the crowd again and saw no familiar face.

"Who are you looking for, Michael?"

"No matter. He's not here."

Paul, always physically expressive, hit his forehead with the butt of his hand.

"Of course. I nearly forgot. The gentleman at the table over there. He asked if I knew you. He wanted me to tell him if you came in. Should I tell him?"

"I looked at a tall, balding Russian-looking man in the far corner. He was kneading the fiber out of a paper napkin with the fingers of both hands.

"Thanks, Paul. Would you ask him to come over here?"

I could see the man rise and move with a quick nervous step to my table. I held out my hand, which he grabbed quickly. I nodded to the other chair at my table.

"Mr. Knight. Thank you. I wasn't sure you'd come."

He smiled with a nervous laugh that only elevated the tension.

"I'm here to deliver a message."

He was speaking English, but the accent made it sound more like Russian.

"And you are?"

"I'm sorry. We've never met. My name is Alexei Samnov. I don't know how to begin so you will believe every word I say. It is that important."

"Perhaps you could tell me how you picked this coffeehouse. Do you know Paul?"

"No. No."

He used the shredded napkin to wipe the beads of sweat that were forming on his forehead. He leaned close enough to whisper and fortunately spoke slowly.

"Can you hear me, Mr. Knight?"

I nodded.

"Professor Leopold Denisovitch once told me about this place. I thought you would know it."

If he lacked any part of my attention before, he had it now.

"What about the professor? Is he all right?"

His hands came up in a gesture of frustration and apparently deep concern.

"I don't know. I don't think so."

"Perhaps you'd better give me the message. Is it from him?"

"No — no."

He scanned the immediate area and moved even closer.

"I am also a professor of art history. Professor Denisovitch has been my friend and my colleague for many years. We are both experts in the work of Vermeer. He recently became involved with a group of people who involved him in something against his will. He's a good man."

"I can save you the anguish, professor. I know about his authentication of the fraudulent Vermeer."

"Ah. I see. I also became involved — in a similar business. It involved authentication of the original of the same painting. The problem is that Professor Denisovitch's painting is causing certain financiers to doubt the authenticity of the original. This is causing concern for the man with whom — for whom I was working. He's a very dangerous man."

"If his name is Sergei Markov, I've met him."

"Ah. You've met Sergei. No. The gentleman of whom I speak is by far more dangerous."

His sincerity sent a new rush of chills coursing the length of my spine.

"What's his name?"

He just shook his head and raised his hands.

"Everyone has a name, professor."

"I suppose so, Mr. Knight. But no one I have ever met knows his. He is simply referred to as 'The Gentleman.'"

That seemed a dead end, so I moved on.

"Is the message from him?"

"Yes."

I wanted at the very base of my being not to hear it, but I opened the door.

"What's the message?"

"He has Professor Denisovitch. That's what I'm to tell you. Actually his man, his agent of violence, a man named Lupov, has the professor. The gentleman is aware of how you helped Professor Denisovitch in London. He knows you have feelings for him. I'm to tell you that the professor will suffer more than you could ever imagine if you do not do what he commands."

I could sense how passionately Professor Samnov detested his role as messenger. At the same time I could feel a steel vice tighten around my own heart.

"What does he want?"

"The painting done by Professor Denisovitch. He knows you have it. Once he gets it, he can have me demonstrate why it's a fraud. Nothing else will satisfy his financiers."

I sat back to try to get a few clearing breaths of air. I had just given the key to the locker containing the painting to Tony Aiello. How in the world could I get it back? And if I did and gave it to this so-called gentleman, what were the chances that Professor Denisovitch would live through it anyway?

I asked my coffee companion that last question. He shook his head.

"I'm sorry. I give you an honest answer. There's little chance either way. When the gentleman has the painting, there's no reason to allow Professor Denisovitch to live."

I could read in his eyes everything from fear to deepest shame. My own fear was becoming engulfed in sympathy for him. He seemed too good a man to be forced to deliver such a message. Unfortunately, it emphasized the truth of every word he had whispered.

I was at a total loss for a next move, or even a response. In a way, that gave me a decision.

"Professor Samnov, you can give this answer to your so-called gentleman. I have no answer. When I do, I'll give it to him."

He closed his eyes. He looked as if he had taken an arrow through the heart. I didn't envy him the task of taking that answer to the big shot. On the other hand, I didn't envy Professor Denisovitch, or myself either.

"How do I get in touch with you, Professor Samnov?"

"I'll be in touch with you, Mr. Knight. I'm sure the gentleman will have more to say. Please excuse me."

He was on his feet and through the door before I could get in another word.

CHAPTER THIRTY-FIVE

I fell into bed that night more unconscious than asleep. My last thought was that if God should grant that I awake in the morning, I had no clue as to what I would do beyond brushing my teeth.

My first stop at about eight thirty was the office and a heart-to-heart talk with Mr. Devlin. It helped to have another person share the pain and indecision, but it would be asking something superhuman to expect him to come up with a solution.

I knew instinctively that his first concern would be for me. I was right. He wanted to throw the whole affair, outside of the specific defense of Peter, into the lap of Dominic Santangelo and let the chips fall, or explode, where they may. It was tempting, but it would be abandoning Professor Denisovitch and opening a bloodbath between the don and his traitorous lieutenant, Tony Aiello.

We sparred with each other over the "right" thing to do until nine thirty-five. At that moment, the game changed forever, and the stakes went up a hundredfold.

The phone rang. Mr. Devlin answered it and handed the receiver across the desk to me. Julie was transferring a call.

One would not need psychic powers to be frozen by the tone of Professor Samnov.

"Mr. Knight, the gentleman has responded to your message. Professor Denisovitch is dead."

I just held the phone in silence.

"There was a news report early this morning of an unidentified Russian found dead in Amsterdam."

"If he was unidentified, how do you know it was Professor Denisovitch?"

"The manner of death was described. It's the signature killing of Lupov. Something he devised for the purposes of the gentleman. There's no point in being more graphic."

Now I was completely baffled. If the professor was the leverage this beast was using to get the painting, the threat just evaporated with his death.

"Then it's over."

"It's not over, Mr. Knight. He is still demanding the painting."

"Or else what?"

The next words I heard produced the most pure panic I have ever experienced. By the time I had subdued the driving urge to scream at the top of my lungs and gathered what wits I could summon, I began to see my next move with crystal clarity.

I got up as deliberately as I could and walked to the door. With every step I willed myself to be in rational command of my emotions.

I knew that Mr. Devlin was sensing my barely controlled panic. I could hear his voice in the background, but the words weren't penetrating until I reached the door. I was finally able to hear him and understand.

"Michael, tell me. What is it?"

I stopped just long enough to answer. I knew exactly what I was going to do, and nothing and no one in this world could stop me.

"Michael. What?"

I stunned myself with the calm deliberateness of my answer. "He has another hostage."

"Who?"

"He has Terry."

CHAPTER THIRTY-SIX

I was driving on autopilot, just pointing the nose of my Corvette through the snarls of traffic and tourists around Faneuil Hall toward the North End. I felt cold as steel and single-minded as a bull in full charge. If I allowed myself one rational thought, I'd have taken a U-turn at any intersection.

I slowed down to a merely dangerous rate of speed on Salem Street. I spun the car hard to the right on Prince Street and skidded to a stop halfway onto the sidewalk. The total lack of a legal parking place was not even a consideration.

I had no idea where Aiello might be, but I figured the Stella Maris Restaurant was my best bet. Tom Burns had tracked Benny there twice, which indicated that Aiello probably called some back-room his office.

It was about eleven in the morning. Fortunately, they had just opened for lunch, which mooted the passionate option of kicking in the front door. I headed straight for the bartender who was halfway down the bar that extended along the entire right wall.

There was a scattering of overstuffed male bodies that looked to me like Aiello's soldiers clustered around several tables. I caught sight of a couple of the familiar goons who had accompanied Fat Tony on his first excursion to the Parker House. Before I knew it, they were on each side of me at the bar.

I looked straight at the bartender.

"I need to see Tony Aiello. Now."

The one on my right put on a smug grin and pushed closer until he was practically leaning on me.

"You need to see *Mr. Aiello*, do ya? You're the creep from that place uptown. I think you better haul your ass out of here, cuz Mr. Aiello didn't say nothin' about no appointment with you."

I turned to look him square in the face. I dropped my voice down to a whisper. "Listen to this carefully. I'll say it just once. When you talk to me, you're talking to Mr. Dominic Santangelo."

He just looked at me with the blank expression of a deer in the headlights.

"I'll say it one more time. I need to see Tony Aiello. Right now."

He nodded to the bartender, who picked up a phone behind the bar and turned his back to talk.

The bartender turned back. "He says take him back."

The goon led and I followed through a door at the back that opened into a large room. There were four or five chairs scattered around the room in front of a battered desk. Behind the desk sat the bluberous figure of Tony Aiello, his chair tilted back almost to the breaking point and his feet propped on the desk.

"So now you come to me, smart guy."

"I have a message from Mr. Santangelo. He says—"

"No, no. That crap don't fly around here. If Santangelo wanted to send a message, he'd send a couple of torpedos that'd make you look like a Girl Scout. You only got in here cuz you got me curious. What do ya want? Say it fast. I'm busy."

It was down to one-on-one, and all the leverage seemed to be on his side. I needed the painting now, and there was no time to muster the troops.

"I need the painting."

He looked at me as if I had just said, "I'd like you to give me the Old North Church, and throw in Faneuil Hall."

A disbelieving grin started to curl his lips.

"The hell you say."

"I do say. And before you get locked into a decision, this is the situation. There's a man who operates a crime network all over Europe. A Russian. He's so powerful that most people don't even believe he exists. Believe me, he exists. He just had Professor Deniso-vitch, the one who authenticated your painting, murdered in a way that would shock even you. He did it because I couldn't meet his demand to give him your painting."

"Yeah. So?"

"So he's still making the demand. This time he has a hostage that means more to me than anyone in this world."

He held up his hands in a "So what?" gesture. "You ain't told me nothin' that's got anything to do with me."

"Then let me do that, because I don't want you to think you're out of the loop. This Russian could make shish kabob out of you. You're not in his league. The entire North End couldn't save you if he decides to come after you. Now get this. If anything even minor happens to the hostage he has now, I'll put him onto the one who has the painting in two seconds. That would be you. Now do you feel included?"

He pushed back from the desk and his feet hit the floor with a thud. The redness around his collar was working its way up his face.

"Listen to me, ya bum. You come in here, in my office, makin' threats about some Russian in Europe. I never even heard of this guy. You think you scare Tony Aiello? You've got another —"

"No, you listen, you ignorant blimp. You're going to find your-self taken apart like a reverse jigsaw puzzle if I don't get that paint-ing into his hands fast."

I could see those words flash across my mind like subtitles. If I had actually said them, my next conversation would have been with Saint Peter. What I actually said was more in check.

"Tony, this is too serious a business to decide in anger. I know you're a big shot around here. I'm not questioning your power or your reputation."

That seemed to bring his temperature closer to normal.

"Let me explain something I learned in Amsterdam. This whole painting business was a fraud. John McKedrick and a Russian, Sergei Markov, were in on it together. John met this Markov when John was apparently your messenger boy to Amsterdam in some business deal. We don't need to go into that."

"Good. Leave it sit."

"Anyway, according to their plan, John brought you the idea of getting hold of this stolen Vermeer painting and using it for collateral to borrow a lot of money for your other businesses. We don't need to go into that either."

"Damn right."

"So you went for it. Now here's the bottom line. The whole thing was a scam. On you. As I see it, the borrowed money was suppose to be wired into your account. It wasn't. It was transferred into some else's account."

"Whose? McKedrick's?"

"I don't know. Someone's. John was killed around the same time the money disappeared."

"That son of a —"

"Here's the kicker. Listen carefully, Tony. The painting, the Vermeer you thought you got — it's a complete fraud. It was painted by Professor Denisovitch. He authenticated it as an original Vermeer. It was just part of the whole scam. It's worth no more than the price of the canvas and paint."

"Yeah? Says you."

He was putting on a front, but I could see the truth exploding in his eyes.

"Says Professor Denisovitch. I met him in London. He told me the whole thing."

"Then let him tell me."

"Tony, I told you he was murdered by this other Russian, the one who's going to take us all apart if I don't get that painting to him."

He sat there in a silent funk trying to process all of this. I gave him a minute, but I had precious little time to give. I had no idea of what Terry must be going through. The thought of it turned my brain to jelly, so I tried to focus on what had to be done.

"Tony, I need the painting. Can we get off dead center."

He looked up at me with an expression like a rock.

"You get nothin'. That picher stays where it is."

I had to play the last trump I had.

"This is it. You are in one deep pile of crap. You owe seventy million dollars to some Dutch dealers. The only thing you have to back it up is a phony painting that isn't worth ten bucks. You got into this bind to betray, probably to assassinate, the Godfather, Dominic Santangelo. The only thing that's keeping him from taking vengeance on your life is an agreement with me and my partner."

I could see the look of shock deepen in his eyes.

"That's right. He's onto you. Between Santangelo and this Russian who's demanding the painting, your life isn't worth as much as that phony Vermeer. And think about this. The only thing standing between you and both of them is me. You hear me, Tony? Me!"

He was looking straight into my eyes, and no words were coming out. It was time to pull the trigger.

"I've got to move, Tony. In ten seconds, I'm out that door. If I leave without that painting, you won't have a chance in hell of seeing the sunset. I'm counting."

I stood the full ten seconds. Nothing moved. I knew it wouldn't as long as I waited.

I held up my hand and turned to the door.

"Good-bye, Tony. If you know a priest, I'd make a quick confession."

With every measured step to the door, my heart pounded more loudly. The question was blaring in silence through my mind: *Without that painting, what can I possibly trade for Terry?*

My desperation nearly reached the panic level when I pulled open the door. I hesitated just long enough to hear a desk drawer open behind me. My first thought was that Tony was going for a gun. Useless as I felt for Terry, I almost didn't care.

I turned around to avoid being shot in the back and said what I thought was my last prayer. I saw Tony on his feet with his right fist clenched. There was no gun.

He started to say something, but he couldn't seem to get it out. He threw something that he had in his right hand. I caught it, and felt as if a cement block had fallen away from my heart.

It was the key to the South Station locker where I had stashed the Denisovitch painting.

CHAPTER THIRTY-SEVEN

I was halfway between South Station, where I had picked up the painting from the locker, and my office on Franklin Street, when my cell phone gave me a start. When I heard Alexei Samnov's voice, I pulled over to the curb on Summer Street to give it my full concentration.

"Mr. Knight, I need an answer. I have to have something to tell — you know."

"It's all right, professor. I have the painting."

I heard a deep sigh of relief. I did not share the feeling.

"Tell me the truth, Professor. If I give it to him, is there a chance he'll let Terry go?"

He breathed another sigh. This time it was empathy.

"Mr. Knight, I'm afraid not very much. I know this. If he doesn't get it, there's no chance at all. Then he'll come after you. "

Apparently I had gotten Terry and myself into this lobster trap where there was no backing out. The only way was forward.

"So how do we do it?"

"I've been contacted by Lupov. It's typical of him. He likes to do his work in seclusion. Do you know the town of Milton in New Hampshire? It's just off Route Sixteen."

"I've been past it. It's on the way to the White Mountains."

"There's a farm. It's on a small road between Milton and Farmington. I can give you directions. He'll be waiting there."

"Did he say he'd have Terry there?"

"He didn't say. He only said look for a barn across an open field. He'll see you approaching. You're to come alone and tell no one. If you don't do this exactly, she'll die. Those are his words."

"That wasn't a question, professor. It's a demand. Terry is to be there. We make the exchange at the same time. That's absolute."

There was a pause.

"I'll try."

"No, tell him. No Terry, no painting. And bring me the answer."

"I'll get back to you. The exchange is this afternoon. Four thirty."

The drive to Milton would take close to two hours based on my ski trips to the mountains around Laconia. Before starting, I made one stop at a stationery store to pick up something that I optimistically thought could give me a slight advantage.

I was overwhelmingly tempted through the entire drive to call Mr. Devlin or Tom Burns. I never felt so alone in my life. I was just afraid that they might make some move that would trigger Lupov to do something to Terry. I couldn't risk it. My only resource for strength and comfort was prayer.

Professor Samnov's directions were flawless — as was his prediction of seclusion. The barn was in the center of at least five acres of cornfield that had been harvested down to the ground. The sun was setting behind the barn. There was just enough light to make out the large barn door facing me as I came to the edge of the pine woods surrounding the field.

I walked to the edge of the field and stopped. It was just four thirty. I was looking across an expanse of cornfield of about half a football field. Nothing was moving.

I shouted, "Hello."

It spooked a flight of crows halfway to the barn, but nothing else.

I called again louder. "Hello!"

I saw the barn door open about a foot. I waited another five seconds before hearing a deep voice with a heavy accent.

"Mr. Knight, you're very punctual. That's good. I hope for the life of your friend that you followed all of my directions as well. You'll please hold up the painting."

I came five feet out into the field and held up the cardboard tube I had picked up at the stationary store to hold the painting.

"Excellent. I'm sure that the painting is in that cylinder because you know what will happen if it is not. You will now walk across the field and place the painting on the ground at this door."

"Not yet. I'll see Miss O'Brien in full view before I take a step."

There was an exceedingly uncomfortable pause before I heard, "Why not?"

The barn door opened a few feet. In the fading backlight, I could see what looked like a female figure in a long coat standing in the doorway. I yelled to her.

"Terry, are you all right?"

There was no response. In a few seconds I heard the man's voice.

"I'm afraid there will be no conversation. The precaution of tape on her mouth. Now you'll walk the painting to the barn door. "

I trusted this snake as far as I could throw the barn, but someone had to make the first move. I was literally dying to get Terry safely in my arms.

I started pacing my way across the open field toward the barn. When I got halfway there, I stopped. I dropped the cylinder on the spot, and I walked back to the edge of the trees. The voice came again with considerably more tension.

"You're playing with the life of your friend, Mr. Knight. You'll follow my directions exactly if you expect her to live. This is not a game."

"No it's not a game, and you don't make all the rules, Lupov. I think you need to get this painting as much as I need to have Miss O'Brien safe. I believe your life could depend on it. I think perhaps your so-called gentleman is unforgiving of failure. Now here are my rules."

I bent down and picked up the identical cardboard cylinder that I had left at the edge of the woods.

"I give you my word, Lupov, the painting you want is in one of these two cylinders. You will walk Miss O'Brien to the cylinder in the middle of the field. You'll pick it up, leave Miss O'Brien there, and walk back to the barn. Miss O'Brien will walk to me."

"You're insane. Why should I trust you?"

I held up the cardboard cylinder in my left hand and lit a Zippo lighter in my right. This was the insurance I bought before leaving.

"You'll trust me because this cylinder in my hand is doused in lighter fluid. If you make one move to harm Miss O'Brien, this cylinder will turn to charcoal in five seconds. If the painting is in this one, it will be charcoal too. How would you like to report that to your no-name gentleman?"

He looked totally perplexed. He had gone from a pair of loaded dice to a pure crapshoot. I had gone from a hopeless long shot to an even-money gamble. I still hated the odds on Terry's life, but they were at least improved.

It took thirty agonizing seconds for him to respond. I had played my last card. There was nothing I could do but wait.

After an eternity, I saw the door creak open wide enough to let two figures pass. In the fading light, I could see that the woman in the heavy long coat was in front. A stocky male figure was immediately behind, holding her by both arms. I still couldn't make out Terry's features. It could have been anyone, but that was my gamble.

I sensed to my amazement that the conscienceless violence that had always given Lupov the commanding hand was in a peculiar way working to my advantage. He had probably never known what it was to face someone who had a terrorizing leverage over him. He had no idea how to respond other than to concede and take his chances.

The two figures walked in slow lockstep toward the cardboard cylinder in the middle of the field. I could feel Lupov's eyes riveted to my face as I held the small flame an inch from the cylinder in my left hand.

When the two reached the middle of the field, I saw Lupov stop and hold the woman with one hand. He slowly bent down and snatched up the cylinder. Now that I had him on command, I pressed it.

"Now let her go. Take that cylinder and walk back to the barn. Hesitate for one second and this cylinder goes up in flames."

I saw him turn and start to move in that direction. I could see the woman's features more clearly now. I was almost sure it was Terry. She seemed frozen to the spot. I yelled at the top of my lungs.

"Terry, run! Here, to me!"

I started toward her, still holding the flame and cardboard cylinder in case Lupov turned with a gun. He was halfway to the barn. I could see him ripping apart the cardboard cylinder. I realized that in a few seconds he'd know he had the painting. The one I was holding a flame to was a bluff.

I dropped the cylinder and lighter and started to run to Terry. She still hadn't made a move in my direction. I couldn't imagine why.

When I got within ten yards of her, I could see her mouth covered with tape. She was actually running and stumbling away from me. I yelled to her again in case she didn't understand, but she fell and tried to scramble all the harder away from me.

I caught a quick glance at Lupov. I could see that he had the painting in one hand. He was just standing there grinning. He had something that I couldn't identify in his other hand. It didn't look like a gun, so I ran the rest of the way to Terry who seemed to be struggling as hard as she could, tangled in the heavy long overcoat, to get away from me.

I reached her and grabbed her in my arms. I could feel her still struggling to get away. Her face was covered with tears, and she seemed to be pleading and pulling away.

I looked up at Lupov who faced me with a vicious grin. He pointed his hand with the object in it at us. I knew it was not a gun, but I instinctively pulled Terry to the ground as if to avoid whatever it was.

I half expected to hear a blast from his direction in case I was wrong about a gun. When it came, I was dumbfounded. It came from the wrong direction. It came from the woods behind me. I braced for the impact, but none came. When I opened my eyes. I saw Lupov reeling backward with a great, dark hole in his forehead. He was dead before he hit the ground.

I held Terry tight and kept repeating, "It's over. It's over. It's over."

Her struggling and writhing finally stopped. She just lay on the ground, shaking her head in a gesture I didn't understand. I held her head steady and worked the tape off of her mouth. When it was off, she just screamed at me to get away, run.

I held her until I could get her to listen to my words and know that Lupov was dead. It had passed.

When it finally sank in, she just lay rigidly on the ground and pleaded with me not to touch her. Her hands were tied behind her, so she couldn't resist as I worked on the buttons to open the long overcoat that had tangled around her. When the last button gave way, I saw what was terrifying her.

My first move was to run to Lupov to be sure he was dead and to work the thing he was holding out of his locked-finger grip. When I got it away, I laid it on the ground and ran back to Terry.

I pulled away all of the folds of the overcoat to expose rows of sticks of explosives. I carefully slid my hand under her back to follow the wires until I felt a small box. I worked with my fingers in the blind to free it from the tape. It finally came loose, and I could pull the wires out of a small radio-controlled detonator.

I carefully untaped each of the cylinders of explosive that surrounded her body under the coat. When the last one came loose, I raced them to the creek just inside the tree line and threw them into the water.

When I got back to Terry, she was shaking all over with chills of cold and shock. I wrapped her in the overcoat and just hugged her until they passed.

I had one last thing to do. I went to Lupov's body and began a search. I found what I was looking for on the third finger of his left hand. I removed it from the body and picked up the painting where it lay beside him.

I helped Terry to her feet and practically carried her to the car.

CHAPTER THIRTY-EIGHT

The ride back to Boston gave me time to think. The heat of the warm car, and the exhaustion from the nightmare caused Terry to sleep most of the way.

In spite of the car's heat, I had the shakes when I realized what Lupov had planned. Once I'd given him the painting, he knew I'd run to Terry. When we were together, one press of the small garage door opener in his hand would have triggered the detonator connected to the explosives taped to her body. We'd both have been blown across the New Hampshire countryside. Again, Lupov would have left no witnesses.

I thanked God that we were both alive, but I also realized that I had someone else to thank. In fact, this was the third time in three weeks that an invisible guardian angel had stepped in to snatch my life out of the hands of a killer. I was remembering the shooting of Aiello's assassin, Vito Respa, in Rockport, then the two thugs in the car that was following me on Charles Street, and now the prince of evil, Lupov. I believe in angels, but I've never heard of one that works with guns.

On the drive back to Boston, I had time to go through the cast of characters for some clue as to who had been watching my back so efficiently. Each time, the thought process led me to the same unlikely conclusion, and each time I rejected it.

I reached another conclusion that I couldn't reject. It would be the worst kind of wishful thinking to believe that Lupov's death was the end of the threat to either Terry or myself. Somehow I had to reach higher. Somehow I had to neutralize the nameless Russian "gentleman" himself. He could hardly afford to leave either of us alive as a loose end, even if he got the painting.

I realized that I was deeply in need of an immediate favor. While I drove, I flipped through my mental Rolodex and came up with Judy Olanski. We were classmates at Harvard Law School and shared an office on law review. Long nights of editing articles and studying for exams, punctuated by slices of lukewarm pizza and reheated coffee, had made us pals of the type who shared Saturday night movies when neither of us had a date.

We had unfortunately let the friendship ties cool since law school. I knew that Judy had practiced law for a few years until our old alma mater had called her back to be a professor at Harvard Law.

I called her old number and thanked God when she answered. I could spare about forty-five seconds of catch-up chitchat before getting to the point. Fortunately that was enough. I could sense that the years had dropped away, and Judy was the old Judy.

"This is not fair, and I don't know how it fits into your life at the moment, but I need a grandiose favor."

"A grandiose one, is it, Mike? I don't know. I'd be good for an *enormous* favor. But *grandiose?*"

I gave her the bare-bones facts—just enough to convince her that it was a matter of life or death that she let Terry stay with her for a few days. There was never a question of her answer. She did, however, question my lifestyle.

"Mike, what are you, some kind of James Bond?"

"Not by a long shot, Judy."

"I think we need a long talk over a cold pizza, Mike."

I signed off to concentrate on the road, when it dawned on me that Judy accepted the guest without ever questioning how much danger it would bring into her own life.

Old friends.

I left Terry with Judy and drove to my apartment. I was taking no chance with Terry, but I was willing to run the risk that it was safe for

me to go home. I hoped that word of what had happened in the wilds
of New Hampshire would not yet have reached the ears of anyone
dangerous. I needed to be at home to get what I hoped would be a
call from Professor Samnov, since I had no way to get in touch with
him.

When I reached home, my first call was to Mr. Devlin. I realized he had no inkling of where I had been since the phone call came
in his office saying that Terry was a hostage.

He sounded as if his day had been tortured with worry. His
relief at hearing my voice and knowing that both Terry and I were
alive poured through the telephone. At the same time, he knew as
well as I did that the danger was merely interrupted, not ended.

We planned to meet the following morning at eight o'clock at
a small hole-in-the-wall coffee shop on Arch Street, just off Franklin.
It was insignificant enough to enable us to ask a third party to join
us without the likelihood of being noticed.

I realized that there were two roads to be traveled, and each was
demanding immediate attention. First, I knew I'd be hearing from
Professor Samnov at any moment. In fact I was counting on it. He
was my only thread of connection to the nameless Russian spider at
the center of the web.

The second road was the defense of Peter Santangelo. The trial
would reach the call of the list for pretrial conferences soon. Soon,
however, was not immediate, and before the spider could touch Terry
or me again, he was priority one.

It was eleven o'clock at night when the phone ringing brought me out
of a dead sleep. Professor Samnov sounded surprised when I answered. I may have been deluding myself, but I thought his surprise
was tinged with relief.

"Thank God you're alive. I wasn't sure. And the girl?"

"Alive."

"Thank God. How did you do it? You delivered the painting?"

"Lupov's dead."

That brought silence for a moment.

"But, the painting?"

"I told you. Lupov's dead. We're alive. It was his every wish that it be the reverse. I have a message for your nameless gentleman. Can you reach him?"

"I'm sure he'll be contacting me when he doesn't hear from Lupov. What shall I tell him about the painting?"

"Nothing. Absolutely nothing. From now on he deals with me directly. That takes you off the hook since you have no information to give him."

"But he'll demand —"

"Let him. You know nothing because you can't contact me. That's your story. That includes any information about Lupov. I'll give him all the information he needs when we meet. Your only function will be to arrange a meeting between us."

I could hear him breathing rapidly and feel waves of fear coming through the telephone. "But if I don't answer his questions —"

"Listen to me, Professor Samnov, you're safe. You're the only one he won't harm. He needs you to convince the moneylenders that this Denisovitch painting is a fraud. That's your life insurance."

There was a pause while the logic of what I said sank in. "Then what shall I tell him?"

"Tonight nothing. You haven't heard from anyone. I need time to put this together. Can you meet me tomorrow, ten a.m.?"

"Where?"

I needed a place that was private but that didn't look like an arranged meeting place in case either of us was being followed. I decided to go with my theory that the most public place can be the most private.

"Park Street Station. It's an MTA station on Tremont Street just down Park Street from the State House. Meet me downstairs by the information booth."

Mr. Devlin and I were the first of our trio to arrive at Charlie's Coffeeshop on Arch Street the next morning. We were both there at ten minutes of eight. We huddled together over Charlie's steaming good coffee and powdered-sugar donuts and put together what we wanted to say to our invited guest.

It was five past eight when Billy Coyne came down the steps out of the cold. He thawed out with hot coffee while Mr. Devlin laid out what we'd put together.

Billy just inhaled the steam rising off of his coffee while Mr. D. outlined the possibility of taking down an infamous, though nameless, international dealer in stolen art, murder, kidnapping, and anything else we could lay at the feet of this no-name Russian gentleman.

Billy finally spoke through the steam without looking up. "Lex, this is Suffolk County. I'm the deputy D.A of Suffolk County, not Interpol. What's this guy done that I could prosecute?"

I made the offering.

"How about this, Mr. Coyne? Receiving stolen property, the Vermeer painting that was stolen from a Boston museum around ten years ago. How about kidnapping of a girl named Terry O'Brien from her home in Boston? How about attempted murder of both Terry and me near Milton, New Hampshire? You could get the D.A. up there involved. They're going to be wondering about the body of a Russian they'll be discovering in New Hampshire. Good for starters?"

He looked up at me with one of those doubtful looks old trial attorneys reserve for young lawyers.

Mr. Devlin stepped in for credibility. "We've got a witness who can lay all of this on the no-name Russian."

"Who's the witness?"

"He's a Russian professor. He can testify firsthand. He may need witness protection. You've got an in with the feds, Billy. I'm sure they're going to be interested in this guy too. This is major league."

Mr. Coyne looked at Mr. D. with more credence than he showered on me.

"Where is this no-name Russian, Lex?"

"At the moment, anywhere in the world. We don't know. I doubt that anyone does."

"Oh, well that should make it easy."

Mr. Coyne looked over at me and then Mr. D. with a slight grin. "I assume you boys plan on paying for these excellent donuts and coffee. Because it looks like that's all I'm going to get out of this little excursion."

Mr. D. leaned over next to his ear. I could just barely hear what he whispered. "Billy-Boy, the donuts are on me, but there's a price. And it's nonnegotiable. Otherwise you pay for your own damn donuts."

Billy looked Mr. D. in the eye.

"And that price would be what?"

"You listen to every word my partner is about to utter. You take that sarcastic, patronizing grin off your face, and you listen. Both ears, Billy."

Mr. Coyne looked slowly over at me. The grin, as aptly described by Mr. D., was gone. I had his rapt attention. I laid out in as much detail as I could what I had put together the night before. I was able to put more grit into my voice for knowing that Mr. Devlin had bought into the idea.

When the three of us walked out of Charlie's Coffeeshop — separately — the ball was truly in my court, with all of the crushing responsibility that old tennis expression implied.

At ten o'clock, I started down that interminable escalator into the bowels of Park Street Station. The morning rush-hour crowd had subsided, but there were still the predictable, self-absorbed patrons of the subway moving along the platforms.

I spotted a heavy overcoat bundled around a tall figure with a fur hat obscuring everything that showed above the coat. I walked over and said "Good morning" to the hat. It lifted enough to let a pair of eyes check me out.

I led him over against a wall that enabled us to be obscured as much as possible by the steady stream of commuters. We may have been under observation, but I was sure that no one could hear us.

"Professor Samnov, is that you in there?"

He mumbled, "Good Morning."

"Time is short, professor. I have some very serious things to say. First, did you hear from your mislabeled gentleman?"

"Yes. He asked questions. I told him I'd heard nothing."

"Good. Professor, listen to me. I'm going to ask you the question of your life."

He slowly raised the hat above his face. After stealing glances in all directions, he focused on me.

"How would you like to be free of him? How would you like to free the world of him?"

His eyes widened in a mixture of disbelief and fear. I might have hit him with his very first inkling of the possibility of turning on the one who had become his puppeteer. He knew better than I what a conscienceless beast we'd be taking on.

He still just stared.

"I'm guessing you're a good man who made one mistake and got sucked in beyond your expectations. My bet is that you've hated every waking moment — and maybe even yourself ever since. Just nod if you're hearing me."

He nodded with a vigor that told me he was saying more than that he heard me.

"Then it's time to break free — maybe even make amends."

The momentum continued, as did the nodding. Now the tough part. I gave it to him all at once, which could have been a mistake.

"I want you to meet with a district attorney. He'll want you to give a statement under oath that he can use to get a grand jury indictment against your gentleman. If the case comes up for trial later, you may have to testify in person against him."

His eyes opened as wide as the circle of his mouth. The fear in his eyes ran soul-deep.

"Listen to me, professor. You'll have protection. You'll be taken into the federal witness protection program. You'll have a home, a completely new life here in the United States. No one will ever find you."

He was still frozen with fear, and I could understand it.

"There is no hiding from him. He knows everything. He can do anything."

"Professor, only God knows everything and can do everything. This is just a man. He has weaknesses."

I could sense his mind racing behind the eyes that just stared into a vacuum.

"Professor, if you help, we can put him away. He'll never hurt any of us again."

His body just tilted back until he was leaning against the wall. He needed time to take it all in. I gave it to him, with one final jolt.

"Keep this in mind, professor. If we do what he wants, if I give him the painting, and you swear that it's not the original, he'll kill us both. That's a certainty. He leaves no loose ends. You know that in your heart. I'm offering you the only way out."

He was looking me in the eye now rather than staring into space. He finally spoke. "I guess there's no other way."

"Then I'm ready to trust you, professor. I'm going to place my life in your hands."

His voice was steadier now.

"What do you want me to do?"

I walked him to Billy Coyne's office.

Billy took both of us into a closed-door session with the United States Attorney. From there, the carefully coached professor made telephone contact with the no-name beast, and all hell broke loose.

CHAPTER THIRTY-NINE

The phone call between the professor and the gentleman was even more turbulent than I expected. The speakerphone broadcast it to the few of us in the room. It was all in Russian, which put the words beyond my understanding, but the heat flowing through the wires could have boiled water.

The professor stuck to the script. He reported that all he knew was that he had contacted me after my meeting with Lupov, and I still had the painting. I fully expected that the "gentleman" on the other end of the line would be unlikely to receive bad news graciously, but I could not have predicted his ferocity.

The professor was severely shaken. If Billy Coyne and I had not been in the room, he would have crumbled. He kept looking to us for the reassurance that we provided with profuse nodding.

The professor signaled that the gentleman was asking about Lupov. When the professor said that he had heard nothing, the tirade started all over again. Not only did he not have the painting, but his obedient servant, Lupov, was not responding to commands.

I was actually enjoying it. Each blast of Russian profanity from the so-called gentleman signaled a wound to his sense of omnipotence. I could read the moment when the professor stopped answering questions, and gently took the first step in our offensive. I assumed that he was telling in Russian that I had left a message. The message, as we rehearsed, was that I was willing to deliver the painting, but only to the gentleman personally and alone according to my instructions.

I expected an outburst of refusal. I was not disappointed.

The professor then relayed my follow-up message, i.e., that I had secreted the painting with instructions for its destruction if I disappeared or suffered any harm. If the gentleman had the faintest expectation of having the painting in his hands, it would have to be transferred my way.

There was a pause on the line. I knew he was weighing his options.

The four of us in the room looked from one to the other. Only Billy expressed a prediction with a "no chance" shake of his head.

Shock spread around the room when the gruff voice came through the phone with what sounded like a question. The professor responded by relaying my precise directions for the personal handover of the painting.

The following morning, I was back in Amsterdam. I knew I could push the gentleman so far, and no farther. I had to pick a hand-off location that he would be willing to risk. My first choice would, of course, have been Boston Police Headquarters off Cambridge Street, but moving from the sublime to the possible, I had chosen a coffeehouse beside the Herengracht, one of the main canals in the center of Amsterdam. It was small — about eight tables — but there was a regular flow of locals in and out, particularly attracted by the selections of marijuana openly offered on the menu.

We had set the meeting for two p.m. I arrived at one forty-five. I took the table against the far wall, just as the professor had specified on the phone. There was a young couple that looked like a reincarnation from the sixties at one table and an old man in work clothes nodding off at another table with smoking apparatus in front of him and a simple smile on his face that indicated that he was in his own world. This was just how I remembered the coffeehouse.

Within minutes, another group of young people took a table at the front and placed their order. I was clearly the only one in the shop who had come for coffee.

At five minutes of two, a couple of men who looked more Slavic than Dutch came in, looked around, and took a table along the side. I tried to catch an accent, but they were silent, morose types — which also said they were not Dutch. I could feel a tightening of every muscle in my stomach. I sensed that the gentleman was already weaseling around my demand that he come alone.

At exactly two, an older, rotund man with a cherubic face and white whiskers that could get him work as Santa in any mall appeared at the door. He was just as the professor had described him.

Without hesitation, he walked directly to my table and took a seat. His smile would charm any child who sat on his knee, but as I looked past the smile into his eyes, I had no desire to climb into his lap.

I opened with a testing jab at his anonymity.

"Is there any name I should call you by during our conversation?"

He smiled and summoned the waitress.

"Choose any name you like. It will be a short conversation and quite likely our last."

He ordered an espresso, and after looking for my nod, made it two. When she left, his voice became low and coarse.

"Mr. Knight, you have no idea of the immensity of the mistake you're making in disrespecting my wishes. You're younger than I thought. Perhaps that explains your willingness to forfeit your life for what I assure you will amount to nothing."

I looked him directly in the eye and reached slowly into my suit coat pocket. I removed the cell phone that I had already used to connect to Billy Coyne. I held it in plain view, which cut off his monologue in mid-intimidation.

"You'll hand that to me."

"Well, maybe not, whatever your name is — Listen, I've got to call you something. Marvin. How about if I call you Marvin?"

The smile had totally vanished and a bit of redness was beginning to color his flawless complexion. He started to speak, but I leaned forward and cut him off.

"No, Marvin. It would not be a good idea for me to hand over the phone. Let me explain something. This phone is connected to someone who has direct access to the painting that brought us together. If we should be disconnected, or if I should say a particular word, he will immediately incinerate the painting. Poof! There goes your financial security. I hear you're called "The Gentleman." Shall we begin again and speak like gentlemen?"

He had that look that Harry Wong gets when he has the first inkling that I might have him in checkmate over a chessboard.

The gentleman settled back in his chair while the waitress brought our espressos. When she left, he spoke in a restrained voice.

"You speak of a business deal, Mr. Knight. I assume you want something. What is it?"

"I've discussed this with your messenger, Professor Samnov. Incidentally, you both surprise me. You both speak English very well. He in particular has practically no accent. How do you manage it?"

I could see impatience welling up in his eyes. He had not come for chitchat. "The professor has been educated all over the world. He's something of a linguist. So am I. Now can we get down to business? What do you want?"

"Now that's complicated. My primary interest is to be free of you entirely. I'll admit I'm at a loss as to how to accomplish that. Right now, I have the painting for protection. But after that —"

While I spoke, I reached into my left pocket and took out something that I thanked God I had had the presence of mind to obtain in the first place. As I reached for the bowl of sugar for the espresso, I "accidentally" dropped the solid object with a thud on the table. My eyes were glued on his, and what I saw — or didn't see — sent chills of alert rampaging.

I reached for the object and clumsily knocked it off the table. It hit with another thud and rolled across the floor toward the front door. Now I knew what I needed to know. I pressed one of the numbered buttons on the cell phone, and sat back in the chair. I addressed my companion in a sentence that I dragged out unmercifully.

"The Dutch . . . I find . . . and you may not agree . . . but then you may . . .make. . . an excellent . . . cup of espresso."

The look on his face expressed irritation at my irrelevant observation. His puzzlement was short lived. Within seconds, a squad of uniformed officers flooded into the coffeehouse. They placed every one in the room under arrest, including me and the staff, saying something about a hard narcotics raid. We were all placed in handcuffs and loaded into separate police vans waiting at the curb.

I was loaded alone into the rear van. As soon as the door closed, I got the ear of the ranking officer.

"The one at my table, he's an accomplice. That's all. Hold him. But he's not the one. The one you want is the fat old man at the middle table. He's in old work clothes. He's the one. Guard him with your lives. He'll be the subject of extradition as soon as possible."

The following afternoon at about two, I was once more grateful to be landing back on American soil. After scurrying through customs with just an overnight bag, I caught a cab under the deft and swift guidance of a driver named Carlotta. She had me at the office of the United States attorney in the federal building faster than I could have gotten there from my office.

I joined a familiar gathering of Lex Devlin, Billy Coyne, Andrew Styles, the U. S. attorney for the District of Massachusetts, and, to my pleasant surprise, Professor Samnov.

The entire room was in a cautiously jubilant mood — even the professor. The gentleman had been caged. The local Amsterdam, police, acting together with members of Interpol, were holding him in custody under maximum security.

The raid on the coffeehouse had been carefully arranged by the U.S. attorney and Billy Coyne with the willing, in fact, eager cooperation of the Amsterdam and Interpol authorities, who recognized an opportunity when it dropped into their laps. The "gentleman" and his scourge of praying mantises were as well known to them as he was anonymous in the United States. The indictment obtained by the U.S. attorney through the testimony of Professor Samnov was the basis for beginning extradition proceedings.

Billy had been on the other end of the cell phone connection I kept open during my conversation in the coffeehouse. When I hit the numbered key on the cell phone, Billy gave the word to the combined Amsterdam and Interpol officers to launch the raid.

Billy was, typically, a ball of curiosity for details.

"What the hell was that loud noise? It sounded like you dropped your teeth."

I explained that I seriously doubted that the gentleman would just walk in and sit down at the table as ordered. On the other hand, I was sure he'd show up. He wouldn't risk losing the painting. That's why I had to be sure the man I was speaking to was the gentleman himself.

"When I complimented him and Professor Samnov on speaking English without an accent, I got an answer. He accepted the compliment, and even explained it as an international education. The fact is — and Professor Samnov, please forgive me — you have a Russian accent that you could cut with a knife. Linguistics is not your forte. The real so-called gentleman would have known that."

Billy, always the realist, put my thin theory to the test. "Suppose he had just decided to accept a compliment? Maybe he even thought that he and the professor had no accent. Maybe he'd never heard the professor speak English."

"All possible. That's why I put it to the real test. That clunk you heard was a ring the size of pipe bowl. It was a mass of silver in the shape of a wolf. I took it off the hand of the assassin, Lupov, in New Hampshire. I dropped it on the table to see his reaction. Absolutely none. It could, in fact, have been my teeth as far as he was concerned.

"Then I 'accidentally' sent it rolling down the floor. The old man in work clothes at the other table fixed on it like the Hope Diamond. I was certain that he recognized it. The stunned look on his face told me he knew where it came from. I was sure he was the so-called gentleman, but Professor Samnov can give a positive identification at the extradition hearing."

My next move was to pick up Terry at Judy Olanski's and drive her home to Winthrop. She looked a little frazzled herself, which, considering the more unusual aspects of our dating history, is to say that she was bearing up amazingly well.

I left her with a kiss and a promise that somewhere in our future there would be a date of the type that normal people enjoy. I'm not sure she believed it, but she seemed pleased with the prospect.

CHAPTER FORTY

Before we went our separate ways from the gathering at the U. S. attorney's office, Mr. Devlin and I got a chance to huddle on a game plan. He told me that Judge Gafni, the assigned judge in the trial of Peter Santangelo, had called a pretrial conference for ten o'clock the following morning. We both predicted that the focus of the conference would be to set a trial date, with Judge Gafni probably pushing both sides for the earliest date that both sides could manage.

So far, our entire defense amounted to putting Peter on the stand to deny everything with a sincere look on his face, and Mr. Devlin's disemboweling the credibility of Three-finger Simone, the prosecution's witness who claimed that Peter had hired him to accomplish the bombing of John McKedrick.

That may sound like more than nothing, but that's just what it was — barely more than nothing, particularly having a defendant who was the son of the man the jury knew as the Godfather.

I had a burning curiosity about John McKedrick's doings the week before that Friday bombing. Terry was of little help since the relationship between her and John had been, thank God, far more superficial than I had first imagined.

I decided, with reluctance, to try a tender source. I called John's parents at their new home. Their phone number had been changed, and when I reached John's father at the new number, he gave me directions to their new home with a lot less enthusiasm than I remembered in the past.

Their old address was in a working-class neighborhood in

Southie. The new address was several notches more upscale in a professional section of Brookline. It was not Beacon Hill, but it was a definite upgrade.

John's mother and father invited me into their living room. In all the years I'd known them, I had never once sat in their living room. We'd always gathered over coffee or beer at the kitchen table.

After condolences were offered and received, I got down to business. "Did you have a chance to see John that week before the 'accident.'"

I noticed people still felt more comfortable with that word. John's mother started to speak, but his father took the lead.

"No. John called to say he was very busy that week. He usually came to dinner on Wednesdays, but not that week."

"Did he say what he was busy with?"

Again his mother opened her mouth, but the words came from his father.

"No. Just work."

"Other than busy, did he seem unusual in any way?"

They looked at each other. His mother got a word in. "Like how, Michael?"

"Anything at all unusual. Nervous, worried, rushed?"

His father took back the floor. "John was always rushed."

I was sorry I'd thrown that last word in. It gave him an easy out. And so it went. We sipped tea—which in itself was a strange shift—while I threw pitches at which neither of them seemed inclined to swing.

I was finally willing to admit to myself that I was drilling a dry well. I stood up to leave. At that point, I decided to ignore sensibilities and salvage something out of the trip.

"I can't help noticing that you've moved to a much nicer neighborhood. If you don't mind my asking, did John leave you money in his will?"

As soon as the words were out, I sensed an even tighter stiffening. The temperature went from a slight chill to frost warnings. The question was so indelicate that I hated myself for asking it, but I reminded myself that the rest of our client's life was hanging on a threadbare defense.

They locked on each other's eyes. John's mother withdrew into a concrete shell, and his father barely got out the word. "Yes."

I wondered about the amount, but clearly it was substantial, and asking the exact dollar figure would be less likely to get me an amount than a clipped change of subject.

So that was it. I took my leave without kisses or handshakes, and went home for what, under the circumstances, passed for a night's sleep.

The next morning, Mr. Devlin and I walked into Judge Gafni's chambers for the pretrial at ten a.m. The First Lady of Prosecution, Angela Lamb, was already there and seated in her smartly tailored, dark pin-stripe pantsuit.

We took two of the other chairs in front of the judge, and moments later, Billy Coyne walked in. He passed between us and the desk with his back to the judge. As he passed Mr. Devlin, he dropped the unopened envelope with the letter to the witness, Simone, from Tony Aiello onto Mr. Devlin's lap and mouthed the words, "I can't."

We both understood. It could be anything from a bribe to intimidation of a witness, and Billy would be the unwitting aider and abettor if he delivered it. The whole show escaped the notice of Angela Lamb, who was beaming her most confident smile at the judge.

Judge Gafni, facing a full day's docket, cut directly to the core. "Counsel, we're here to set a trial date. I'll just say this. It's not even general knowledge that the defendant is still alive after an attempt on his life his first night in prison. Every minute he spends in lockup is a test of the security of the system. I want this trial to begin as soon as possible. Miss Lamb?"

"We could begin tomorrow, Your Honor. We've been ready since the indictment came down."

I suppose that that could have been said without smarminess — but not by Ms. Lamb.

Mr. Devlin spoke quietly and sincerely. "Judge Gafni, I don't think in forty years at the bar I've ever delayed the court's proceed-ings."

"That is not only your reputation, but also my experience, Mr. Devlin."

"Thank you, Judge. With that as a prologue, I'm going to ask the court for three weeks. This is a far more complicated case than it seems on the surface. Our interest in Peter Santangelo's life is also paramount. But I also have to be concerned with where he'll spend the rest of his life after the trial. May I say on my honor that we need three weeks to accomplish justice here."

The Judge nodded at Angela.

"Judge, I've heard arguments based on law, on precedents, and on facts. I have never heard a credible legal argument based on 'honor.'"

Judge Gafni turned his chair to face Angela directly.

"That's a pity, Miss Lamb. I wish that I could credit the bar with making more arguments on the honor and worthiness of its mem-bers. Because I'll tell you this from the heart. The honor and the word of a lawyer who's earned my respect means more to me than all of the precedent you can pile up on that desk. This case is set for trial three weeks from next Thursday. Thank you, Counsel."

CHAPTER FORTY-ONE

My first port of call the next morning was the Suffolk County Probate Clerk's office to check on John's bequest to his parents. It was not one of my usual haunts, but I wasn't a total stranger to its civil servants.

There were other clerks at the counter, but I waited until Pat McCarthy was free to chat about the Bruins's recent trade for a center, the Red Sox's chance of acquiring a reliever, and whether or not I might see John's will, which I assumed was at least in the process of being probated since his parents seemed to be already living on his bequest.

Pat, ever the pessimist, just shook his head about the Bruins's trade, predicted a dry winter for the Sox, and checked his computer regarding John's will. It seems that John left no will. I found it amazing that John, a lawyer, had left an estate of many millions of dollars from his scam on Tony Aiello, but no will. Not impossible, but still amazing.

I was back in the office that afternoon catching up on calls. I was interrupted by a call from John's parents. His father, as usual, was taking the lead, but they were both on the line, and they both sounded close to panic.

As before, they gave precious little information, but they practically pleaded with me to come back to the house. I agreed to go right over.

I knew something had happened to change the dynamic when they led me past the living room and directly to the kitchen table.

They were clearly shaken and ready to ask for help. Mr. McKedrick led off, but this time, they both seemed willing to loosen up. "Michael, I'm sorry. The way we treated you the last time —"

"Don't worry about it. I'll help you any way I can."

They looked at each other as if neither of them knew how to start.

"Start anywhere. What happened?"

Mr. McKedrick held his wife's hand and spoke for them both. "Last night we had a phone call. A man said he worked with John. He had a heavy accent."

"A Russian accent?"

"Yes. It could have been. He said his name was Sergei Markov."

The mere sound of that name drove an icicle into my heart.

"What did he want?"

"He said that John took money that belonged to him. A great deal of money. He thinks John gave it to us. He's demanding that we give it back to him. He's talking about seventy million dollars. Dear God. Where would we get such an amount? Where would John get such an amount?"

Ah, dear people, if only you knew that your little boy, Johnny, was working a hardball hustle in a league that would make your nose bleed.

I guess that would have been unkind. I softened it by finessing the question. "Let me be honest. I'm going to help you. In fact, I may be the only one on God's earth who can help you. I know more about this than you do, but I need a few more pieces. For example — and here's where you get to be totally honest — how much did John leave you?"

Mrs. McKedrick started to speak, but her husband put his hand over hers and broke in. "Five hundred thousand —"

"Whoa." I cut him off in mid-figure.

"I'm going to say this as gently as I can. Just don't let the gentleness suggest a lack of urgency. This Markov who called you is the most passionless killer you could ever conceive. It's likely that he's coming here to take your money and kill you. If I involve myself in this, I add my name to his kill list. If I get one more whiff of you two playing dodgeball with my questions, I'll be out of here. That didn't come out quite as gently as I intended, but do you both get my drift?"

Judging from the size and clear focus of their eyes, they took my meaning.

"Again, how much did you get from John?"

Mr. McKedrick volunteered what for the first time sounded like a straight answer. "Five hundred thousand dollars, Michael."

"Mr. McKedrick, you didn't buy this house for five hundred thousand dollars."

"No, no. We had some savings, and we took a mortgage for the other three hundred thousand. John has been wanting us to move for years, so —"

"I understand. But Markov won't. Did John tell you about any other money before he died?"

"No, he didn't"

The flow and directness told me I was getting truthful answers.

"All right. How did Markov leave it with you?"

"He said he'd call us tomorrow morning. We were to be ready to turn the money over to him. What should we do?"

"Listen to me very closely, folks. I want you to do this. No more, no less. When Markov calls tomorrow morning, you're to tell him you need until the evening to get the money together. He'll be suspicious. Tell him it's not in liquid funds. It's with a stockbroker. You'll have to work on getting it into transferable form. Tell him to come here to your house tomorrow night at nine o'clock. You'll have as much as you can for him then. Are you all right so far?"

"What if he doesn't accept that?"

"He won't. Tell him you have no choice. You're both in ill health. You can't travel. But you'll meet him here. He'll argue, but stick to the story. Nine o'clock, here. I was going to suggest that you sound scared, but I think that'll come across without trying."

They looked at each other and hesitated.

"Listen to me, folks. There's more to the plan, but that's all I want you to know right now. It'll help you play the part better if you don't know the rest. Trust me."

They both walked me to the door with profound thanks. I hadn't actually done anything yet, but I guess they were clinging to the hope that I might.

There was one question that had been nagging at me since I got their call that afternoon. I toyed with saving them the embarrassment, and then decided that with all that was at stake, a little embarrassment was a small price to pay.

"One last question. Clearly, you were not in a frame of mind to trust me with your problems the last time we got together. Now you are. What made the difference?"

Again they looked to each other before Mr. McKedrick managed to get out, "The call from Mr. Markov. We were really terrified. We remembered that you had always been a good, loyal friend to our son."

I had always thought so. John and I had been very close friends, and they both knew that. So why the freeze and then the thaw? The frightening call from Markov was an answer, but I didn't think it was the right answer.

Once more I was face-to-face with the theory that I had rejected every time it reared its head. This time, I couldn't shake it. I not only accepted my previously rejected theory, I made every move thereafter depend on it. The terrifying thought was *God help us all if I'm wrong*.

CHAPTER FORTY-TWO

The next morning I got Tom Burns on the phone.

"Tom, I need two of your best men with a rifle for this one."

"Sounds interesting. What did you get yourself into this time, Mike?"

"Same case. Here's the deal. John McKedrick's parents live in Brookline. I'll give you the address. You'll want to scout it out yourself, but here's the layout. Their house sits back from the street behind about sixty feet of driveway. Woods on both sides and across the street. This is Seclusionville."

"Sounds cozy."

"On a good day, yes. Tomorrow, it could mean they're sitting ducks. There's a man coming to see them at nine o'clock tomorrow night. He's coming to collect money they don't have. This guy thrives on violence with no limits. I want you to have your men positioned across the street in the woods with rifles just in case. I need two, so at least one will get a clear shot."

"That's possible, Mike. As long as the action stays outdoors."

"That's my job. I'll do my best to keep the confrontation in front of the house."

"I understand. Any other instructions?"

"Yes. This is important. I want your men to hold their fire until the last possible second consistent with the safety of the McKedricks. That's why I need good riflemen with judgment."

"I never give you less than the best, Mike."

"I know, Tom. That's why I'm calling you instead of the police."

By nine o'clock the next night, the sun had been down for some hours. The moon was a tiny sliver and cast practically no light.

I had arrived at the McKedricks' about eight. This time we were back in the living room, at my suggestion, with the lights out. I wanted a full view of as much of the street as I could see through the bowed window.

They were nervous as cats, sitting on the couch facing the street, each holding the hands of the other for strength. I was confident without seeing anyone that Tom had had his men in position since the sun went down. I could have told the McKedricks about them, but something told me they'd play their parts better if they didn't have that crutch to rely on.

The minutes were endless before nine o'clock, but the seconds seemed like hours after nine. At quarter past nine, I felt every muscle go into full freeze. In the darkness on the far side of the street, I saw a deeper darkness that took the shape of a black sedan moving at a creep with no running lights. It passed without stopping and continued down the street.

I whispered to the McKedricks, "It's time. Come on. Just exactly the way I told you. Most important. Not a word out of either of you. No matter what. I do the talking."

I waited until I saw the same black shadow return from down the street and stop just beyond the driveway. I saw a sole figure get out of the car. I was betting that Markov would come alone. He had nothing to fear from the McKedricks, and I doubted that he wanted another living soul to hear what he was there for.

I opened the front door and stood back in the darkness while I ushered Mr. and Mrs. McKedrick out the door into the circle of light thrown by lamps on either side of the door. They stopped according to my directions at the top of the three front steps and looked as if they were scared out of their wits. I knew that would give Markov the sense of control of the situation.

I let his footsteps approach to within fifteen feet before stepping out onto the front landing beside them. He stopped where he was. It was a slight jolt to his anticipation, but he quickly regained the dominating attitude. The light caught the barrel of the Austrian Glock in his right hand.

"Mr. Knight, I should have known you couldn't keep out of this. You McKedricks, who else did you tell?"

Mr. McKedrick leaped in with an answer. "No one. I swear."

I hoped my right hand was hidden behind Mr. McKedrick's back when I gave him a smack between the shoulder blades, soft enough to prevent him from leaping, but firm enough to remind him that he did not have a speaking part in this scene.

"They told no one else, Markov. This is not something they want made public."

"That had better be true, Mr. Knight. I'm actually glad to see you. We have a score to settle. But one thing at a time. How much money did you people bring?"

My hand rested on Mr. McKedrick's back like a hand puppet, just in case he became loquacious again.

"I can answer that, Markov. Not a dime."

That brought a pause, which was good. It also brought a raising of the Glock to a firing angle, which was not good.

"I think you better explain that."

"Certainly. Not a dime means you don't get one damn cent."

His eyes focused on me, but he could pick off the three of us in rapid-fire succession. My comfort level was descending rapidly.

I could see Markov becoming more agitated.

"You people are being sadly misled by this lawyer. This is not a negotiation. There is no bargaining. Once more. You will listen carefully. One of you will go into that house. You will return immediately with enough money to convince me not to fire a bullet into the heart of the other."

I grabbed the back of the shirt of Mr. McKedrick. It was now soaked with perspiration in twenty-degree weather. He started to speak. I tightened my grip until he just stood with his mouth open.

Mrs. McKedrick was sobbing uncontrollably. It was heart wrenching to feel her pain, but I knew at least that she couldn't speak.

I raised my voice to be sure to carry to the woods across the street. "There's nothing here for you, Markov. This is your last chance to leave these people alone."

He raised the gun to shoulder height and aimed directly at Mrs. McKedrick's heart. "Say good-bye to your bride, Mr. McKedrick."

I saw his finger begin to tighten inside the trigger guard. Why in God's name did I tell Tom to wait until the last instant?

I knew I had waited too long, but I let instinct or panic dictate one last futile move. I used the grip I had on Mr. McKedrick's shirt to drive him sideways into Mrs. McKedrick. They both tumbled headlong onto the landing, as a gunshot louder than anything I had ever heard concussed in my eardrum.

I landed on top of them and just held them both down under me. When a stillness followed, I looked up at Markov to prepare for the next blast of the Glock.

He was not there. I waited for my eyes to begin to adjust before I could see Markov's body splayed across the lawn on his back.

On his back. He fell backward, not forward. The shot came from in front of him. It had to come from inside the house.

I crawled slowly to my feet with my eye on Markov. As I got closer, I could see by the position of his body that he was dead.

The danger had come to a sudden halt, but now it was my turn to feel sweat running down my back. I knew now that my theory had proven true. The very thought of what I was seeing exposed was making my knees buckle.

While Mr. and Mrs. McKedrick helped each other to their feet, I walked back into the circle of light on the porch that made everything in the dark inside the open door to the house invisible. I didn't need to see inside. I knew to the very bottom of my heart who was there.

From where I stood, I forced the only two words I could utter through constricted vocal chords.

"Hello, John."

CHAPTER FORTY-THREE

I stood frozen to the spot for what seemed like a lifetime before I heard the voice that I thought I'd never hear again.

"Hello, Mike."

The figure that walked slowly through the door into the light had John McKedrick's face and body, but I had to touch him to be sure he was substance and not spirit.

It was the strangest moment of my life. Ever since that Friday intended rendezvous for dinner, if anyone had asked what I'd give to have my friend John standing in front of me, I'd have said, "Anything." Now here he was, and my mind and heart were tugged in a dozen different directions.

My sense of rejoicing was dampened by feelings of anger for the pain of mourning that he had put me through and, I suppose, hurt pride for the lack of trust he had shown in not letting me in on his little secret.

There was no time for sorting out all of the conflicting feelings, many of which I was not proud of. They were finally all submerged under one overwhelming realization. John McKedrick was standing in front of me. It must have hit us both at the same moment, because I suddenly found that we had our arms around each other. I was gripping a friend that I thought was gone forever. I held on as if I could prevent ever losing his presence and friendship again, and neither of us could stop the flow of tears.

We let the moment last, because we both knew that there were things to be done that couldn't wait, things that might mean that the old closeness would never go back to the way it was before.

Most immediately, we helped John's parents into the house. We needed to talk before the outside world intruded, and there was no better place than the McKedrick kitchen.

Whatever else needed explaining, there was one burning question that I couldn't postpone. "John, what happened that Friday?"

He pulled his kitchen chair up closer to me. "Mike, the most painful part of this whole thing was having to let you think I was dead. I wanted so much to let you in on it, but I really believed you'd be safer if you didn't know."

I could see him looking closely at the mostly healed scars on my face from the bombing, and I could read the pain in his eyes.

"If I'd known that you'd be injured, I'd never —"

"I'm good as new, John."

He smiled, but his eyes were still full of regret.

"Tell me about it, John. We don't have much time. Your old buddy, Markov, is still decorating the front lawn. We have to call the police, but I need to know some things first. What happened that Friday night?"

He leaned back to collect his thoughts. When he spoke, I knew that every word was the gospel truth.

"I need to put it in context, Mike. You've been right for years. The longer I stayed with Benny Ignola, the dirtier it made me. I could feel myself slipping into that slime. I began to hate myself for it. Every time you told me to get out, I knew I had to do it. The problem was how? I spoke to Benny about getting out. He said he'd ask Tony Aiello. He came back and said Tony told him that if I wanted out, there was only one way. A trip to the bottom of Boston Harbor. I knew where too many bodies were buried and who buried them. It made sense, Mike. It's all business. That meant I had to find my own way out."

"Which was?"

"I had a connection with Markov and the two Dutch financiers you met in Amsterdam. Aiello had me dealing in diamonds over there that he'd smuggle into the United States. I knew Aiello was planning to take over the family from Dominic Santangelo. His problem was that he couldn't kill the head of the Boston family without the permission of the heads of the other families. The so-called Commission. He had to convince them that he could make more money than Santangelo.

"That's when I came up with the idea of using a Vermeer painting as security to enable Aiello to borrow a lot of money from the Dutch financiers. Aiello could use the money to double his business in drugs and all the rest of it. That would impress the Commission."

He saw the wave of disgust that must have passed through my eyes when I heard the dirtiest word in the English language — drugs.

"Hold on, Mike. Hear the rest of the story. Aiello would never see the money. I pretended that I was still representing him. I got our old Professor Denisovitch to paint a copy of the Vermeer that had been stolen from a Boston museum. He could authenticate it as a genuine Vermeer. The Dutch financiers were willing to loan Aiello money on that security."

"That much I know."

"All right, Mike, here's what you may not know. When it came time to transfer the borrowed funds from the Dutch to Aiello's account, I just had to give them the number of my own account instead of Aiello's. They didn't suspect anything. Seventy million dollars was transferred electronically into my account in a foreign bank. Aiello never got a dime of it. That was my ticket out. Then I had to disappear in a way that would prevent Aiello from coming after me. He has contacts all over the world."

"And the way to do that was to fake your own death."

"I needed a witness that was believable. That's why I had you meet me in the parking garage. I know now I should have told you what was happening."

"Why didn't you, John? You and I were like brothers. You couldn't trust me?"

John shook his head.

"It wasn't that. Believe me, Mike. I knew there'd be hell to pay when I disappeared and Aiello was stuck with a debt for borrowed money he never got — and couldn't repay. I really thought you'd be safer if you weren't in on the deception."

I had to think that one over, with precious little time to do it. My first conclusion was that I disagreed with John on his decision not to take me aboard, but I also couldn't doubt his sincerity in thinking I'd be safer on the outside.

"How did you pull it off, John? All I remember is walking toward your car."

"I had one of the Mafia hoods who was supposed to be good at that sort of thing rig the car. He put a protective plate in front of the driver's seat. He told me to open the door and jump just as I turned the key. That part worked out. What didn't work out was that the force of the blast went through the front grill and hit you. I never dreamed anything like that would happen. I never even knew you were injured. As soon as I was out of the car, I was picked up in another car and out of there. I didn't hear about your injury until the following week."

My mind was racing to put together John's version with what little I remembered of that day.

"So who was in on it, John?"

"I worked all that week to put it together. The only ones I told were the man who rigged the bomb, the pick-up driver, the boys in the ambulance. I had them standing by at the entrance to the garage so they'd be the first on the scene. Who else? Matt Magarrity at the funeral home. Oh, and that garage attendant who was watching when you came into the garage. He signaled the ambulance and hustled me into it right after the explosion. That was it, with the exception of my parents. I had to tell them."

"And whose body did you use."

"No one's. There was no body. You remember the whole thing was run with a closed casket, supposedly because of the injuries."

"How did you get these people to go along?"

"Money. Remember, I had Aiello's money at that point. They were acquaintances to start with, but they were also well paid."

Since John had raised the subject, I satisfied another curiosity.

"What about the money, John?"

"Ah, now there's a subject. If I gave it back, whom would I give it to? Tony Aiello? What would he use it for? To flood the city with more drugs. Should I give it back to the Dutch financiers? They'd loan it out to someone else to build a criminal empire. They keep their own hands clean, but they finance some of the worst scourges on earth. No, Michael, I don't think so. You know, as I look back on my life defending Benny Ignola's clients, the loansharks, the drug pushers, the pimps, I can say to myself in all honesty that because of my existence the world is worse off. Now I've got the time and the means to change that. I'm going to find the places in the world where it'll do the most good without it being detoured into the pockets of corrupt politicians. That's going to be my life."

Time was really getting short now. The police had to be called before a suspicious amount of time lapsed after the shooting of Markov. But I still had two questions that needed answers no matter what.

"John, I have to know this. You know that Mr. Devlin and I got mixed up in this when Peter Santangelo was indicted for your murder."

"I know, Mike. That came out of left field. That was Aiello. He saw the chance to make Santangelo look bad before the Commission. The last thing those boys want is the notoriety of killing a lawyer in a pubic place. If he could hang it on Peter, it would look as if Mr. Santangelo couldn't even control his own son. That was the reason for the frame-up. He got Three-Finger Simone to confess to the bombing and cut a deal with the D.A. by fingering Peter. You know our crusading district attorney. She'd cut a deal with Jack the Ripper if it would get her a headline prosecution."

"So it seems, John. Now to my last question. In all of this mess, thank God, I've had a guardian angel. One with a gun. First when Vito Respa came after me up in Rockport. Then again when Aiello's men had me trapped on Charles Street. Then again tonight. Unbelievable as it seemed, I've been getting this creeping suspicion that you've been my angel all three times."

I looked into his eyes that for the first time seemed to have lost the tinge of guilt. I thought I saw the beginnings of a smile.

He looked down at the table and spoke in a low voice.

"Mike, I've been ashamed of most of what I've done since I joined Benny years ago. I needed to make this break, and I swear to you I couldn't see any other way out. That doesn't mean I was proud of it. But I'll say this. The money I took has given me the ability to assemble a network of people to work for me who've been my eyes and ears — and my hands when it was necessary. I gave the orders, but they're the ones you can thank. It may have been unorthodox, but thank God you're alive here tonight. When did you know?"

"When I realized that there was no one else in the world who cared about me enough to commit murder to save my life."

He started to say something, but it wouldn't come out. He used his hand to wipe something out of his eyes and reached over to squeeze my arm. I put my hand on top of his.

"I didn't think I'd ever get to thank you, John."

He just shook as head, and I knew what he meant.

I leaned closer to his ear. "Just one more question, John."

He looked up at me.

"I know what you're going to ask, Mike. I've been wanting to say this for weeks. Terry O'Brien and I were friends. That's all. When I realized that my two best friends were falling in love, I couldn't have been happier. I knew that at least something really good came out of all this. I may not be physically at your wedding, Mike, but there'll be no one more deeply there in spirit. Does that answer your question?"

What a scene. Now the two of us had liquid running down our cheeks, and neither one of us was ashamed of it. A couple of tough guys, right?

CHAPTER FORTY-FOUR

While Mr. McKedrick called the police to report that "someone" had shot a man in front of their house, I used my cell phone to wake Mr. Devlin with the most shocking news he had heard since this odyssey had begun. John was alive.

"How shall we handle it, Mr. Devlin? Do you want to notify Angela Lamb? And, of course, Mr. Santangelo."

He thought for a moment before coming back.

"No, Michael. Neither one. I want you to be at Judge Gafni's courtroom at nine tomorrow morning. We've got to tie this up with no loose ends. Here's what I want you to do."

At exactly nine the next morning, Judge Gafni's bailiff, Keiran O'Toole, called "All rise." The judge took his place on the bench. Mr. Devlin and myself were at defense counsel's table and a very hyped up and totally in the dark Angela Lamb took her accustomed position at prosecution's table.

The judge looked in our direction first.

"Mr. Devlin, you're the one who called for this session. I've displaced several other matters on my docket. I trust this is worth it."

Mr. Devlin rose to his feet.

"Oh, I think you'll call this a most extraordinary day, Judge. I have a motion and a witness."

"I'm all ears, Mr. Devlin."

"Thank you, Your Honor. My motion is for an immediate dismissal of the charge against Peter Santangelo."

That dropped Angela's jaw at least half an inch. Her head spun toward Mr. Devlin fast enough to give her whiplash. Whatever her flaws, lack of a quick mind was not one of them.

Judge Gafni took it with more equanimity.

"You say you have a witness, Mr. Devlin. Please enlighten us."

"Thank you, Your Honor. I'd like to call to the stand the corpus delecti of this first degree murder charge — Mr. John McKedrick."

Angela's head spun around in the opposite direction toward the door of the courtroom, and even the judge's eyebrows lifted. John walked into the courtroom as if he had never been dead a day in his life. The skin of Angela's face drained of every drop of blood and her eyes followed John's walk to the witness stand as if Elvis had just walked into the courtroom.

The judge looked back at defense counsel.

"I assume you have an explanation for this, Mr. Devlin."

"I do, Your Honor. I have just one question of this witness. Could we have him sworn in?"

The judge's clerk did the swearing, and Mr. Devlin took the floor.

"Are you the John McKedrick who is supposedly the person who died in a bombing incident allegedly ordered by my client, Peter Santangelo?"

John was the soul of composure.

"I am, Mr. Devlin."

Angela's perplexity radiated from every pore of her blanched face. She seemed fixed in one position.

I saw that glint in Mr. Devlin's eyes that told me he could in no way resist hammering the last unnecessary nail in Ms. Lamb's case.

"And would you tell the court, Mr. McKenna, are you in any sense of the word dead?"

The judge was on his feet and striding toward his chambers without allowing time for an answer.

"I'll see counsel in my chambers. This witness is not excused."

Ms. Lamb, Mr. Devlin, and I gathered in chairs around the judge's desk.

"Mr. Devlin, you did not overstate the matter. This is an

extraordinary day. I'm looking for an explanation from you, Miss Lamb."

"Flustered" is the only word that comes close to poor Angela's state at that moment, and the word doesn't even come close.

"This comes as a complete shock to me as well, Your Honor. I had absolutely no idea."

That statement needed no backing up beyond one look at our shaking Queen of Prosecution.

"Then, Mr. Devlin, let's hear it from you. I want this done in chambers before the press goes shooting off half-cocked."

Mr. Devlin gave a brief account of how the assumed corpse of John McKedrick had returned to the world of the living. He wrapped it up neatly.

"The most immediate piece of business is your ruling on my motion to dismiss the charge of murder against my client, Peter Santangelo."

The judge looked at Angela simply as a matter of courtesy. "If I may ask an absurd question, Miss Lamb, do you have any objection to the motion?"

She stalled for a few seconds to see if there was any possible straw to be grasped. The judge gave her an incredulous look.

"Miss Lamb, that was practically a rhetorical question."

"Yes, Your Honor. I can't — think of an objection."

"No. I'd think not. The motion is granted. The indictment is dismissed. I want to do this in open court. Is there anything else at the moment."

Angela bounced back in admirable style.

"Yes, Your Honor. I want you to issue a bench warrant for the immediate arrest of John McKedrick."

"Interesting, Ms. Lamb. On what charge?"

"Fraud on the court, to begin with. There may be other charges."

"Very well, I'll issue the warrant. Any objection, Mr. Devlin?"

Mr. D. just raised his hands in submission.

"He's not my client, Your Honor. No objection here."

The slight smile on his face told me that he and I were sharing the same thought.

Our little troop marched back into the courtroom, where we discovered with a glance that the witness chair was empty. The judge called the bailiff, Keiran O'Toole, to the bench.

"Where is he, Keiran? I told him he was not excused."

Keiran, in his Irish brogue, reported that Mr. McKedrick had had the need to make use of the men's lavatory facilities and had left the courtroom merely for that purpose.

The judge sent Keiran to fetch back Mr. McKedrick. Keiran returned in a minute to report, I believe to the surprise of no one, with the possible exception of Angela, that Mr. McKedrick was nowhere to be found.

The judge made short work of granting the motion to dismiss the indictment against Peter, and we left the courtroom. On my way out, Keiran took me by the sleeve and led me over to a corner.

"Mr. Knight, he left you a message."

"Keiran. You let him walk right by you."

I smiled when I said it, and Keiran smiled when he replied.

"And shall I give you the message?"

"I'd appreciate it."

"Mr. McKedrick wanted me to say to you in these very words, 'May the road rise up to meet you, and may the wind be always at your back.'"

I felt a lump the size of a grapefruit come up in my throat. I just patted Keiran on the shoulder by way of a thank you, and he understood.

I knew that was John's way of saying good-bye, and that I might never see him again. I think he was also telling me exactly where I could find him if I ever needed him. I think he wanted me to put that old Irish blessing together with my knowledge of where John's ancestors were buried in the west of Ireland.

I said a reciprocal prayer for my once friend and brother, and left the courtroom.

CHAPTER FORTY-FIVE

I got as far as the courthouse steps when my cell phone rang. It was Mr. Devlin.

"Michael, we've got one more loose end to tie."

"I know. Can we do it?"

"Who knows? I have to try. I want you there. Meet me in an hour at Matt Ryan's church."

I walked up the steps of the Church of the Sacred Heart with a sense of impending closure. This was where it began, and by the grace of God, this was where the last act would play out.

Based on the lack of cars out front, I assumed I was the first one there. I relished those few moments of quiet peace before the altar — the first still moments I could remember for some time.

Monsignor Ryan came to the pew and sat beside me. I told him the news about Peter. That brought a heartfelt smile. Then I asked him not to mention it to Mr. Santangelo if he should arrive next. That brought a dark cloud. I think he knew exactly why I made the request.

"How is he, Michael?"

I knew he meant Mr. Devlin, and I knew he was not looking for a glib answer.

"In the mornings, he's flint and steel. By the late afternoon, I see a weariness that wasn't there before. He'd never admit to it, but it's there, and it worries me."

Monsignor Ryan put a great knuckled hand on my shoulder. He looked at me as if he were reading my thoughts.

"You love him, don't you, Michael?"

I smiled. "It shows, does it? Yes. I admire him. I respect him. But most of all, I guess I love him. My own dad died when I was very young, and —"

"Don't for a minute think that he loves you any less, Michael. You're awfully good for him."

I could just nod in thanks. There was nothing he could have said that could have gone so straight to my heart.

There was a sound at the back of the church, and we both walked back to meet Mr. Devlin. A minute later, Mr. Santangelo appeared. I remembered what a stake in my heart it was the first time I saw him in that church, and recognized what I thought was the absolute Icon of Evil. Now he looked like just an ordinary older man who was aging fast.

Monsignor Ryan led us back to the office. We sat in our usual seats. Mr. Santangelo was the first to get to business.

"What do you want to tell me, Lex?"

Mr. Devlin rubbed his eyes with the palms of his hands. I knew that meant that he was searching for a place to begin.

"Dominic, I'm going to make a deal with you."

"I thought we had a deal, Lex."

"Consider it a renegotiation."

"I'm listening."

"How much is Peter's life worth to you?"

That question stunned him.

"Are you looking for a fee, Lex? Ask any amount you want. If I can pay it, I will. If I can't, I'll get it."

"In other words, any amount."

"Did you ever doubt it?"

Mr. Devlin stood up and walked over to lean against the edge of Monsignor Ryan's desk.

"No. I didn't. But I'm not talking about money. That being so, does the same upper limit hold?"

Mr. Santangelo was openly at a loss as to where this was going.

I knew, and I'm sure Monsignor Ryan knew. Nevertheless, Mr. Santangelo nodded in the affirmative.

"Dominic, you and I lost each other many years ago. You can say we took different paths. That wasn't it. We became different people. I'm going to be blunt here. I'm no angel, but you willingly followed a life so despicably evil that I said to myself I'd have no part of it or of you."

The lines on Mr. Santangelo's forehead said that Mr. Devlin's words were causing direct pain, and I wondered how much more of it the don would take.

"I was wrong, Dominic. I didn't hate you. I never did. We were brothers, you and me and Matt."

He took a pause that was more than a breath. His voice was tighter when he could continue.

"All these years. I hated what you were doing, and how it almost killed our brotherhood. Now Matt, our brother, this priest, has opened a door for us. I want to walk through it, and I'm calling on you to do the same."

"You talked about a deal, Lex. What do you want me to do?"

Mr. Devlin leaned forward to speak even more directly to Santangelo.

"I'll give you back your son, Dominic. That's my part."

Mr. Santangelo looked somewhat taken back, almost hesitating to believe it.

"How, Lex?"

"As I say, that's my part. It's a promise. I can do it. I'll explain in a minute."

A cloud seemed to lift tentatively from Mr. Santangelo's face, but he allowed Mr. Devlin to stay on track.

"And my part, Lex?"

Mr. Devlin leaned even closer.

"Become the man I knew forty years ago."

Mr. Santangelo looked away. Ten seconds later when he looked back, he was the aging man I saw when he came in.

"How can I —?"

Mr. Devlin looked directly into his eyes and I knew that he had never faced a jury that he more deeply wanted to win over.

"You've been wronged, Dominic, in the most painful way. Your lieutenant, Aiello, is a traitor of the worst sort. He attacked you through your son. I can tell you this. The danger to you and Peter from his insidiousness has passed. That's a story we can tell later. There's another danger. You have control now. What will you do? Will you take blood revenge because you can? If that's what you choose, you'll break the bonds that are beginning to grow again between us. Make no mistake. That's the price."

Mr. Santangelo looked directly into Mr. Devlin's eyes.

"Why do you defend this Aiello?"

"I don't, Dominic. I'm defending you, and me, and Matt, and what we had before."

He looked at Mr. Devlin for what seemed an eternity before speaking.

"What do you want me to do?"

"Aiello's defeated, Dominic. Let him leave. Alive. Back to Sicily if he chooses, but alive."

Mr. Devlin pulled his chair over to sit and face Mr. Santangelo directly. "This has to be your free choice, Dominic. Hear me. Peter's indictment has been dismissed. He's free to go. You can bring him home when we finish."

Mr. Santangelo was on his feet as if some new life had revitalized his body. Mr. Devlin stood to face him.

"It's true, Dominic. You have your son."

Mr. Santangelo looked as if he wanted with all his heart to embrace Mr. Devlin, but there was still a mountain between them. I could see moisture forming in Mr. Santangelo's eyes. I was surprised to see that this Godfather was capable of tears.

"Dominic, we're old men. There isn't much time. I want to meet you in heaven, and I don't want it to be in anger."

Their eyes were locked. I watched the tension slowly drain out of the face of Mr. Santangelo. His arms came up, and so did Mr. Devlin's. It was as if some greater power was pulling them together. They stood with their arms around each other as they might have done forty years ago to celebrate a knockout win by Matt Ryan, and their arms only opened to enclose Monsignor Ryan in the circle.

They never noticed when I left the room. This was their time. And besides, there was a young lady I'd promised a date without one single murder or kidnapping all evening.